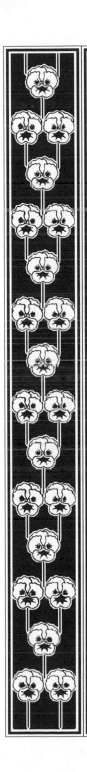

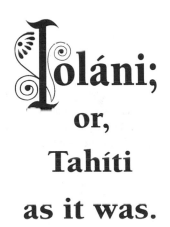oláni;

or,

Tahíti

as it was.

A

ROMANCE

BY

Wilkie Collins

EDITED AND INTRODUCED BY

Ira B. Nadel

PRINCETON UNIVERSITY PRESS

PRINCETON, NEW JERSEY

Copyright © 1999 by Princeton University Press
Published by Princeton University Press, 41 William Street,
Princeton, New Jersey 08540
In the United Kingdom: Princeton University Press, Chichester, West Sussex

Library of Congress Cataloging-in-Publication Data
Collins, Wilkie, 1824–1889.
Ioláni, or, Tahíti as it was : a romance / by Wilkie Colline ;
edited and introduced by Ira B. Nadel
p. cm.
ISBN 0-691-03446-X (cloth : alk. paper)
I. Nadel, Ira B., 1943– . II. Title.
PR4494.I56 1999
823'.8—dc21   98-28620

This book has been composed in Berkeley

The paper used in this publication meets the minimum requirements
of ANSI / NISO Z39.48-1992 (R 1997) (*Permanence of Paper*)

http://pup.princeton.edu

Printed in the United States of America

10 9 8 7 6 5 4 3 2 1

✿ CONTENTS ✿

ꙮ ACKNOWLEDGMENTS ꙮ

Glenn Horowitz, bookseller *extraordinaire*, first alerted me to
the existence of the *Iolāni* manuscript and put me on the track
of studying the work. While he graciously tolerated my frequent
intrusions, I have, in turn, always found constant delight in his
friendship. Faith Clarke, the great-grandaughter of Wilkie Col
lins, and her husband, William M. Clarke, have generously supported the publication of the manuscript and encouraged, as
well as corrected, my work from the beginning. Their assistance
and support has been inestimable. Andrew Gasson has been a
tireless champion of the work of Wilkie Collins, both as bibliog-
rapher and Chair of the Wilkie Collins Society (London); his aid
in identifying various details has been immensely helpful. Catherine Peters, through her research and publication on Collins,
has long established the principles of accuracy and clarity so
essential for understanding his career and life. Norman Page
also assisted through his critical and editorial work on Collins.

Robert Brown of Princeton University Press has waited patiently for this work and maintained his enthusiasm for the
book ever since it was first proposed. A. Deborah Malmud has
been an able editor directing the manuscript through to publication. Pamela Dalziel has guided me through the thickets of
editorial theory and practice through her own distinguished
work and personal encouragement. The University of British
Columbia's Social Science and Humanities Awards Committee
has also generously aided this edition. My children, Dara and
Ryan, newly won fans to Wilkie Collins's sensation fiction, have

been constant supporters, although like others they could never quite satisfactorily answer the question, "What's a Victorian novelist doing in Tahiti?" This edition provides a clue.

✸ INTRODUCTION ✸

Wilkie Collins wrote his first novel while at tea. Only now, over
a century and a half later, is it being published. He was in fact
a twenty-year-old apprentice with the London tea merchants
Antrobus & Company when he started the original manuscript
in 1844 at their office in London's Strand. It was never accepted
by a publisher and was rarely seen again until it suddenly sur-
faced in New York in 1991.

The story of the manuscript's existence is itself a mystery
worthy of Collins. It begins with the 1845 rejection of the work
first by Longmans and then Chapman and Hall. The manuscript
then appears to have dropped out of sight until possibly 1870,
when Collins recalled it in an interview for *Appleton's Journal*.
The manuscript resurfaces in 1878 when he presumably presents it to Augustin Daly (1838–1899), an American theatrical
impressario; it does not publically appear, however, until the
end of the century when it is offered for sale in March 1900 as
lot 605* (there was an unasterisked lot 605) from Daly's library
and acquired for $23.00 by George D. Smith, a young book
dealer who would later become a principal agent for Henry
Huntington. Smith soon offered the Collins manuscript in his
catalogue for $100.00, noting that the novel "would well repay
publication."[1]

Smith sold *Ioláni* to the Philadelphia collector Howard T.
Goodwin, who had the Pfister binding made for it. Goodwin's
sudden death in 1903, however, allowed the manuscript to appear at auction for a second time, in the Philadelphia rooms of
Stan V. Henkels (as item 32 of the Goodwin sale), where it was

purchased by Joseph M. Fox, a Philadelphia lawyer who became the first backer and partner of the Rosenbach Company. Until 1991, the manuscript remained in the Fox family. But despite its frequent transfer at auction, *Ioláni* escaped the notice of literary scholars and biographers, who until recently have been unaware of its existence.

Why should Daly have been the recipient of Collins's earliest work? The answer is not difficult. A prominent New York theatre producer noted for his productions of Shakespeare in America, Daly was principally responsible for Collins's success on the American stage. In 1870, Daly commissioned Collins to adapt *Man and Wife* for the New York stage, but he was disappointed when he received the treatment and diplomatically urged Collins to make changes. When Collins ignored the request, Daly announced that he would adapt the novel himself. Collins was upset at this state of affairs and disliked trusting his reputation to the producer, urging Daly not to advertise the production as a collaboration.

Ironically, Daly's adherence to the novel was more faithful than Collins's. His adaptation was a hit, running for ten weeks, due in part to casting the popular American actress Clara Morris in her first starring role. In a grand gesture, Daly sent Collins a thousand dollars at the end of the run, despite Collins's withdrawal from the project.[2] In 1873, Collins embarked on a reading tour of the United States and that fall, coinciding with his visit to New York, Daly planned his own production of Collins's *The New Magdalen*, his novel about a reformed prostitute. Collins cooperated in a minimal way; in Manhattan, Collins attended only a few rehearsals, being too preoccupied with his readings and travels to give more time. However, he did attend the premiere on 10 November 1873 and took a celebratory bow after the second act. His enthusiastic reception set the tone for the remainder of his public appearances characterized by adulation, praise, and acceptance.[3] Following opening night, on 11

November 1873, Collins gave a much applauded New York reading and by the close of his tour, for which he earned approximately £2,500 (not even close to the £20,000 Dickens earned in 1867), he was venerated in America.

Other collaborations between Daly and Collins occurred or were proposed, especially in the fall of 1878, when Daly visited Collins several times in London. There is no evidence, however, to confirm whether Collins gave Daly the *Iolāni* manuscript or whether he simply lent it to him in the hope of future publication or adaptation for the stage. Although we know that Collins was particularly sensitive about the stealing of his copyright in the United States, my own belief is that in the fall of 1878 or in February-March 1879, just before Daly returned to the U.S. after a sojourn to Paris, Collins presented Daly with the manuscript of *Iolāni* in gratitude for his theatrical efforts. It is unlikely Collins gave him the manuscript earlier because he most assuredly did not take it with him to America for his reading tour in 1873; and if it *had* in some fashion reached Daly before 1878, he might have been tempted to auction it in October that year when he was forced, by his business debts, to sell off his library in New York. The sale took five nights to complete, earning a precommission total of $9969.63 and profit of $8,500.00 after expenses, according to Daly's brother in his biography of the impressario.[4]

The transmission of the manuscript to America simultaneouly insured its preservation and disappearance. When it suddenly appeared on the rare book market in 1991, the manuscript created something of a sensation; its purchase by a private collector in 1992 created something of a mystery.

I

An early work, *Iolāni* is nevertheless the embryo of Collins's later fiction. Thematically dramatizing the abuse of power—in this work, the victimization of women by patriarchal figures—

the novel initiates a lifetime critique of corrupt authority and individual oppression. The construction of plot reflects Collins's understanding of suspense as a key device, while his use of dramatic scenes, forcefully depicting a variety of battles and encounters, skillfully integrates with the development of character and displays his ability with action. An exciting pursuit in Book III, concluding with a body cascading down a deep ravine, is but one thrilling example.

Vivid descriptive passages develop the exotic appeal of the Tahitian landscape, the setting of the novel, enlarged by lush descriptions and knowledge of Tahitian customs. A fascination with crime, especially in the paradoxes of the criminal mind, finds remarkable expression in the evil priest and eponymous hero, Ioláni. Throughout the novel, Collins probes the psychology of his villain and victim, anticipating his later absorption with the mind of such demonic figures as Robert Mannion of *Basil*, Count Fosco in *The Woman in White*, or Dr. Benjula in *Heart and Science*.

Complementing the complex presentation of evil in the novel is the complex presentation of women who are assertive, independent, and aggressive—but at a price. Idía, the mother of Ioláni's child, jeopardizes her life, as well as that of her friend, Aimáta, in her determination to escape from Ioláni and save her son from the Tahitian practice of infanticide. But despite her suffering, she does not weaken and becomes the first of Collins's many independent women who resist mistreatment by men. But Collins does not disguise her ambivalence. In spite of the constant threat of death from Ioláni, Idía laments her lost love: "her thoughts still wandered, mechanically, to the passionate lover of Vahíria; rather, than, to the inexorable tyrant of the Temple and the Field" (128). The ambiguity of Idía displays Collins's circumscription of the radical through a subversive doubleness of self. Yet the plot requires that Idía remain an outcast, eventually poisoned by Ioláni and a sorcerer.

Restraining the youthful, enthusiastic style of the novel is Collins's omniscient narrator, part moralist, part conversationalist. The voice, which will diminish in his later fiction, is here solicitous in its interruptions, seeking the reader's patience with his method, as in Book II Chapter VI, when he explains why he pauses to provide a lengthy physical description. Such a rhetorical strategy has the critical effect of encouraging reader sympathy. The novel relies strongly on such a narrator who elaborates descriptions, limits dialogue, and restricts subplots, which Collins, in his more mature fiction, will replace with limited descriptions, enlarged dialogue, and multiple plots.

Collins's organization of *Iolâni* into three books with individual chapters, a division many of his later novels will replicate, indicates his early conception of novelistic structure as a set of discrete episodes or scenes mirroring a theatrical model. Collins uses such divisions of the story, which lack transitions or bridging passages, to control suspense, disrupt events, shift chronology, and occasionally mislead readers. Such a structure in his first novel suggests Collins's early adaptation of dramatic principles to enhance his story-telling, developed, for example, in *No Name*, with its divisions into "Scenes" and "Between the Scenes." Of his more than twenty-five novels, only *Antonina* and *Hide and Seek*, in fact, have no divisions other than chapters. Collins's second published novel, *Basil*, contains an important declaration on the alliance between the novel and drama already enacted in *Iolâni*: "the Novel and the Play are twin-sisters in the family of Fiction; that the one is a drama narrated, as the other is a drama acted."[5]

The action, method, and theme of *Iolâni* illustrate elements Collins enlarges in his later work. From independent women and descriptive landscape detail, to the psychology of villains and the hypocrisy of moralists, Collins's first novel provides a glimpse of the method and materials he will later elaborate. Analysis of character—including the sympathetic treatment of the villain—while often revealing its contradictory nature, shown in the midst of triumph to be unsure and in the course of despair to be heroic, is evident. Courage and determination in the face of danger, which will define the tension between good and evil in his later work, is manifest in his first attempt at fiction, *Iolâni*.

II

Collins began the 160-page holograph manuscript of the novel in the autumn of 1844, some three years after leaving school. His situation at Antrobus & Company had been made possible through his father's friend, the banker Charles Ward of Coutts Bank; Antrobus was a relative of one of the Coutts directors and knew Ward, who recommended the young Collins. In 1842 Antrobus acknowledged his respect for the talent of Wilkie's father, the painter William Collins, by paying 200 guineas for a portrait of the three Antrobus daughters, which was exhibited at the Royal Academy.

Wilkie Collins's position at Antrobus & Company was most likely as an unpaid apprentice rather than a salaried clerk.[6] He remained there from January 1841 until May 1846, when his father, acknowledging his son's desultory labors, had him admitted as a law student at Lincoln's Inn. Not surprisingly, Collins did not take his work seriously at Antrobus & Company, which Frank Clare's indifferent performance of his job at a London tea merchant in Chapter IX of *No Name* echoes. Zackery Thorpe, Jr., who spent three weeks at a tea broker in *Hide and Seek*, comically explains the problem: "they all say it's a good opening for me, and talk about the respectability of commercial pursuits. I don't want to be respectable and I hate commercial pursuits."[7] Collins preferred vacationing in Paris to working at a London desk and sought distraction through writing. Diligence was offset by composition, industriousness by creativity, although Collins defensively reported that whenever Mr. Antrobus "found me tale-writing, I was always able to show that I had finished everything I had been given to do."[8] His most important communication with Antrobus was often in the form of requests to extend his various trips to the continent and gain additional vacation time away from the office. As he explained to his friend Edmund Yates, most days at Antrobus were spent trying his hand at "tragedies, comedies, epic poems and the usual literary rubbish invariably accumulated about themselves by 'young beginners'"—all this instead of dealing with "invoices, bills of lading, and the state of Chinese tea markets."[9]

During this period, Collins also composed "a novel of the most wildly impracticable kind, on the subject of savage life in Polynesia, before the discovery of the group of islands composing that country by civilized men."[10] His father, already proud of his son's journalistic publications, submitted the manuscript of *Ioláni* on 25 January 1845 to Longmans, who kept the manuscript for two months, originally suggesting they would publish the work if William Collins would pay *part* of the costs. Despite a favorable reader's report, Longmans finally rejected the novel on financial grounds, adding, however, that if William Collins would bear the *entire* cost, they would consider publishing the work. William Collins, in a letter of 8 March 1845, declined.[11] The manuscript was later submitted to Chapman and Hall (at 186 The Strand), who also rejected it, although, on the basis of what he felt was its impending acceptance, Collins confidently asked his parents for a loan of £100 to extend a vacation in France to include Nice. "Could you not send me £100," he roguishly asks, "upon the strength of my M.S. and Chapman and Hall? . . . Life is short,—we should enjoy it. I am your affectionate son[,] W.Wilkie Collins.—you should humour me!____." Later, on that same journey, Collins reminds his parents that he has not disobeyed their injunctions about economy: "You said you hoped I should make my Cheque last for my *trip*. It *has* lasted for my *trip* but not for my *return*."[12]

In an 1870 interview, Collins recalled *Iolàni* as an unsuccessful blend of Gothic romance and South Seas adventure:

> The scene of the story is the island of Tahiti, before the period of its discovery by European navigators! My youthful imagination ran riot among the noble savages, in scenes which caused the respectable British publisher to declare that it was impossible to put his name on the title page of such a novel. For the moment I was a little discouraged. But I got over it, and began another novel.[13]

When returning the work in 1845, the Longmans reader intimated, according to Collins, that "the story was hopelessly bad, and that in his opinion the writer had not the slightest aptitude for romance-writing."[14] Collins further recounted that he met "the worthy man years after at a dinner party, when *The Woman in White* was running through *Household Words*, and I remember that neither of us could forbear from bursting out and laughing at the *rencontré*."[15]

Collins had, of course, been attracted to writing from early in his life, not only by meeting such authors as Wordsworth, Henry Crabb Robinson, and Coleridge, who visited the family in what was then rural Hampstead, but by his early readings in which he prized not only Scott (his mother's favorite) and Byron, but also Marryat and Cervantes. Curiously, Scott indirectly delayed the marriage of Collins's parents: the opportunity of William Collins to paint the arrival of George IV on his official visit to Scotland in July 1822 postponed his proposed marriage to Harriet Geddes, but the chance to paint memorable events in the company of Sir David Wilkie, Andrew Geddes and, briefly, J.M.W. Turner could not be refused. On the trip, William Collins was thrilled to meet Scott. In order to hasten his marriage, however, William Collins had his fiancée join him from London and they were married in Edinburgh on 16 September 1822. Twenty years later, in the summer of 1842, the eighteen-year-old Wilkie took a leave from the tea company and joined his father on a return trip to Scotland, traveling to Edinburgh and the far north, eventually to Shetland, where William was to provide the illustrations for the Abbotsford Edition of Scott's novel *The Pirate* set in Orkney and Shetland. Memories of the wild and romantic scenery remained with Collins throughout his writing career, and one coastal hamlet gave him the title of a novel published more than twenty years after: *Armadale*.

III

On the surface, little explains Collins's choice of Polynesia as the setting of his first novel beyond a love of the unusual, which he would repeat in his second novel, *Antonina*, set in fifth-century Rome, and expand in works like *Hide and Seek* with Zackery Thorpe, Jr.'s, voyage to the wilds of America, *The Woman in White* with Walter Hartright joining an expedition to search for ruins in Hondouras, and *The Moonstone* with the storming of Seringapatam and the Indian jugglers. In 1877 Collins would recapture his interest in Polynesia in his short story, "The Captain's Last Love," similar in setting, and character to, but not taken from, *Iolâni*. The plot of the story involves an English sea captain who falls in love with a priest's daughter on an isolated island. A volcanic eruption on the nearby main island, rather than a bitter war, destroys the idyllic Polynesian world and romance between the two. Aimáta, the young woman in *Iolâni* whose assertiveness saves the heroine and her child, reappears in the 1877 short story as the "Nymph of the Island," who captivates the sea captain at the threat of his life from her sorcerer-priest father. The captain's attempt to rescue his love from the sinking island fails, although not before he sees a vision of her beckoning to him. Distraught at his loss, the captain returns to England, "his heart dead to all new emotions; nothing lives in it but the sacred remembrance of his last love" the narrator solemnly declares.[16]

The sorcery, setting, descriptive detail, and name of Aimáta link "The Captain's Last Love" to *Ioláni* but do not explain why Collins should renew interest in Polynesia in the fall of 1876 when he wrote it. Possibly, he rediscovered the *Ioláni* manuscript, which revived his curiosity in the South Seas. His great love of sailing and the sea, which he thought diminished his bouts of rheumatic gout and which he enjoyed on his frequent trips to Ramsgate, may have also renewed his desire to tell a story of the sea. Or, it may be that at age fifty-two, Collins began to reminisce. In 1876 he published *The Two Destinies*, which uses background material from his 1842 trip to Scotland with his father, as well as detail from Sir Walter Scott's *The Pirate*, which his father illustrated. Such memories may have triggered his recall of *Ioláni* and its world of Tahitian romance.

Collins's inspiration was unlike that of Melville, who based his first novel, *Typee, A Peep at Polynesian Life*—first published in London by John Murray in 1846—partly on his apparent captivity in the valley of the Typee in the Marquesas Islands of Polynesia in July 1842, during four years spent sailing in the South Pacific. Collins chose Polynesia for its exotic appeal only. Interest in the South Seas was fueled in London by the 1774 publication of John Hawkesworth's popular redaction of the logs of the Pacific voyagers, especially those of Captain James Cook, who explored Tahiti in 1769. The exploits of Captain Bligh and the mutineers of the *Bounty* in Tahiti in 1789 also absorbed the British. Bligh's *Narrative* (1790 folio ed.) stimulated such efforts as Mary Russell Mitford's narrative, *Christina, the Maid of the South Seas* (1811) and Byron's last completed poem, *The Island* (1823). Harriet Martineau's *Dawn Island, a Tale* (1845) and later works by Robert Louis Stevenson and Conrad highlight the vogue of the South Seas adventure story.

Early discoverers of Tahiti originated an idealized view of the island. The reports of Captain Samuel Wallis, the first European to set eyes on Tahiti in June 1767, suggested parallels between the Tahitians and the ancient Greeks, viewed by the eighteenth century as gifted children who lived at the dawn of civilization. The French navigator Louis de Bougainville, who visited Tahiti in 1768, a year before Captain Cook, also compared the Tahitians to Greek gods. For the eighteenth century, the idea of the noble savage personified the belief in the nobility and simplicity of Nature, which deists believed would reveal God to man when properly understood. Consequently, the noble Tahitians were closely identified with the tropical luxury of the island, confirming the link between the noble savage and his natural setting. Bougainville and Joseph Banks, the scientist who accompanied Captain Cook, both associated the Tahitians with such primitives of classical mythology as the inhabitants of Elysium. By 1801, classicists were reversing the comparison. In that year the classical scholar Richard Payne Knight compared the Greeks to the Tahitians in his *Analytical Enquiry into the Principles of Taste*. Significantly, the classical world permeated the European imagination of the South Pacific.[17]

Morally, the Tahitians exhibited a naturalness unseen in Europe. They became a deist's argument against the necessity of Revelation, since they possessed "a knowledge of right and wrong from the mere dictates of natural conscience," wrote John Hawkesworth.[18] Morality for them was a matter of social custom, a quality often satirized in various eighteenth-century poems like "An Epistle from Oberea . . . to Joseph Banks" by

John Scott. But others believed that natural virtue supplemented the paradise of landscape and human beauty suggested by the early accounts of travelers.

Tahiti was also a healing island, and seamen rotten with scurvy would regain their strength after several days there (largely because of the abundance of fresh fruit). Various travelers reported Tahiti as Paradise before the Fall with the inhabitants in a state of perpetual innocence intensified by stories of trees that grew bread (Tahitian breadfruit) and palms that supplied milk. Banks added that Tahiti was "the truest picture of an Arcadia of which we were going to be kings that the imagination can form" (in Smith, *E.V.*, 26). Banks also envied the sexual freedom of the people and claimed that the Tahitian women were the most elegant in the world. The clothing in particular followed nature in design and color.

The arrival in England in July 1774 of Omai, the first Tahitian to visit Great Britain, created a sensation. Former guide and interpreter for Cook, Omai was received with honor and mingled with fashionable society. Reynolds painted a full-length portrait of him, revealing an acceptable and even fashionable noble savage with a deep gaze and flowing robe set in an idealized exotic landscape and posed in a classical gesture with an outstretched right hand, suggesting affinities with antiquity. Satiric poets of the day, however, soon found Omai and the noble savage idea irresistible material. One work, in fact, called for Omai's return to England after his departure in 1776 because the English lacked natural men and Tahitian fashions must immediately displace those of Italy. While the painter William Hodges was introducing Tahitian motifs in his Italianate landscapes, poets were adopting Tahitian customs to lampoon the veneration of anything Italian which they thought dominated stylish society.

But Tahiti also had a dark side, expressed through prostitution, infanticide, and licentiousness, especially as practiced by the Areios tribe. The British understood these developments as the passing of the Golden Age that Tahiti may have once possessed. The island suddenly became a symbol not of the ideal of human happiness but of its transience. Early engravings, as well as later European art, repeatedly emphasized this theme, which subsequent missionaries and anthropologists confirmed. Yet Bougainville called Tahiti "*la Nouvelle Cythère*" and the island became notorious in the European popular mind as a land of free love. Chapbooks and engravings, especially in France, frequently detailed the erotic attractions of Tahiti. The 1824 visit to England by King Kamehameha II of the Sandwich Islands (Hawaii) increased British fascination with Polynesia, intensified by the sudden death of the king and his queen within weeks of their arrival in Britain.

Of greater importance for Collins's interest in Tahiti, however, was the 1797 landing of members of the London Missionary Society. These Evangelicals, sent out to convert the "pagans" to the doctrine of Christ, faced civil wars in 1799 and 1809 that curtailed most of their activities; but by 1815, with Pomare II in power, peace returned and Christianity flourished. Between 1815 and 1837 the missionaries exerted great political, as well as social, control over the kingdom, replacing infanticide, polygamy, and violence with moral and religious order. A monotheistic theology centering on good deeds leading to salvation substituted for the omens, idols, and sorcery of the Tahitian gods, who promoted war as well as indulgence.

In 1816 William Ellis (1794–1872), an ordained missionary for the Society, left England for Tahiti, where he would serve for the next six years. He not only learned Tahitian, but introduced the first printing press to the South Pacific, taught the Tahitians to raise various fruits and plants and, most importantly, gained their trust. In 1822 he visited Hawaii and in 1823 became part

of the first white men to circle the big island of Hawaii. By 1824
Ellis returned to England and enlarged his journal of Polynesian
life by adding observations and comparisons to life in Hawaii.
In 1825 it appeared as *A Tour Through Hawaii* and went through
five editions in three years. In 1829 Ellis published this information with what he collected on other South Pacific Islands, notably Tahiti and New Zealand, under the title *Polynesian Researches*. This two-volume edition was enlarged and published
as four volumes in 1832–34. This second edition, owned by
Wilkie Collins, is the origin of the plot as well as the characters
of *Iolâni*.[19]

The selection of Ellis by Collins as the source text for *Iolâni*
has as much to do with religion as it does with travel. Ellis's
Christian interpretation of Tahitian life both satisfied and disturbed the young Collins, whose awareness of Ellis most likely
originated through the Evangelicalism of his parents, who believed churchgoing so pleasurable that they and the family often
attended twice on Sundays. Harriet Collins converted to
Evangelicialism in 1811, snatched as a young girl from beginning a perilous career as an actress by a clergyman and his wife,
who prepared her to become a governess. William Collins was
an enthusiastic Sabbatarian and Evangelist who tolerated no
desecration of the Sabbath, which his friend, the artist John Lin-
nell, tested when he tied up some peach trees on a Sunday to the
horror of Collins.[20] Duty, earnestness, hard work, prayer, and
belief in God were the attributes of Collins's faith. The portrait
of the pious Zackeray Thorpe, Senior, and his enforcement of
Evangelical precepts in *Hide and Seek* (beginning with the sadis-
tic Sabbatarianism of the opening chapter) and the satiric presentation of Miss Clack's Evangelicalism in *The Moonstone* suggest the reaction of the young Wilkie Collins to evangelical
strictures, which his parents promoted, and the London Missionary Society institutionalized through its goal of spreading

the "knowledge of Christ among heathen and other unenlightened nations."[21]

Nonetheless, Collins read Ellis's *Polynesian Researches* carefully and accepted its indictment of immoral Tahitian life. Yet, while he agreed with the orthodox Christian critiques of Tahiti, finding the child-killing, disrespect of marriage, and constant fighting reprehensible, Collins also found himself greatly attracted to the sensational, Gothic, and dramatic aspects of the Tahitian society Ellis recounted. Quite intentionally, Collins set his novel in "Tahiti, as it was," to quote the subtitle of *Iolâni*, the period of pre-Christian omens, sorcery, and talismans. This decision not only anticipates his rejection of the conservative Evangelicalism of his parents, but anticipates his focus on the sensational, which frames the domestic in his fiction.

Ironically, but significantly, Collins turned an Evangelical account of Polynesia on its head, using the irregular features of its culture as the very source material of his first book. Drawn to the London missionary's account, Collins bypasses the morality of Ellis to discover in its opposite the story of his novel. Additionally, Collins changes the character of the enlightened King Kamehameha II of Hawaii (who was sometimes called Iolâni), into a vicious and villainous priest, another example of the reversal or inversion of sources by Collins, a habit he repeats in many of his later novels.

Ellis becomes a conduit through which Collins finds not the programmatic view of the Evangelicals but the unfettered world of licentious action and emotional intensity that became the hallmarks of his more developed sensation fiction. *Iolâni* elaborates the very qualities Ellis judges as pagan, turning them into the virtues of Collins's fiction. In a curious way, this reworking of sources parallels how Collins applied his father's aesthetic of the "correctness of observation"[22]: rather than use this technique mimetically, Collins alters it to stress the accurate pres-

entation of sensational detail and emotional crises in his writing. Just as the religious is read as the dramatic in Ellis, so, too,
is nature seen by Collins as sensational rather than natural.

The importance of Ellis for Collins begins with the protago-
nists' names each taken from *Polynesian Researches*: Idía, the
woman who fathers Iolâni's child but escapes from the priest,
Aimáta, her youthful friend and charge, and Mahíné, the rebel
leader and later husband of Aimáta, are all borrowed from Ellis.
Historically, Idía was the mother of Pomare, a Tahitian king
exiled to the nearby island of Eimero, although he triumphantly
returns; Aimáta was a young princess, the only daughter of Pomare and his queen and introduced as a six-year-old in Ellis's
history; at her marriage some years later, she possesses a "disposition volatile" yet "superior intellectual endowments." At
the death of her brother in 1827, she became queen of Tahiti. Mahíné was the chief of the Eimeo and Huahine tribes of
Tahitians.[23]

Iolâni incorporates additional statements from Ellis concerning language and its oral, rather than written, tradition. For example, a note in Collins's hand appearing on page one of the
manuscript, explaining that "the vowels of the Polynesian language are sounded in the same manner as in the Italian. Thus,
the proper names at the head of the present chapter should be
pronounced as if written—*Eolahne* and *Edeah*," derives from
I:8–10 of Ellis's first volume, where he observes that "different
Polynesian dialects abound in vowel sounds perhaps above any
other language" and that they reject "all double consonants,
possessing, invariably[,] vowel terminations, both of their syl-
lables and words. Every final vowel is therefore distinctly
sounded" (I:8–9). Furthermore, Ellis explains that "I-dí-a" is
pronounced "E-dee-ah," "Ai-má-ta" sounds like "Eye-mah-ta,"
and "Ma-hí-ne" vocalized as "Mah-he-nay" (I:10). Iolâni's name
is noticeably absent from the pronunciation list but appears

later in the final volume of the history referring to a Hawaiian king rather than a Tahitian nobleman (IV: 450–55, 471). Ellis adds that *lani* means heaven or sky.

Most interesting is Ellis's account of Kamehameha II (spelled Tamehameha by Ellis), the Hawaiian king who died in England in 1824. In describing his origins and names, Ellis notes that he was generally called *Rihoriho*, a contraction of *Kalaninui-ri-horiho* from *Ka lani*, the heavens. He also had a variety of other names, adding that "the most common of which was *Iolani*. The word *lani*, heaven or sky, formed a component part in the name of most chiefs of distinction" (IV:446). The title of Collins's novel is, therefore, an ironic acknowledgment of the remarkable Hawaiian king whose journey to England ended tragically.

The character of the actual king and Iolání, however, differ greatly. Ellis idealizes the king, calling him "good-natured, except when he was under the influence of ardent spirits"; he had an inquisitive mind, and knew much about the customs and society of North and South America, although he had never visited there (IV:446). Ellis and a Mr. Bingham were his teachers and witnessed his moral character develop into that of a fair-minded ruler whose one weakness was drink. The reasons for his trip to England, Ellis offers, were to meet the king or the chief members of the government in order to confirm the secession of the Sandwich Islands, although he sought to place himself and his islands under British protection. Ellis then rebuts the suspicion of the Sandwich Islanders that their king might have been poisoned in England in revenge for the death of Captain Cook, part of a plot to regain control over the islands.

The Iolání of Wilkie Collins's novel shares the same name but little else. Collins's figure is the archetypal powerful and evil priest, head of a group of fanatical Tahitian followers who blindly accept his decisions and sacrifices. Vindictive, the priest pursues the independently minded Idía who has borne his child but escaped his reign to avoid committing infanticide. Accompanied by her young friend Aimáta, Idía flees to a neighboring village as a cascade of events follow, including wars, sorcery, visions, and deaths. Even a wild man of the jungle appears.

In representing Tahiti, Collins discovered how he might blend the attractions of the Gothic romance (originating in his reading of Gothic fiction and Scott) with a fascination for the exotic. He could not resist engaging a world defined by the unknown and unexpected; in this the Tahitians excelled. "No place in the world," writes Ellis, "in ancient and modern times, appears to have been more superstitious than the South Sea Islanders, or to have been more entirely under the influence of dread from imaginary demons or supernatural beings" (I:361).

Ellis was the sourcebook of not only plot and character but theme, since he emphasized the unorthodox morality of the Tahitians and the immoral practice of infanticide, critical elements in Collins's story. The history of Christianity in "civilizing" Polynesia is one of the key dimensions of Ellis's text, which in Volume I contains chapters with such subtitles as "Ch. X, Infanticide, Numbers destroyed; Universality of the crime—prevalence of polygamy"; "Ch. XIV, Polynesian idols,—Human sacrifices—Demons, incantations, sorcery." Ellis stresses the spiritual customs of the islands, notably their reliance on the will of the gods: "if they were favourable, conquest was regarded as sure; but if they were unfavourable, defeat, if not death, was certain" (I:303). Enchantment was used to shape their ultimate decisions, while the supernatural became the means to learn their sanctions.

Criticism of Tahitian marriage practices, dislike of Tahitian indolence, offense at their violence, and disagreement over their treatment of women are the moral views Collins borrows from Ellis—as well as an appreciation of the picturesque landscape. The moral center of *Iolàni*, however, is its abhorrence of infanticide, which the young Collins found, as did Ellis, intolerable. Ellis provides details on its causes and acceptance in Tahitian culture, noting that it is the worst consequence of idolatry. And although the almost universal practice was "one of the indispensable regulations of the Areoi society, enforced on authority of those gods whom they were accustomed to consider as the founders of their order," it was not limited to that group (I:252). However, Collins again alters his source to suit his ends. Ellis states that both parents agreed with the killing of their child, the mother performing the deed, the father preparing its grave (I:250). In *Iolāni*, the murderous savagery is the father's alone. And no less than two thirds of Tahitian children, writes Ellis, "were massacred" in the "generations immediately preceding the subversion of paganism" (I:251–52). Not a mother from those generations escaped responsibility—a condition that may have sparked Collins to create the unorthodox character of Idía, who refuses to commit such a deed.

Graphic details of the infanticide accompany Ellis's remarks (I:253–55), although he ironically points out that if the child lived ten minutes or half an hour, it was safe. And in a statement that provides the source for the plot of *Iolāni*, Ellis writes, "there were times, when a mother's love, a mother's feelings, overcame the iron force of pagan custom, and all the mother's influence and endeavours have been used to preserve her child" (I:255). Nonetheless, there were numerous "struggles between the mother to preserve, and the father and relatives to destroy, the infant. This has arisen from the motives of false pride," he adds (I:255). The reasons advanced for justifying this deed were (a) orders from the Areoi gods; (b) the transient duration of marriage where infidelity, not allegiance, ruled (marriages could be dissolved whenever either party desired it); and (c) unacceptable progeny from those of inferior rank (I:255–56). Ellis also observes the degradation of women in Tahitian society, admitting that "their sex was often, at their birth, the cause of their destruction" (I:257). The only purpose in rearing children was to fish, to fight and to serve at the temple, all male activities. Part of Collins's reason for writing *Ioláni* may have been a youthful protest against the mistreatment of women—a theme, of course, his later fiction both depicts and condemns.

Collins criticizes marriage in Tahiti—at best a temporary social arrangement—as early as page 7 in his novel, when the narrator observes that except for a few extreme situations, "Marriage was considered by the greater portion of the inhabitants, either, as a tie to be broken and reorganized at will, as a ceremonious pandar [sic] to the fleeting passion of the hour, or, as a privilege so circumscribed by the pride of rank and possessions, as to oppose every obstacle to the few desirous of using it aright" (7). The implied support of marriage by the narrator is ironic, however, given Collins's later disavowal of the institution while privately supporting Caroline Graves and Martha Rudd, the latter with whom he had three children. Polygamy, practiced more by the Tahitians than by the Hawaiians, Ellis relates, would later become strikingly appealing to Collins.

What Collins did object to was Tahitian indolence, a cliché enlarged by Ellis in his narrative. The phlegmatic behavior of the Tahitians becomes the source of a good deal of their problems. Or as Ellis explains, their "indolence . . . was the parent of many of their crimes, infant-murder not excepted, and was also a perpetual source of much of their misery." The balmy climate, the source of their "luxurious indulgence," "strengthened their natural love of ease" and "nurtured those habits of excessive indolence" (I:450). This was offset, however, by violence. Captives in battle were usually murdered instantly, unless kept for slaves. The dead bodies were ritualistically pierced and jaw bones frequently removed. Others used the dead bodies as rollers over which they dragged their canoes. Perhaps the most gruesome application was that of cutting a hole in the dead body large enough for a warrior to thrust his head through to form a grotesque poncho: "with the head and arms of the slain hanging down before, and the legs behind him, he [the warrior] marched to renew the conflict" (I:310). Collins describes no similar act but he does outline the grim treatment of dead bodies followed by a human sacrifice to secure the return of the "occupations and amusements of peace" (I:311). Other details taken from Ellis include descriptions of war canoes, defensive battlements, and the *heiva* or grand dance performed in the presence of the king to celebrate a victorious peace. Warriors danced, while priests supplicated the gods and the war weapons were retired—until the next quarrel.

One product of the Tahitian wars and sacrifices was the supposed wild men living on the interior mountains of Tahiti. Ellis reports that in 1821 he actually saw one of these men who was "comparatively tame," although his "aspect was agitated and wild" (I:305). Collins makes use of the wild-man motif in *Ioláni* but as a form of rescue and, in a reversal of plot, salvation. The independent Idía, who rebels against the powerful Ioláni, rejecting the practice of infanticide, reverses the conventional view of Tahitian women as subservient and malleable. The energetic and active Aimáta, co-conspirator, sets the pattern for a series of forceful and unorthodox women in Collins, from the vengeful Goth, Goisvintha, in *Antonina* (whose children have been murdered by the Romans and who must hide from male persecutors, as does the heroine of *Ioláni*) to the aggressive Margaret Sherwin in *Basil*, the independent Marian Halcombe in *The Woman in White*, and the inquisitive Valeria Woodville in *The Law and the Lady*, possibly the first female detective in a full-length novel. The presentation of women in *Ioláni* anticipates what Mr. Pendril, the lawyer in *No Name* observes: "The women are few indeed, who cannot resolve firmly, scheme pa-

xxx   *Introduction*

tiently, and act promptly, where the dearest interests of their
lives are concerned."[24]

Other sources for names and incidents in *Ioláni* include Mary
Russell Mitford's popular 332-page poem, *Christina, the Maid of
the South Seas*. A verse tale of the mutinous Bounty leader Christian, who fathers a child with an island woman named "Iddeah,"
the book-length poem of four cantos stresses the lush environ-
ment of Tahiti, the fearful practice of ritual infanticide, and the
constant threat of war. The narrator at one point in Canto 2
exclaims:

> Iddeah,—O, what frenzied tears!
> A living pledge of love she bears,—
> Slaves to their superstition wild,
> The Arreoys will destroy my child!
> With its first breath will seize their prize,
> Unfathered, unrevenged it dies![25]

Anticipating a device Collins would later use in his fiction,
Mitford inserts actual documents to support her poetic interpretation of the adventures set on Pitcairn's Island in the South
Seas and includes numerous notes. "Fitzallan's Narrative" in
Canto III, for example, appears as a counter to the improbable
nature of the story. A detailed description of the canoes used by
the natives, taken by Mitford from *Captain Cook's First Voyage*,
appears on pages 206–7 and may be one source for Collins's
information about the canoes used by Ioláni and others in his
novel. Details from *Bligh's Voyage to the South Seas* and Cook's
Last Voyage Round the World also appear in the poem, as well as
references to human sacrifice, Tahitian women, and infanticide.
The Narrative of the Bounty by Bligh, appearing in a folio edition
of 1790, also mentions a character named Iddeah, with variant
spellings including "Iddea," "Ideea," and "Itia." It also details
the practice of killing the firstborn at birth. Sir John Barrow's

Account of the Mutiny of the Bounty (1831) was another possible source, as well as Captain Basil Hall's *Fragments of Voyages and Travels* (3rd series in 9 vols., 1831), which was in Collins's library.[26]

More importantly, the use of these texts indicates how Collins built a foundation of the dramatic and sensational upon the factual, a characteristic of his later work as well. His subsequent reliance on textbooks, lawyers, physicians, and even scientists for the details that would be transformed into the fictional action of his novels begins with his research on the life and customs of Tahiti for *Iolâni*. His father's obsession for working with originals—noted in the son's memoir—is analogous to Collins's determination to ground his work on such documentary sources such as Ellis's *Polynesian Researches* for *Iolâni*, Gibbon's *Decline and Fall* for *Antonina, or The Fall of Rome*, John Elliotson's *Human Physiology* for *The Moonstone*, or the case history of Madame de Douhault found in Maurice Méjan's *Recueil des Causes Célèbres* for the plot of *The Woman in White*.

IV

The full title of *Iolâni* is *Iolâni; or, Tahiti as it was. a Romance*, the subtitle immediately disclosing the setting, time, and origin of the story. Having grown up with a thorough education in the work of Mrs. Radcliffe and Scott, Collins clearly understood and enjoyed the Romance. He quickly learned to appreciate the imaginative terror, focus on suspense, element of surprise, and frequent fear that characterized the Gothic romance. A letter from 1842 records his delight at reciting "the most terrible portions of The Monk and Frankenstein" to a horrified aunt and her family.[27] Mrs. Radcliffe was particularly central: Collins's mother, Harriet, was a fan of her work and copies of *The Mysteries of Udolpho* and *The Italian* were in her son's library. Inter-

estingly, both works employ "Romance" in their full titles, sig-
nalling to the reader the character of the story before the first
page.

Implicit in the phrase *romance* is a world of invention, not
realism, akin to the definition Dr. Johnson supplied in his *Dic-
tionary*: "a tale of wild adventure in war and love." But Radcliffe,
and by extension Collins, use the term as Scott was to define it
in his 1824 "Essay on Romance" for the *Encyclopedia Britannica
Supplement*: "a fictitious narrative in prose or verse; the interest
of which turns upon marvellous and uncommon incidents."[28]
Incident, not character, the traditional formula of romance,
highlights the texts of both Radcliffe and Collins where the improbable as well as the unexpected, the violent as well as the
remote co-exist. Collins found the category useful and borrowed the term for such later titles as *Antonina, or the fall of
Rome: a romance of the fifth century* (1850), *The Moonstone: a
Romance* (1868), and *The Two Destinies: A Romance* (1876).
And to his satisfaction, *Bentley's Miscellany* ended its review of
Antonina with this statement: "The author, in his first work, has
stepped into the first rank of romance writers."[29]

Implied in the use of "Romance" in the title of *Iolâni* is the
addition of the exotic through the reference to Tahiti in the title,
linking the mystery of the South Pacific with the features of the
Gothic romance. Disappearances, supernatural occurrences, the
extreme presentation of feelings are all foreshadowed by the category of romance, which richly confuses the alien and the familiar, the natural and the unnatural. What Radcliffe's work accomplished, and what Collins in his early (as well as later) texts
explores, is the separation of female desire into power and eros
represented by the heroic Idía, in conflict with the masculine
will to power, embodied by the violent priest of the war god
Oro, Iolâni. One representation of this male power is that the

title of the novel is the name of the villain, the only Collins work with that distinction.

The Gothic romance sets the tone for *Iolâni*, with Mrs. Radcliffe the primary and Scott the secondary influences. Collins closely follows Radcliffe's pattern of a persecuted, beautiful, but solitary woman in a picturesque but threatening landscape, as he details the frantic escape into the wilderness of the lovely Idía with the child of Iolâni. Aided by her young friend and female charge, Aimáta, and later protected by a king, Mahíné, Idía nonetheless faces threats, attacks, and natural dangers in her escape from the vengeful and powerful priest. The idea of religion being associated with such behavior recalls *The Italian; or, The Confessional of the Black Penitents: A Romance* (1797), Radcliffe's late novel, where the imprisonment and escape of the heroine from the mountain convent of San Stefano and the exposure of the tyranny of the Church, anticipate Collins's critique of the abuses of Tahitian religion and customs before the arrival of Christianity. Indeed, part of Collins's implicit theme is the value of Christianity for the Tahitians, a distinct emphasis in Ellis's history of the island. Beauty—of the landscape as well as the characters—plus terror—of the jungle as well as the villains—establish the atmosphere of both Mrs. Radcliffe's fiction and that of *Iolâni* where passion inflames behavior.

Another parallel between Radcliffe and Collins is the heroine, importantly a mother, and one who resists, acts, and initiates. Idía, like Emily St. Aubert in *Mysteries of Udolpho* or Ellena in *The Italian,* displays the virtues of fortitude and endurance. But Collins also reveals the subjectivity of his heroine, sometimes at the expense of the plot. This subjectivity opposes the codes of morality and society, which in Radcliffe and Collins is often made up of mysterious conspiracies and deceptive if not immoral actions. Idía, disempowered by the formal levels of society, nonetheless seeks her independence and freedom at any cost, rejecting sexual dominance and economic dependence, foregoing any element of social privilege or protection. This behavior sets a pattern for the major heroines of Collins's later fiction which a passage in *Ioláni* summarizes:

> In women, more universally than in men, the necessity for action generates the power. Their energies, though less various, are more concentrated and—by their position in existence—less over-tasked than ours; hence in most cases of extremity, where *we* deliberate, *they* act; and if, in consequence, their failures are more deplorable, their successes are, for the same reason, more triumphant and entire. (20)

In *Ioláni*, only the courageous King Maháni saves Idía from her nightmare fate; he defends her from the violence of Ioláni, whose future becomes enmeshed in a political battle with the king for land. Terror becomes a narrative device in *Ioláni*, driving the plot as it moves into the theme of pursuit and capture. *Ioláni* is a Tahitian Gothic romance, blending a documentary source text with the subjective imagination and supernatural elements of the Gothic.

For Collins, Scott represented the historical in fiction and the successful union of fact with imagination. In using Scottish history to fashion his stories, Scott showed Collins how to employ actual events in an imaginative construct. Hence, the reliance but not dependence by Collins on Tahitian history as represented by Ellis and the accounts of the "Bounty." But typically, Collins located a foundation for his imaginary adventures in the actual narratives of Tahitian life. By successfully emulating the technique of Scott through the incorporation of history in his story, Collins blended the improbable with the documentary and succeeded in uniting what would become the distinguishing feature of his later, sensational fiction: the domestication of the Gothic through the terror of the everyday.

Understandably, there have been until recently few accounts of *Iolâni* and none that deal with the text.[30] But now, with the publication of the novel more than one hundred and fifty years after its composition, that will change. *Iolâni* stands as the important beginning of a writing career that spanned forty-seven years and more than thirty-five titles. It is the crucial first work of an author distinguished for his dramatic, sensational, and popular writing.

NOTES

1. George D. Smith in Wilkie Collins, *Iolâni, The Original Autograph Manuscript* (New York: Glenn Horowitz Bookseller, [1991]), 13.

2. Marvin Felheim, *The Theatre of Augustin Daly* (Cambridge, Mass.: Harvard University Press, 1956), 102.

3. Clyde E. Hyder, "Wilkie Collins in America," *University of Kansas Humanistic Studies* 6 (1940):50–58.

4. Joseph Francis Daly, *The Life of Augustin Daly* (New York: Macmillan, 1917), 306.

5. Wilkie Collins, "Letter of Dedication," *Basil*, ed. Dorothy Goldman (1852; Oxford: Oxford World's Classics, 1990), xxxvii.

6. Catherine Peters, *The King of Inventors: A Life of Wilkie Collins* (London: Secker & Warburg, 1991), 55. All references to this edition unless otherwise noted.

7. Wilkie Collins, *Hide and Seek*, ed. Catherine Peters (Oxford: Oxford World's Classics, 1993), 45.

8. Wilkie Collins, *Men and Women*, 5 February 1887, in William M. Clarke, *The Secret Life of Wilkie Collins*, rev. edition (Stroud, Gloucestershire: Alan Sutton, 1996), 45. The location of Antrobus & Co. may have actually stimulated Collins's literary ambitions. Next door, at 445 The Strand, were the publishers of *Saturday Magazine*. Close by were *Punch*, the

Illustrated London News, Bell's *Life in London*, the *Observer*; Chapman & Hall's various monthlies were at 186 The Strand. In August 1843 Douglas Jerrold's *Illuminated Magazine* (320 The Strand) published Collins's first signed article, "The Last Stage Coachman," a sure catalyst for the literary desires of a young writer shortly to begin his first novel.

    9. Collins in Edmund Yates, "W. Wilkie Collins," *The Train* (June 1857), rpt. in Yates, *Celebrities at Home*, 3rd Series (London, 1879), 355.

    10. Collins in Yates, *Celebrities*, 355.

    11. William Collins to Longmans, 8 March 1845, British Library add. ms. 42575 f.158.

    12. Wilkie Collins (WC) to Harriet Collins, 30 September 1845. Pierpont Morgan Library, MA 3150 19.

    13. WC in George W. Towle, "Wilkie Collins," *Appleton's Journal* (3 September 1870), 279.

    14. WC in *Men and Women* (5 February 1887), 281, cited in Peters, *King of Inventors*, 65.

    15. WC in *Men and Women* (5 February 1887), quoted in Clarke, *Secret Life*, 47.

    16. Wilkie Collins, "The Captain's Last Love," *The Spirit of the Times* [NY] (23 December 1876); *Belgravia* 31 (January 1877), 263, 274. Collins retitled the story "Mr. Captain and the Nymph" when he reissued it in *Little Novels* (1887). The story appears as "The Captain's Last Love," in Collins's *Mad Monkton and Other Stories*, ed. Norman Page (Oxford: Oxford World's Classics, 1994), 333–54, but as "Mr Captain and the Nymph," in *Wilkie Collins: The Complete Shorter Fiction*, ed. Julian Thompson (New York: Carroll & Graf, Inc., 1995), 563–77.

    17. Bernard Smith, in *European Vision and the South Pacific, 1768–1850* (Oxford: Clarendon Press, 1960), henceforth referred to as *E.V.*, and in his *Imagining the Pacific* (New Haven: Yale University Press, 1992), expertly surveys the method and importance of the European vision of Polynesia. Also useful is Neil Rennie, *Far-Fetched Facts: The Literature of Travel and the Idea of the South Seas* (Oxford: Clarendon Press, 1995). The standard account of Tahiti, masterfully detailing the history of the islands, is Douglas L. Oliver's *Ancient Tahitian Society*, 3 vols. (Honolulu: University of Hawaii Press, 1974).

    18. Hawkesworth in Smith, *E.V.*, 27.

19. Melville, who also owned the book, refers to Ellis's *Polynesian Researches* in his "Preface" to *Omoo*, while Harriet Martineau's 1845 novel, *Dawn Island, A Tale*, similarly draws from Ellis. The name of the heroine is Idya, who flees to a remote part of the island to escape sacrifice with her lover and her protector, a priest of the island. Collins's copy of Ellis is recorded as item 39 in *Catalogue of the Interesting Library . . . Of the Late Wilkie Collins* sold at auction by Puttick and Simpson on 20 January 1890.

20. Peters, *King of Inventors*, 8; Dorothy L. Sayers, *Wilkie Collins*, ed. E. R. Gregory (Toledo, Ohio: Friends of the Toledo Library, 1977), 43.

21. Richard Lovett, *The History of the London Missionary Society 1795–1895* (London: Henry Frowde, 1899), 30.

22. Wilkie Collins, *Memoirs of the Life of William Collins, Esq R.A.* (1848; London: E. P. Publishing, 1978), II:316.

23. William Ellis, *Polynesian Researches*, 2nd ed. enlarged, 4 vols. (London: Fisher, Son and Jackson, 1831–32), II:560–62. All references to this edition unless otherwise noted. For information on Mahíné see I:246.

24. Wilkie Collins, *No Name*, ed Virginia Blain (Oxford: World's Classics, 1986), 92.

25. Mary Russell Mitford, *Christina, the Maid of the South Seas* (London: Rivington, 1811), Canto 2, Verse XXIV:74.

26. Also listed as item 39 in *Catalogue of the Interesting Library . . . of the Late Wilkie Collins* (1890).

27. Wilkie Collins to William Collins, postmarked 24 August 1842, Pierpont Morgan Library, MA 3155. The aunt was Catherine Gray.

28. Samuel Johnson cited in Sir Walter Scott, "Essay on Romance," *Encylopedia Britannica Supplement VI* (Edinburgh, 1824), 435; Scott, ibid.

29. *Bentley's Miscellany* XXVII (April 1850), 378, in *Wilkie Collins, the Critical Heritage*, ed. Norman Page (London: Routledge & Kegan Paul, 1974), 42.

30. Among those who record the discovery of the text are Catherine Peters in the 1992 paperback reprint of her Collins biography, *The King of Inventors* (London: Minerva, 1992), and in Appendix C of the 1993 Princeton University Press American edition of the book; William M. Clarke, in his 1996 revision of *The Secret Life of Wilkie Collins* (Stroud, Gloucestershire: Allan Sutton, 1996); and Lillian Nayder in her 1997 introductory study, *Wilkie Collins* (New York: Twayne, 1997).

✒ EDITORIAL POLICY ✒

In the absence of other textual witnesses, the manuscript copy of *Ioláni* necessarily becomes the only copytext. The editorial policy of this first edition of the novel is to provide an accurate reading text of the work and to indicate all deletions, cancellations, and emendations of wording. In some instances, as on page 127, line 13, Collins removed, crossed out, or altered individual words or sets of words as he wrote or revised the manuscript. Because this is Collins's first attempt at novel writing, it is important to see Collins at work, drafting, revising, and altering his material. All wording variants, deleted from the text, are therefore recorded with the lemma repeated only for purposes of identification. For example, the deletion of a word, now illegible, following "disposed" on page 137, line 1 is presented thus: disposed] disposed ⟨*illegible*⟩. Angled brackets ⟨ ⟩ indicate deletions. Square brackets [ ] indicate an editorial insertion. A revision occurring in the same line as an earlier reading is marked "[*altered in same line*]."

The edited text also reproduces Collins's inconsistent spelling, because it conveys the immediacy of his manuscript composition and sense of process in creating the story. Similarly, I have maintained his unorthodox punctuation, which has a rhetorical and emphatic role in the text. Capitalization, paragraphing, and dashes remain as Collins presents them. Unintentionally omitted accents, however, have been added, and the spelling of "Tahíti" (also spelled Tahìti by Collins) has been used throughout. The altered accent on Tahíti appears too infrequently to justify disruption to the reader.

✸ BIBLIOGRAPHICAL DESCRIPTION ✸

The bound manuscript, entirely in the hand of Wilkie Collins, consists of 167 leaves: four gatherings with two extra free end papers bound in at the front of the volume and two at the back. The first gathering consists of 52 leaves; the second of 39 leaves (folios 53–91), with one leaf apparently tipped in on the stub of a previously canceled leaf numbered 57 in the manuscript; the third gathering of 44 leaves (folios 92–135) and the fourth of 28 leaves (folios 136–163).

Folios 1–52 consist of the title page, a blank leaf, a leaf containing an epigram, and folios 1–49 in Collins's foliation; folios 53–91 correspond to folios 50–88 in Collins's foliation; folios 92–135 to 89–132 in Collins's foliation; folios 136–163 to folios 133–160 in Collins's foliation.

The leaves are cream in color and measure 25.4 cm. x 20 cm. Four watermarks can be identified: a small fleur-de-lis, a large fleur-de-lis, "BUNE," and "1844." Horizontal chain lines for all four types of paper are artificially imposed and are 2.5 cm. apart.

The manuscript is bound in a brown leather, Pfister binding measuring 26 cm. x 21 cm. with a gold stamped spine, which reads: [raised band 20.5 mm.] IOLANI AND IDIA [raised band 20.5 mm.] COLLINS [raised band 20.5 mm.] [raised band 20.5 mm.] [raised band 20.5 mm]. The inside boards and endpapers are a light marbled pink.

❧ NOTE ON THE TEXT ❧

The uniform neatness of the manuscript suggests that it is a fair copy, since corrections, emendations, and cancellations are at a minimum. The clean copy reflects none of the hesitations of a first draft with its accompanying insertions, deletions, revisions, or structural changes. Nor are there any notes suggesting the length of episodes or chapters, all features of the manuscript for *Antonina*, Collins's second novel, now at the Harry Ransom Humanities Research Center at the University of Texas at Austin. *Antonina* remains his first published novel (London: Richard Bentley, 1850), but not his first written. The manuscript of his third novel, *Basil*—at the British Library—is also corrected, revised, and reworked, a characteristic of his later manuscripts as well. The manuscript of *Iolàni* is most likely the fair copy that possibly circulated among Longmans and, later, Chapman and Hall.

Book I

"In secret we met—
In silence I grieve,
That thy heart could forget,
Thy spirit deceive."

Byron

(1)

Chapter I
Iolâni and Idía.

The last days of summer were near at hand, as one night, (while Tahiti was yet undiscovered by the voyagers of the North) the desolation ~~and ride~~ of the great lake Vahíria was brightened by the presence of two human beings — a man and woman — who were listlessly wandering along its rugged and deserted shores.

It was a strange and, to most hearts, an unalluring place. Looking upward from the spot occupied on this particular occasion by the woman and her companion, the eye encountered a long and almost unbroken range of mountains, whose jagged sides, though occasionally checquered by a clump of dwarf trees, or a patch of parched, ~~scanty~~ verdure, were for the most part bare and precipitous in the extreme. The different masses that formed the chain, were generally but little distinguishable, the one from the other, ~~and were scarcely to distinguish~~ either in form or elevation, but were relieved from absolute sameness, by the presence of the immense Orohéna (the loftiest mountain in the island) that farther in the distance, rose like a beacon over the tops of the inferior ranges. Lower, between the mountains and the lake, stretched large, dense tracts of forest land; and beneath these again, lay in the utterest confusion, mass upon mass of basalt rock, wild and jagged in form and reaching down almost to the water side; while, the waves of the Lake, but partially lightened by the rays of the young moon and preserved ~~from~~ at most points from the wind by their natural guardians of forest and rock, looked wilder and gloomier than all beside, as they stretched forth dull and stagnant — here utterly lost in darkness, there faintly gleaming in the pale and fitful light. Truly, it was a desert and fearful spot. Hardly could the mind imagine from the appearance of those barren mountains, that their farther sides overlooked every variety that Nature could bestow — every charm that the seasons could dispense, and the blessed sunlight watch over and adorn.

Not a human habitation was to be seen on the borders of Vahíria. The natives generally, had a dread of the place and

---

* It may be necessary, perhaps, at the outset of our narrative, to inform the reader that the vowels of the Polynesian language are sounded in the same manner as in the Italian. Thus, the proper names at the head of the present chapter should be pronounced as if written — Eolahne and Edeah.

CHAPTER I

Ioláni and Idía

The last days of summer were near at hand, as one night, (while Tahíti was yet undiscovered by the voyagers of the North) the desolation of the great lake Vahíria was brightened by the presence of two human beings— a man and woman who were listlessly wandering along its rugged and deserted shores.

It was a strange and, to most hearts, an unalluring place. Looking upward from the spot occupied on this particular occasion by the woman and her companion, the eye encountered a long and almost unbroken range of mountains, whose jagged sides, though occasionally checquered by a clump of dwarf trees, or a patch of parched, scanty verdure, were for the most part bare and precipitous in the extreme. The different masses that formed the chain, were generally but little distinguishable, the one from the other, either in form or elevation, but were relieved from absolute sameness, by the presence of the immense Orohéna (the loftiest mountain in the island) that farther in the distance, rose like a beacon over the tops of the inferior ranges. Lower, between the mountains and the lake, stretched large, dense tracts of forest land; and beneath these again, lay in the utterest confusion, mass upon mass of basalt

---

*It may be necessary, perhaps, at the outset of our narrative, to inform the reader that the vowels of the Polynesian language are sounded in the same manner as in the Italian. Thus, the proper names at the head of the present chapter should be pronounced as if written—*Eolahne* and *Edeah*.

rock, wild and jagged in form and reaching down almost to the
water side; while, the waves of the Lake, but partially lightened
by the rays of the young moon and preserved at most points
from the wind by their natural guardians of forest and rock,
looked wilder and gloomier than all beside, as they stretched
forth dull and stagnant—here utterly lost in darkness, there
faintly gleaming in the pale and fitful light. Truly, it was a desert and fearful spot. Hardly could the mind imagine from the
appearance of those barren mountains, that their farther sides
overlooked every variety that Nature could bestow—every
charm that the seasons could dispense, and the blessed sunlight
watch over and adorn.

Not a human habitation was to be seen on the borders of
Vahíria. The natives generally, had a dread of the place and
shunned it with the utmost perseverance. Their strange superstition had stored it for them, long since, with the spirits of the
dead and the daemons of a bloodshed and crime. Here, also,
had been occasionally seen those wretched outcasts of humanity—the wild men, who haunted the loneliest fastnesses, at that
period, of the mountains of Tahíti. These unfortunates, whose
former existence in the Pacific Islands is well known even to
the European traveller, were either confirmed and dangerous
madmen, or victims marked by the relentless Priesthood of the
land, for human sacrifices, who had escaped a horrible and
often undeserved death, by embracing the melancholy alterna-
tive of perpetual exile from their kind.

Of the two wanderers in this solitary spot, the woman was, in
appearance, the most impressive and uncommon. Her face,
thoroughly southern in its dusky, monotonous hue, and its
soft, intelligent expression, possessed the additional attraction
of an almost European regularity and refinement of feature. Her
figure was taller and more slender than the general order of female forms among the population of the Islands, and was set off

to the utmost advantage, by the simple and yet luxurious dress in which she was habited. No envious apparel concealed the delicate rounding of her shoulder, or the soft, regular heaving of the bosom below. The forepart of the sort of double shawl worn by the Polynesian women, she had cast over her shoulder, so that it fell gracefully back upon the long, white tunic that hung beneath; while, her beautiful and deep black hair, partially gathered up by a chaplet of flowers, streamed over all, in exquisite contrast with the snowy whiteness of her habiliment. Of her companion, it may be sufficient to say, that his appearance was chiefly remarkable from his great stature and from a commanding and dignified expression of countenance.

The connection existing between these two individuals, though considered as a serious moral infraction of the laws of society, in civilized countries, excited, among the luxurious people of the Pacific Islands, neither indignation, nor contempt. Saving in a few instances of extreme and extraordinary attachment, Marriage was considered by the greater portion of the inhabitants, either, as a tie to be broken and reorganized at will, as a ceremonious pandar to the fleeting passion of the hour, or, as a privilege so circumscribed by the pride of rank and possessions, as to oppose every obstacle to the few desirous of using it aright.

In the present instance, on the woman's side, unhallowed love was the simple and necessary consequence of the proud position of her companion among his people; for it was no other than Iolāni, Priest of Oro[,] the War-god, and brother of the King, whom the lowly-born Idía had won to the desert solitudes around the shores of the Lake.

Cunning, was the great principle of this man's life. It had supplied him with the means of securing every variety of iniquitous triumph, without a chance of failure or detection. In no character could more vile and dangerous elements be more se-

cretly and securely lodged than in his. His natural malignity of
disposition, was shielded by the most indomitable patience and
contrivance. His cruelty, was refined by invention and aided by
caution; and his fiery passions, were concealed by the most
consummate hypocrisy and set off by the most ensnaring eloquence of speech and demeanour. The peculiar charms of Idía,
caught at first sight, his sensual fancy, and he won her affections, as he had won the affections of all others before her, in
security and triumph.

His last—perhaps for the time—his best beloved, was a
woman, whose strong and many affections, destined her to a
troubled existence either of turbulent joy or of overwhelming
sorrow. Unlike the generality of her sex in the Pacific Islands,
her emotions ran invariably into extremes, and the delusive impulse of the moment, decided her as dangerously as invariably,
in every action of her life. From the moment when she had
given her love, freely, truly and unsuspiciously, to the deceitful
Priest, every thought of her heart was unconsciously dedicated
to him alone. She looked at him, not as what he was, but as
what he should be. To *her*, he was all in all—the one, bright
perfection, that it was a delight to gaze upon and love. For,
while it is the doubtful superiority of the mind, in much, to
behold but an insufficiency; it is the humbler and happier faculty of the heart, in a little, to acknowledge an abundance.

And so she wandered on with him, through the solemn
hours of that beautiful night, careless of the dangers with
which superstition had stored the place, while her beloved was
by her side, and revelling in her brief season of happiness, as
securely as if misery had fled the habitations of earth, and guile
had departed for ever from the human heart!

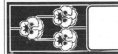

CHAPTER II

Aimáta and Home

It is summer and early morning. The young sun, whose rays, scarcely penetrate as yet, the solemn darkness of the groves and forests, shows beautiful and bright, on the meadowlands at the mountains['] feet. The sea-breeze has just arisen and hies it hither and thither, among the inland adornments of the Islands of the South. It refreshes the fruits, it awakens the flowers. It carries with it its own fitful and delicate music, in the pattering of the falling dewdrops, as it shakes them merrily from their topmost haunts in the great trees and their smallest hiding-places in the fresh, sweet-smelling grass. It sings softly among the loose thatching leaves by the side of the hut, and murmurs pleasantly through the fissures in the rocks and the light brush-wood, at the entrance of the forest dells. It is a messenger of pleasure—a welcome and familiar friend to the happy people of the land. They go forth to meet it with joy, for it is the harbinger, to the Islanders, of merriment and day.

Removed from the straggling village and some miles distant from the coast, stands a solitary habitation, in the pleasantest spot of the more inland portion of the Island. Its rude door is drawn back, but, as yet, no one passes the entrance. At last, a tame turtle-dove flutters out and is followed, in its morning flight, by a young girl.

Singing its soft, monotonous song, the bird flies over the white coral pavement before the house, over the garden plantation and meadowland and into the scattered wood, that stretches almost to the hill-side beyond. Carolling and laughing to herself, the girl still follows her companion. Her simple robe, disarranged by the rapidity of her motion, discloses a supple and delicate form, unrounded by maturity as yet, but tempting to look upon, even now. Onward she wends, wherever her play-mate leads her. Now, she lingers over the wild-flowers at her feet. Now, she starts up and looks for the presence, or listens for the voice, of her gentle favourite. Now, she bounds rejoicingly along the pathways of the wood, or pauses, enamoured of its music and its brightness, by the streamlet that glitters at her side. Here, she playfully chides the briars and creepers that op-pose her advance. There, she laughs with innocent delight, as some small, sudden peep of forest scenery, more beautiful than all she has hitherto beheld, appears before her. Bright and happy as at her setting out, looks she on her return, when she rests at last at her habitation and watches in the soft, clear distance, her favourite's homeward flight.

As she sits listening there, the sound, from the neighbouring vallies, of the cloth-maker's mallet, mellowed and harmonized by distance, rings merrily upon her ear. Now, its pauses are filled by the noise of the woodman's axe—now, by the voices of the journeyers to the village beyond—now, by the rippling of the stream, that runs through the garden of the hut.

She looks downward to the pathway among the trees, that leads to the village. Beautiful, in her unrestrained inartificial attitude of repose, what Eve in her innocence, was to the Para-dise around her, that seems she, to the charms of the land that she lives in and loves. The most artless gaiety and grace of child-hood and the most alluring softness and bashfulness of youth, mingle on her countenance; whose attraction, appears not in regularity of feature, or fairness of complexion; but, simply, in the youth and innocence—in the enchanting variableness and suddenness of its every expression. No wearing and anxious contemplations are her's. Her thoughts rise upon her mind, only to startle and delight, and never linger there long enough, to weary, or confuse. She is still as God made her; unpolluted by misery and unmarred by man.

Already, the village pathway is trodden by many feet. Sometimes, a company of women pass before her eyes, their bright-coloured garments glittering in the sunlight, that has already penetrated the spaces between the trees. Sometimes, a troop of fishermen are seen, bending beneath the weight of the spoil that they have taken in the night; and sometimes, a young warrior—impatiently furbishing his maiden arms and longing for the field of battle from his inmost heart—swells the ranks of the journeyers through the woodland avenue. All these, as they pass, the girl watches with careless delight, until a solitary woman appears among the trees; and then, an expression of the utmost interest and joy takes possession of her countenance, for she recognizes her one guide and companion, in the night-wanderer by the shores of the great Lake.

Slowly and wearily, Idía paces onward. There is a strange mournfulness at her heart as she gains the hut and returns Aimáta's impatient caress. There is a sorrowfulness, mingled with the gentleness of her expression, as she listens to the girl's animated narrative of her chase after the turtle-dove. A strange feeling of discomfort and inexplicable foreboding of she knows not what, is overcasting her mind, now that she is in her own abiding place. There is no visible reason for its assailing her, but it still hangs over her, in spite of her efforts for its removal. Is it an affectionate fear for the future of her young charge? Is it conscience, hitherto unnoticed and unknown at last, asserting its existence within her? Is it a warning from her guardian angel of some calamity in store?—

She sinks down upon the soft grass floor of the dwelling.

Silent and abstracted, she notices not the pleasant array of fresh gathered fruits, that Aimáta is arranging before her. The girl proposes question after question, but remains unanswered still. She exercises many a cunning art, attempts many an innocent stratagem, to entrap her sorrowful companion into merriment as enduring and as lively as her own, but in vain. At last, she relinquishes her purpose in despair. She curbs her natural gaiety, and sitting down, she nestles her head on the bosom of Idía, and looking up lovingly and hesitatingly in her face, she invites her attention to one of the wild, poetical legends of the land; which, she has now perfectly acquired, and which she tells in a half whisper, sometimes, pausing to watch its effect upon the woman's demeanour. A tear has gathered in her eye as the girl pursues her task, but she speaks not, moves not, yet; and the story-teller ends her tale, and is still unrewarded by success.

Alas! In the dark recesses round the Lake Vahíria, and in her midnight communings with Ioláni, the Priest, Idía has lost, for ever, the charm—once so treasured in possession of Aimáta and Home!

CHAPTER III

The Birth in sorrow

Between the inhabitants of the lonely dwelling, there had sprung up, in spite of disproportion in ages and difference in sympathies, the strongest attaching ties. When only assumed for convenience sake, there is no hypocrisy so perishable—when arising from mutual esteem, there is no sincerity so enduring—as female friendship; and this rare and beautiful affection existed in its utmost truthfulness and purity, between the woman and her charge. Of the parents of Idía, one, had died, and the other, had departed for the dwellings of a distant and stranger tribe. She had discovered the child Aimáta, forsaken by her natural guardians, almost in her infancy, and had taken pity upon her forlornness and sheltered and cared for her, herself. In a land, where the domestic ties were often but carelessly recognized, such an event as the abandonment of offspring—though uncommon, was not unknown; and Idía retained undisturbed possession of the girl, up to the time of her introduction to the reader. A better protector, the forsaken child could not have obtained; for as yet, her guardian, had not lost the honest, affectionate sympathy of the people of the land. She was beloved and reverenced by the women, and but seldom visited, by the merciless contempt, so frequently bestowed by the men, upon the female population of this island. To the one sex, she was endeared by the unvarying gentleness and humility of her demeanour. To the other, she was estimable, in the earlier portions of her existence, from her superiority (apparent, though unaccountable) to the women around her; in the later, from her intimate connexion with the high-born and powerful Ioláni, High Priest of Oro.

In this man, centered the one, important difference of feeling, between the woman and her charge. For, persuade as eloquently as she would, Idía could never conquer the girl's aversion to the presence and even the name of the religious principal of the land.

This disagreement, fatal as it might seem to be, and might in truth have been, in many cases, wrought no evil influence on the attachment between guardian and guarded. Aimáta's aversion to the Priest, invincible as it was, was a sorrowful but never an insulting dislike, and awoke, consequently, pity and astonishment, rather than anger and contempt, in the heart of Ioláni's beloved. She was so submissive, so affectionate to her protector, so innocent and uncomplaining in the long solitudes she was now doomed to encounter, that to scorn or forsake her must have been almost too much even for humanity's refined capacity for crime.

Such then were the positions of Idía and her young charge, in the season of their happiness, when their lives were passed in that dreamy monotony of pleasure, so spiritless, when described, so delightful, when experienced. Her usual round of innocent amusements, still sufficed to occupy Aimáta's hours of solitude; and Idía's meetings with the Priest, were as frequent and as undisturbed, as at the first. Thus, the days—those days to be spent in rejoicing to be remembered in woe—glided quietly onward. But a change was rapidly approaching in the fortunes of the girl and her guardian, and in the hour of travail, that was already at hand for the woman, lay its destined signal of commencement for both.

The day that ushered in the event which forms the subject of this chapter, was one of the most beautiful, of the beautiful season that still lingered over the Islands of the South. At some distance from the dwelling of Idía, in a sort of half cavern, half arbour, lay sleeping—sheltered from the noontide heat—the girl Aimáta. The place was situated on a hill, and raised, by a rocky eminence, considerably above the regular and public footway. How its present tenant could have gained such a position, was a marvel; for there existed no visible means of ascent to the strange resting place she had chosen. In her restless slumber, her light clothing had become so discomposed, as to leave the upper part of her form—so delicate in shape, so enchantingly soft and dusky in hue—almost entirely uncovered. Her long hair, drooped over and partially concealed her neck and bosom. One hand, (on which she had pillowed her cheek) still grasped a profusion of the flowers she had gathered in the morning, some of which, clustered in exquisite confusion, over the lower portion of her countenance. The other, rested upon her hip, as if sleep had overcome her, at the moment when she had attempted to arrange the garment that had fallen from her side, in its appointed place. There she lay, in the beauty of innocence and youth! The worthy child of the softest of climates and the loveliest of earthly lands!

Suddenly, however, she started from her sleep and hastily gathering her vesture around her, hurried to the entrance of the cavern.

Two well-known voices, raised in anger and agitation, had struck upon her ear, from the pathway immediately below her. She looked cautiously out. In a few minutes, Ioláni the Priest passed beneath; his swarthy countenance, terrible to look upon in its deep, concentrated expression of fury. She could hear him, muttering to himself and laughing horribly and unnaturally, as he sped onward in the direction of the villages on the coast. She waited until he was out of sight, and then, swinging herself down the almost perpendicular sides of her natural hermitage, by means of the bushes and projections of rock, with extraordinary fearlessness and agility; she ran forward, in the opposite direction to that taken by the Priest.

She had proceeded but a short distance, before she encountered Idía, standing alone, in a rocky recess by the roadside. The woman's deep, olive complexion, had changed to a ghastly paleness; her eyes, wandered wildly backwards and forwards, over the landscape before her; and her hands were pressed on her forehead, as if a deep, dreadful agony had suddenly assailed her. The instant she perceived Aimáta, she seized her almost roughly by the arm, and dragging her close up to her side, spoke a few words in her ear in a harsh, moaning voice. The next moment, the girl fell at her feet and burst into a passion of tears.

What this intelligence was, and why it affected so fearfully both narrator and listener, can be only satisfactorily explained to the reader, by an instant's investigation of one of the few revolting points in the Polynesian character—the deplorable prevalence among the people of the crime of infanticide.

This reproach to the nation, was intimately connected with, if not entirely originated by, a sect of licensed libertines who have existed, under different names, in the Pacific Islands, from the earliest known periods, and whose extraordinary institutions, it will be our duty to revert to, at a future opportunity. Among the rules of this atrocious society, to the prohibition of marriage among its members was added the regulation, that their children should be invariably destroyed at birth. This point of law among the Areoi body, in particular, soon became a point of convenience, among the people, in general; either the poverty, the pride, or the barbarity, of the parents, being the three principal causes of the destruction of the offspring. If a man's possessions were but scanty, if the results of his labour, were precarious and trifling, the impossibility of rearing his children in comfort and plenty, was considered reason sufficient for their death, the instant they entered the world. If a chieftain of rank, contracted an intimacy with a woman from the lower orders of the people, the results of such a connexion, were deemed unworthy of the father[']s care; and were, consequently, destroyed at birth. In the case of a long war, when the ranks of the male members of the population decreased with ominous rapidity, this authorised system of infanticide, was of necessity, partially checked; as the number of children, that from motives of convenience, affection, or need, were generally spared, would, in such a crisis, be unable to supply the sudden and unusual deficiency. So thoroughly, however, among these deluded people, was natural affection overpowered by the insane dread of overpopulation that had induced the ruling powers to authorise infanticide in the first instance, that the frequent remonstrance and resistance of the mother, against the savage intentions of the father and the male relations, was regarded, either as a matter of ridicule, or of downright insult and offence; and the wretched parent, had the misery of seeing her offspring murdered before her eyes, unless she could by any means prolong its existence a quarter of an hour from its birth; in which case, the law decreed that it was thenceforward to be permitted to live.

Such, (briefly analyzed) was infanticide in the Pacific Islands; and such was the crime, to which the Priest had tempted the wretched woman, who had entrusted to him her priceless though simple dowry of affection and truth. Her indignant and positive refusal of his iniquitous demand, instantaneously converted the careless cruelty of his intention towards his unborn offspring, into settled and malignant hatred towards the mother. The woman's charms, had long since, begun to pall upon him. Satiety—crime's safest pathway to the heart—had already urged him to cast her off; but so patient, so doubly affectionate, had she grown with him in spite of his scarce-concealed indifference, that even he, villain as he was, could not forsake her, without some shadow of a pretext. The opportunity for abandoning her she had now provided, by her reception of his proposal, herself; and he seized it with impatience and delight.

But his evil intentions did not end here. The most dangerous period to the offender, is the half hour that follows the offence; for, though the heart create[s] enmity, it is the mind that perfects its work. Thus was it with the Priest. The triumph of having gained his end sufficed him in the honour of parting, but, no sooner had he addressed himself to his solitary journey, than other thoughts began to work within him.

He had been scorned and defied—*he*, the man of power and celebrity, whose nod had, until now, been a command, whose slightest word a law—and by whom?—By a woman!—By an inferior creature in the scale of beings—a household drudge—an appointed slave to the sensuality of man! The meanest husbandman in the island, would rage to have such an indignity as he—the brother of the King, the War-god's Prophet and Priest—had just undergone!

She had not entreated for the child. She had not humbled herself to him for the favor of its life. She had threatened and despised him. It was too much to bear.

Revenge—safe, speedy, ample revenge—he was determined to have; but how should he effect it? Should he attempt the destruction of his child, at the hour of its birth? This, would be fulfilling his first object as well as satisfying his vengeance; and that, moreover, (as the custom of the country ensured) at no peril to himself. To think with him was to act and he immediately turned and retraced his steps.

In a short time, he gained the women's track, and as he halted for an instant, to watch them unobserved, another inspiration, more Satanic than the first, flashed over his mind.

The girl Aimáta, was now hastening to maturity. She was the woman's beloved—her comfort and delight in all seasons. She was innocent and fair and even now, in the first dawn of maidenhood. What a tool for his vengeance might he make of her! How admirably, here, would his lust second and sweeten his revenge! How surely would all that grief left unpreyed on in the detestable Idía, be thus devoured by Jealousy! Here, was truly a tremendous and long-lived process of retribution discovered at last! Bide but the convenient time, and all was sure. Be wary and determined in his attempt, and triumph and success must be his!

Determining thus, the villain set forth again to dog the steps of his victims—now, lurking among the foliage, when they stopped to glance back; now, closing upon their track, when they entered the woods; now, falling far behind, when they emerged upon the plains; but never, for an instant, allowing either to escape his eye.

Meanwhile, the women had been as diligent in preparing for their safety, as the Priest in compassing their downfall. Helpless though Idía might be under the sudden infliction of misery that had befallen her, her helplessness was of the moment, alone. A stern determination had already grown within her, to preserve the child, though she perished in the attempt. The vileness of the Priest[']s proposal, had horrified but had not overwhelmed her; and the desperation of purpose, of a woman whose affections have been outraged without cause, arose, erelong, to fortify her heart against everything that was selfish in emotion or enervated in thought.

And the poor girl—whose innocence, was already marked by the spoiler for his prey; who had been taught to expect a future companion and employment, in the yet unborn child—even *she* seemed to have learned from the hour of sorrow, a determination beyond her years. Dependant upon others, as she had been all her life, by the force of circumstance, she stood forth at this moment a host in herself. In women, more universally than in men, the necessity for action generates the power. Their energies, though less various, are more concentrated and—by their position in existence—less over-tasked than ours; hence in most cases of extremity, where *we* deliberate, *they* act; and if, in consequence, their failures are more deplorable, their successes are, for the same reason, more triumphant and entire.

In a moment, Aimáta perceived that it was her duty now, to govern and not to obey. She led—almost dragged—the woman out of the highway, into a track in the woods, that conducted along the hills towards a deep and distant ravine, bounded on one hand, by a precipitous mountain side, and on the other, by the vast tract of forest land which they had just traversed in effecting their escape. In the distance, at the opening of this natural division between mountain and mountain, you caught here and there, at chasms in the rock, bright, beautiful glimpses of the villages and country below, terminated by the sun-bright ocean that stretched out far beyond. Here, in a cavern formed by the juncture of several immense masses of basalt, Aimáta halted; for a strange presentiment had come over her that their footsteps were tracked by the Priest.

She looked in Idía's face. A slight flush as if of pain, or anxiety, overspread her cheek, and a low, half moaning, half sobbing sound, came from her lips; but she seemed as morally insensible—as incapable of speech, or perception, as ever. The girl drew her towards a portion of the cavern overgrown with moss and wild flowers and breaking a cocoa nut that had fallen from the trees above, she fetched a little water in the shell; and kneeling down by the sufferer, comforted and wept over her.

And thus—patient and gentle creature!—when Death withers the softness on thy cheek and the brightness in thy happy eye; when thy spirit lingers at parting from its loved and beautiful abode, and they that have rejoiced in thee, stand mourning by thy side—thus, shall the ministering angels kneel round thy bed and comfort and weep over *thee*!

The hours lagged on. The husband-man's axe was heard from the vale, and the harmonies of the breeze, from the verdure above. The shadows, one by one, began to appear upon the rocks, and the hot, dusky haze, had already vanished from the distant sea; but the fugitives yet lingered in the cave; and the sufferer, mourned, and the soother, comforted still.

A little longer—and the woman now moved restlessly backwards and forwards on her moss couch. Her eyes flashed and dilated. Her low wailings began to deepen into groans, and she tore at the moss and wild flowers by her side. Then, she raised herself a little and dragged her vesture from her bosom, as if suffocating with heat, beseeching the girl, in a piteous voice, to have mercy upon her—to bear with her yet a little while—to stay there with her till the hour of death _____

❧ ☙

Comfort it, care for it, Aimáta! There are none in the Island to welcome it but thou. Chide it not for its weeping, for its birth was in sorrow. The pilgrimage of earth is a pilgrimage of woe; what marvel then, that the journey at its outset, is undertaken with a tear?

See how the sunbeams glitter on its form, how they stray over the delicate tracery of its little limbs, how they nestle on its round, dimpled cheek!—And the air—viewless though it is to *thee*—how gently, even now, is it stealing over the infant's bosom; how lightly is it hovering round the infant[']s lip! While Nature itself seems luring it to smile—Oh! who shall hesitate to aid so blessed an attempt!

The shadows had lengthened and multiplied; the cool land-breeze of night had already arisen upon the earth; and the sun was fast sinking in the distant ocean, when Aimáta, who was still fondling the child, suddenly stopped in her occupation.

There was a distant rustling among the bushes above. It might have been the fall of a cocoa nut or of a loose piece of stone. She listened again.

After a short interval of stillness, it sounded once more—nearer this time. The noise, too, was more protracted. She flew to Idía almost distracted with terror. The rustling was approaching, and her ear, practised in refined perception from her childhood, detected now, that the sound was caused by human footsteps. They spoke together for a few moments. The woman's tones, were commanding and calm, the girl's, agitated and imploring—The next instant, Aimáta disappeared with the infant, in the direction of the plains.

Idía raised herself and looked towards the opening. Suddenly someone obscured the last ray of sun-light, that was streaming through the mouth of the cavern. She knew him, at that distance, by his lofty and noble stature, and (as he came nearer) by the bitter scorn on his lip and the stern ferocity in his eye. It was the Priest.

"Away!, Away"! she cried, as he approached, "what dost thou here? Get thee to thy sorceries and thy gods; for the child is saved! That which was mine own, I have preserved in spite of thee! He is born! He lives! He shall grow in beauty and in strength! He shall shame thy heart by his comeliness when thou lookest on him! He shall speak in the councils of the brave! He shall yet go forth among the warriors of the land! He is saved! I have seen him! My beloved one, mine own"!

She laughed hysterically, and there was a terrible wildness in her eye, as she motioned him to be gone.

But he still came slowly on, muttering to himself, with a

ghastly revolting smile on his lip, and an expression of mingled lust and ferocity in his eye. As he looked round the outer portion of the cavern, he hardly noticed the woman; and having completed his survey, he proceeded towards the inner recess.

There was a pause—a brief silence; and then, she could hear him groping his way in the dark places beyond her, and calling softly and enticingly—"Aimáta! Aimáta"!

A horrible suspicion flashed across her mind. She looked round towards the mouth of the cave. Where was Aimáta? Should the girl return, while the Priest was there!—It was too terrible to think of. She turned again to the dark recess. "Aimáta! Aimáta"! He was persevering in the search!

She attempted to rise. She could just stand, when supported by the sides of the cavern; so she staggered, aiding herself by the projections of rock, to the entrance of her place of refuge; and there, she set herself to watch. If the girl returned back, she might make her a sign to fly, and so, she might yet preserve her.

"Aimáta! Aimáta["]! Even now she could her his deep, quick breathing. In another instant, he stood by her side. As he looked on her, his fingers mechanically grasped at the air, as if he thought her already within his murderous hold. He advanced, clutched her fiercely by the arm, hesitated for an instant, and then, casting her from him and laughing and muttering to himself, he passed from her sight in the direction of the high lands above; still calling, at intervals,—"Aimáta! Aimáta"!

The sun had gone down. The brief Twilight of the South soon faded and passed away, and forth from the face of the waters, rose the still, soft moon; but the girl came not. A long hour had passed since the departure of the Priest, and Aimáta had not appeared!

Had he met her in the woods? Idía's heart sank within her at the thought. In miserable expectation and dread, she watched on. A few minutes more, and now, she saw by the moonlight, the figure of the girl advancing wearily and cautiously towards her from below.

She gained the cavern. Her long absence had but arisen from an excess of care. The infant was sleeping in her arms, and the bright, happy smile, had already returned to her innocent face. She stole softly up to Idía, and placing her offspring in her possession, she kissed her cheek. At that action, its old gentleness and tenderness returned to the sufferer[']s heart; and a last, faint return, of the beauty that was vanishing from it for ever, flickered on her countenance, as she bent down her head and wept over the child.

❧ ❧

The End of Book I

Book II

"Thirst of revenge, the powerless will
Still baffled, and yet burning still!
Desire with loathing strangely mixed
On wild or hateful objects fixed,
Fantastic passions! mad'ning brawl!
And shame and terror over all"[1]

Coleridge

CHAPTER I

From Present to Past

Another year had passed over the Island, as Idía halted by the shores of the Great Lake, at the same spot as that described at the introduction of this narrative, and almost at the self same hour of the night. On this occasion, however, she was not accompanied by the Priest, but by a woman and a child.

After pausing for a few moments of rest and deliberation, the little party entered a canoe that had been left on the shore, and paddled swiftly and cautiously towards one of the extremities of the Lake, where the rocks rose precipitously from the very water[']s edge and the forests beyond them, were most immense and impenetrable. On arriving at their destination, the vessel was suffered to drift past the steeps with the current, while the elder woman, seated at the bow, minutely examined, by the help of the soft brilliant moonlight, every variety in the precipitous shore, as they glided past it. Suddenly, she made a sign to her companion at the other end of the bark; and the next instant, by a stroke of the paddle, its sides grated against the rugged surface of the rocks.

At this particular spot, the forest vegetation had found a bed of earth at the top of the precipice, and having taken in its luxuriant increase, a downward direction, it now hung so low, as almost to touch the waters beneath, and wholly to obscure a wide natural archway, formed at this point, in the rock. Forcing aside, with great difficulty, these natural obstructions to their landing, the voyagers entered a little creek, whose strip of shingly beach had once been accessible from the forest beyond, by a wild gloomy dell.

At present, however, from the yearly and unrestrained aggression of briar and tree, this woodland cavity had become all but impassable; and the only practicable approach to the inlet *now*, was from the Lake.

From their hurried and anxious demeanour, the women could have had but one object, in seeking such a place, at such a time,—concealment. Having dragged the canoe up on the shore and safely disposed their small provision of baked bread fruit—two arduous achievements in such a situation as their's, where the moonlight scarcely penetrated the tangled masses of brushwood overhead, and the actual space of dry land was contracted in the extreme, they sat down in their strange hiding place—the younger woman and the child, nestling together; the elder . . . .

The reader will already have anticipated that Idía's companions in her vigil by the waterside, were no others, than the companions of her hours of misery in the lonely cave. Still a girl, in years and in feelings, Aimáta was now a woman in form and beauty. With *her*, Time had visited but to adorn; with the other two, his approach had been ever to harm. The child, at its birth so promising, was now weakly and diminutive in form, and strangely sad and un-childlike in appearance. Of the mother[']s former attractions, scarce a vestige remained. Her pale, pinched lips, sunken eyes and wan, haggard cheeks presented a mournful contrast, to her former self. There was the charm of expression in her still; but, the charm of feature, was gone for ever.

Ere, however, we proceed farther, it will be necessary to notice the more important incidents of the year that has passed, since the birth of Iolání's ill-fated offspring.

Some days after the scene in the cavern, Idía and Aimáta departed with the child for another district of the Island; such a proceeding, being their only apparent prospect of escape, from the machinations of the Priest. By travelling only in the night, and keeping themselves carefully concealed in the day, they contrived to elude Iolàni's efforts to prevent their escape, with the utmost success; and reached their destination in safety. The part of the country they had chosen for their retreat, was governed, at the period of their arrival, by a young chieftain, as the representative of the authority of the King, whose ancestors had been celebrated, not only for their military prowess, but for their attachment and service to the crown, for several reigns. The present ruler, however, though lenient in the exercise of his authority, and beloved by the whole body of the people, was the secret, but bitter enemy, of the reigning King and his principal assistants in the government of the Island. An insult from Iolàni, originated his disaffection to the royal cause; its confirmation, being occasioned by the refusal of the King (who acted under fear of his wily brother) to do justice to the injured party. The chieftain was too wise to resent this outrage immediately. He returned to his district without even a word of remonstrance, and patiently awaited the occasion for retribution; the time of Idìa's arrival in his domains, being the time of his return from this unsuccessful application for justice, to the ruling powers.

The fugitives had remained long enough in their new abiding place, to enlist the sympathies of the people for the sorrows, of the one, and their admiration for the beauty, of the other, when Iolàni discovered their retreat, and imperiously demanded them from Mahìné, (their protector) as rebels against his authority, and insulters of his high and holy office. Delighted, at the opportunity thus afforded him of thwarting his ancient enemy, the chieftain refused compliance with the application of the Priest, until he had succeeded, before a council of the elders of the land, in proving his charge. It may be necessary to add, that Mahíné was further moved to this bold determinating by his attachment to the girl Aimáta, and his fears, from the known character of Ioláni, that if once delivered into his power, she was lost to him for ever.

Too chary of his power and influence, to trust either, to the perilous ordeal of false accusation, the Priest abandoned his first plan for obtaining possession of the fugitives. To expose himself as a sensualist, was rather to heighten than to diminish his reputation, among the sensual inhabitants of the land. But, to risk detection as a liar and hypocrite, would be for one in his situation, a fatal mistake. His cunning still held the rule over his revenge, and he knew by experience, that the safest guarantee of success, is to await the opportunity and not to make it.

It would have been an easy task for him, by using his influence with his brother, to have obtained by force, that which was denied to dissimulation; but, there were three valid objections to such a course of proceeding. The first, was the necessity of embroiling the country in war, by thus compassing his wishes. The second, was the loss of his popularity from the people's attachment to his victim; as well as the risk of his power and existence, should they be vanquished in battle; and the third—even supposing that might, would as usual, triumph over right—was the certainty, that by thus satisfying his vengeance, he would secure rather a martyrdom for Idía, than a triumph for himself.

And here, let it not be supposed impossible, that so trivial an offence as Idía's, should excite in the heart of Ioláni, so deadly a determination for revenge. He was a man who either hated, or loved to excess. He possessed no inferior emotions; or rather, no emotion excited within him, was matured in mediocrity; if it past not away in its very birth, it at once became a dominant passion. In the present instance, mere indifference, immediately ripened into implacable hate. Whatever he now saw, or felt, affected him now, but in one way. Actions and incidents the most indifferent, he unwittingly distorted into direct encouragements of his one, absorbing desire. Sleeping, or waking, in labour, or in rest, slowly, surely and incessantly, he fed the fire that was burning within him. He had none to partake; and, consequently, none to weaken its intensity; for, it was a remarkable feature in his character, that he had never trusted a confidant, nor reposed himself on friend. The virtue of never betraying a comrade, is a common human quality; but, the virtue of never betraying oneself, is the rarest of superiorities. This accomplishment, necessary to a good man, is indispensable, to a villain; and it was possessed to perfection, by the Priest.

Neither let it be imagined, that in thus dilating, upon the political cunning, of the rulers and the talent for stratagem, among the people of the Pacific Islands, we represent a capacity for intrigue—a quick, ready intelligence of character, too refined to exist in any other than a civilised community. Wanting, as the inhabitants of Polynesia are, in all that is loftiest and most abstracted in intellect; in those mental qualities, that circumstance can originate and experience direct, they are far from deficient. Their policy, has had its Machiavelli; and their battle-field, its Caesar; though, their religion, has never possessed its Luther; nor their language, its Homer. As a nation, of the *actual* mental virtues, they have few, if any: of the *doubtful*, they have many, if not all.

Foiled, but not intimidated, Ioláni departed from the chieftain's territory. Never had his reputation among the people, stood so high as at the present moment. The circle of Idía's partisans in her native place began already to narrow. It was given out, that the Priest had scorned to prove that, which should have been believed, from such a man, upon assertion. There was a rumor, that on his return from Mahíné's District, the

King, indignant, at the chieftain's disrespect towards his brother, had offered him his army to lay waste the obnoxious territory, and that Ioláni had preferred rather to suffer the indignities that had been heaped upon him, than to embroil the people in war, and thereby, make the innocent suffer for the guilty. Such a thing had been unknown before. It was the first instance of consideration for human life, having overpowered the desire of satisfying private enmity, that had happened in the Island. Warriors of rank and renown, hurried to Ioláni in crowds, to offer him the service of private assassination; but, with the utmost gentleness and dignity, while their attachment was praised, the method they had taken to prove it, was severely rebuked. Soon, the Priest's conferences with his gods, became longer and more frequent; and it was whispered abroad, that his outraged dignity would be avenged by spiritual interposition, and not by the interference of man.

Meanwhile, in Mahíné's District, matters hardly went on so smoothly as usual. In his love-wanderings with Aimáta, the chieftain was as gentle as was his wont; but, among his councillors and warriors, his manner became peevish and gloomy. His late triumph over Ioláni, had made him long for more important successes against his ancient enemy; and he chafed at the obstacles, that prudence, obliged him to offer to his own desires. He dropped vague hints on the imbecility and uselessness of the King, and on the advantage that would accrue to his people and himself, from an enlargement of their district. These hints were not lost on those to whom they were addressed; and the wise among the fighting men, began already, in secret, to furbish their arms.

The great mass of the people, too, though ignorant of the treason that was hatching among their betters, had become indolent and discontented, and, therefore, ready for the watchword of rebellion, whenever it should be called. Their chieftain's attention towards them, had latterly somewhat abated. Strange men had been seen wandering among them; and some, went so far as to declare, that Ioláni was of their number. There was a mystery about this which they could not comprehend, and this want of penetration on *their* part, and the evident existence of it on the part of the intruders, galled them to the quick. In addition to this, many of their war-chiefs, had of late, been more than usually vigorous, in demanding from their agricultural possessions, those tributes which an unjust custom permitted them occasionally to exact. These, and many other causes, contributed to raise a spirit of murmuring among them that Mahíné observed with delight, as adapting them admirably, to aid his seditious purpose. Victory over the King, would not only secure the ruin and downfall of the Priest, but gain him the throne. Ambition and enmity both urged him to attempt so glorious an achievement. He could count upon many of the disaffected from different parts of the country and from other islands. The muster of his own fighting men was—notwithstanding the long peace—considerable and effective; and he looked forward to the result of his enterprise as sure, could the suffrages of the people and the favor of the gods, be obtained ere it was commenced.

For some months more, matters went on as usual in the Island, until the summer had again come round, and the schemes, that Ambition and Vengeance, had so long and so craftily fashioned, were ready to work.

About this period, a personal application to the King was again made by Mahíné, in the matter of his old quarrel with the Priest. His petition, as he hoped and expected, was treated with disdain; and he left the royal dwelling, with the threat, that his own power should right him, as the mediation of the rules of the land, was unjustly denied to him, a second time. That same day, picked bands of marauders from the chieftain[']s district, made incursion on the territories directly watched over by the King, sacked and pillaged the dwellings of the industrious husbandmen, with remorseless cruelty, and returned in triumph to their camp. The demand from head quarters, for their delivery to the government, was refused; and the messengers who bore the requisition, were beaten and most savagely ill-treated, in the presence of the rebel chiefs. These acts of violence, were immediately avenged by the royal party. The once peaceful villages along the coast, became scenes of riot and bloodshed; and the peasantry, abandoning their possessions, crowded with their women and children, to the camps of their respective rulers. The King's flag was sent round the island to gather together his fighting men[;] Mahíné left no means untried to spread treason in the land, and the solemn preparations incidental to the commencement of war, were begun on each side.

A human sacrifice was first offered by both parties. By the one, to conciliate the gods in favor of their treachery; and by the other, to obtain their aid, in the righteous cause of defending King and country. Then, on Mahíné's side, might be seen the hurried and desperate preparations of men in rebellion, for the great crisis of their lawless attempt. Bands of desperadoes from other islands, athirst for blood, craving for slaughter, fighters for the great cause of carnage, landed at the shores and crowded to the rebel camp. The same utter recklessness of consequences, the same glory in the Present and defiance of the Future, animated all ranks and all tempers. It was terrible, to see the apathy of the gentler among the population—the women and children—to the prospect of rapine and bloodshed, that now opened before them. Among some, wild hilarity—awful at such a period—reigned supreme. Others, watched in stolid astonishment, the preparations for the battle. Here, might be seen a woman, adorning with childish delight, the warrior[']s gear. There, you beheld young girls hurrying joyously about the camp, and increasing by their presence, the wild infuriate glee of the fighting men impatient for the battle. Hard by the streams of blood from the sacrifices both of man and beast, were children playing with the horrible remnants of the offerings to the gods; their shrill cries, now drowned by the war of voices from the camp, now by the yells of the tortured men and animals, now by the screams of the half infuriate priests, prophesying success to the rebels and heaping the most hideous imprecations on the enemy's head. Then, in the distant wilds, startling the awful loneliness that hung over the forsaken villages, was heard the hurried tread of fresh recruits hastening to the camp. Forth from the woods and solitudes, their fierce countenance showing wan and ghastly in the moonlight, (for they travelled by night) tramped the husbandman, his bludg eon armed with shark's teeth on his shoulder; the chief, with his three bladed iron-wood sword and his turban-formed fillet of cloth wound over his brow; and the young men, with their spears and slings. On they sped, singing their wild war-songs, and exulting in the prospect of the fight! Onward! onward! swelling with every hour, the ranks of ferocity and crime, they hurried to the gathering place; and the heart of Mahíné leaped within him, as he watched them pouring in, from the pinnacle of the camp!

This scene of riot and debauchery, lasted for several days. The preparations for war—always complicated and many in the Pacific Islands—were, on this occasion, particularly dilatory, on both sides. The solemn observances, however, went on with the utmost regularity, until the final human sacrifice to commemorate the starting of the warriors, was all that was wanting, at last.

With the King's party, at the period described above, the gathering for the battle was accomplished with comparative discipline and order. The confusion, usual among the people on such an occasion, was hardly observable in the royal camp, for the minds of the populace were concentrated upon one serious design—the apprehension of the last victim for the wargod; the doomed wretch, being no other, than the unhappy object of the former love and present enmity, of the great Priest.

While the altars were yet reeking with the primary sacrifices, he called together the whole mass of the populace, and commanded them, with fiery eloquence, to obey the requisitions of his god and capture, as the victim that was to close the ceremonies of war, the ill-fated Idía. He left no attempt untried to arouse their passions and to flatter their bravery and cunning. He represented his former unwillingness to avenge himself of the woman's offence, as the result of a direct communication from the idol, commanding him to reserve the ill-doer for its own will and pleasure. He solemnly declared, that the appointed hour was now come, that the god called for this sacrifice at last, and that their success in the battle that was near at hand, depended upon that offering alone. The effect of this appeal was instantaneous. The wild energy of his language, the mingled dignity and agitation in his demeanour, his poignant outward sorrow, that the idol could only be appeased by the death of one whom he had once loved, and now sincerely pitied and forgave, fired the hearts and aroused the reverence of the superstitious crowd around him. Detached parties of the most experienced spies that the camp possessed, started off immediately, to the stronghold of the enemy. Alive, or dead, they were determined to possess themselves of the victim, though they openly hunted her to the rebel ranks.

Two days passed away; and on the third, the pursuers returned, dispirited and shamed. They had, at first, attempted to capture the woman by stratagem, in order that she might be slain in triumph at the altar of the god; but their efforts had been of no avail. They had then, openly attempted, by bribes, to

incite the more disaffected of the villagers, to the betrayal of her
hiding place; but, the answer of everyone they attempted to
corrupt, was the same—"She had left their camp, and they
knew not whither she had gone". That she could have escaped
from Tahíti, was impossible; for the King's canoes had, latterly,
watched the ocean round Mahíné's territory, to intercept all
communication with the neighbouring islands. On their way
homeward, they had searched every lurking-place with care; a
few of their comrades, who were still on the watch, might discover the victim yet; but, for *their* parts, they had utterly failed.

And but little wonder was it, that their undertaking proved
abortive. While Ioláni had sent forth his spies, Mahíné had not
been idle, in using the same advantage, with regard to the councils of the King. His emissaries, had attended the Priest[']s con-
vocation of the people, and, without delaying to hear more than
the main point of the harangue, hurried back with their intelligence to the rebel camp; for, they judged that the chieftain,
from the woman's intimate connexion and great influence with
his beloved, would be anxious to preserve her from the vengeance of the relentless Priest.

They had deemed rightly. Mahíné, the moment he heard
their tidings, commanded the presence of Idía and her companion; but neither were to be found. One of the spies, had incau-
tiously communicated his intelligence to some idlers round the
outskirts of the camp. It had spread with wild rapidity, from
one to the other, & had reached the ears of Idía and the girl.
They were sought for by order of the half distracted chieftain,
but without success. It was supposed, that they had taken advantage of the confusion in the village, and effected their escape. All that could be discovered of them, was the little that
was soon afterwards gathered from a half-witted old man, who
declared, that he had seen them pass him on the borders of the
forest, and that he had been commanded, by the woman, to

give this message to Mahíné—"Be of good courage; I am guard-
ing her for *thee*; battle it quickly and stoutly, and Aimáta shall
be thy reward."

The scene described at the commencement of this chapter,
will sufficiently hint to the reader, the destination of Idía's
flight. Horrified at the crime and confusion attendant upon the
preparations for war, and fearing for the innocence of the girl,
among such a host of wretches as surrounded her, she had for
some time contemplated taking refuge from the uproar of the
villages, in the silence of the woods. The intelligence of the fate
in preparation for her, immediately determined her in this purpose. She was appalled, but not overpowered, at so terrible a
display of Ioláni's malignity. Danger and distress had done their
utmost for her, and whatever their form, they now came as
companions and not as strangers. She felt her position in an
instant. None knew so well as she, how deep and how successful was the cunning of the Priest. When dependant for protection on others, she was open to betrayal; but, when trusting to
herself, she was sure that her concealment was safe from discovery, either by force, or fraud, and could be frustrated by
chance alone. She only waited to consult the wishes of Aimáta,
whose situation was less perilous than her own, before she set
forward on her flight. The girl, terrified at all she saw and heard
under the protection of her lover, hesitated not an instant in
her choice; and they started for the woods, together.

In choosing Vahíria as her place of refuge, Idía seized her
only chance of preservation from the impending danger. There
were caverns by the shores of the Lake, known only to the
Priest and herself; and as there was but little chance, at such a
critical period for his country, that Ioláni could be spared to
prosecute the search himself, this was the spot of all others,
that offered them the greatest security. For some days, they
lurked about the different nooks and crannies by the waterside,

gathering, as best they might, a scanty supply of provision; and that labour accomplished, they betook themselves to the strange hiding place, described at the beginning of the present chapter.

Ioláni, though furious at the result of his undertaking, was neither discouraged, nor dismayed. He saw that the ill-success of the search for the victim, had diminished the interest of some, in the sacred ceremonies, and had dispirited others. To risk a battle now, was, consequently, almost to ensure defeat. He found, from intelligence received from the spies, that the enemy had concluded their offerings and were on the point of marching upon him. A consultation was held with the chief warriors, the result of which, was the organisation of a strong party of skirmishers, picked from the desperadoes of the forces, for the purpose of embarrassing the advance of the rebels. To this band, the slightest prospect of pillage and bloodshed, was as sufficing an incitement to engage, as was the ascertained favor of the god, to the general members of the army. After having proceeded about ten miles, (half the distance between the two districts) they encountered, in the wilds of the forest, the first rank, or advanced guard, of the enemy. Assisted by superior knowledge of the ground, they slaughtered them to a man; and the main body of the insurgents, ignorant of the actual number of their assailants, and unable to act in any force in so confined a space, were seized with a panic and retreated to their stronghold, in great confusion.

This good fortune, seemed to secure Ioláni's success in the object dearest to this heart. In all probability, considerable time would elapse, before the rebels were again enabled to take the field; and in that period, ample opportunity would be afforded, to hunt down the fugitive and sate his revenge. The people were more than ever devoted to his cause. They looked upon their success in the skirmish, as a direct manifestation of the

favor of their god; and the cry for the victim, rose louder and
louder, among all ranks. On the evening of this day of victory,
Ioláni commanded a second attendance, on the following
morning, before the Temple walls, to hear the result of another
supplication to the god and to ascertain if he still willed the
sacrifice of the victim he had demanded on the former occasion; for, the Priest declared that his hope of saving the woman,
by appeasing Oro with other offerings, was the sole motive of
his venturing a second application to the oracle of War.

So far, then, had this intricate entanglement of events advanced, when the populace prepared on the eventful morning,
to attend the solemn invitation of the Priest. A reckless triumph
and delight ruled all their hearts, and the once formidable insurgents, were now thought of with disdain. How wise was this
contemptuous estimate of the energy of the rebels, will hereaf-
ter be seen.

CHAPTER II

The Answer of the Oracle

The building consecrated to Oro, the deity of the battlefield, was, in outward appearance, simply, an extensive mass of heavy stone wall; saving, on the side nearest the sea, where a sort of pyramid of huge stones, ascended by steep, rugged steps, broke the otherwise monotonous regularity of the structure. On this elevation, were placed the images of the inferior idols of war, which on great and unusual occasions, were displaced for the feared and formidable idol of Oro, himself. It was generally understood by the people, that the sacrifice they hoped to behold, was to take place immediately in front of this erection; a method of proceeding, adopted by the wily rulers of the land, on account of its originality, and consequent power of producing unusual excitement in the hearts, and unusual reverence, in the demeanour, of the assembled populace.

The absence of great attraction in the Temple, itself, was fully compensated by the exquisite beauty of its situation. It stood about a mile from the sea-shore, where a slight rising in the ground, gave it an imposing and commanding position. The borders of the sea—in general studded with rocks—were, at this particular spot, bare of any such appendage; and the view of the noble ocean, already speckled thickly by canoes, was uninterrupted. Between the beach and the green sward before the Temple, lay the gardens of the natives, beautiful in their adornments of fruits and flowers, and contrasting delightfully, with

the sameness of the smooth sands beyond. Then, came the deli-
cious calmness of that portion of the sea protected by the coral
reefs, and farther on, making a break in those natural guardians
of the shore, lay two little islands, far out on the ocean—each
with its canopy of tall cocoa-nut trees, and its surface of cool,
pleasant verdure; and then, farthest and noblest to the sight, its
limitless expanse of waters, gleaming in the glorious sun-light,
and its mighty waves roaring in triumphant grandeur over their
sturdy barrier of rock, stretched the magnificent Pacific.

Strangled with moss and wild flowers, and topped with every
variety of foliage, the rocks that on either side, girded the distant shore, wore an aspect of softness and fertility that blended
enchantingly with the milder characteristics of the inland scenery. The immense tracts of woodland that backed the Temple,
broken here and there, by the appearance of a little village, and
pierced in every direction, by avenues and footpaths, formed a
pleasant prospect, in their coolness and repose, after the glare
and animation of the sea-ward view; while, the mountains afar
off, beautified by the distance, and surrounded by the smooth
fertile hills, lost their barrenness and looked sunnily and softly
down, on the happy vallies at their feet.

And, now that the sun had fairly arisen over this gay and
beautiful place, sauntering carelessly along the paths and avenues, the population of the district wended towards the Temple. The bare-headed old man and the flower-crowned girl; the
warrior in his vesture of brilliant red and yellow and the young
mother in her garments of simple white; trooped happily onward from every passage in the woods, and arranged themselves before the altar of the war-god. No sign, however, of the
commencement of the ceremony appeared as yet; and the light-
hearted people, straggling downwards towards the gardens, betook themselves to their amusements without a gesture of impatience at the unexpected delay.

What thought had *they*, for the solemnities they had assembled to witness? The Past and the Future were nothing to
them—the Present, was all they troubled themselves for, and
trying must it indeed be, if they met it with a complaint. Idía
and her flight, were alike forgotten, in the freshness and sunshine of the morning; and the miseries of the battle to come,
were veiled and hidden in the animation and gaiety that preceded its approach. What to them were the tears of days gone
by, and the grief that might still sadden their dwellings? They
lived and laughed on at the rise of the day; and there, was their
armour of proof, against the ills that might happen at the fall.

On they straggled; some, to their repose in the shade; some,
to their morning[']s bath, in the fresh water streams, that ran
downward to the sea. Forth sallied the old, to their seats on the
turf, and away went the young, to their love-walks in the avenues. Fresh comers, gave every instant fresh animation to the
scene. Every one joined freely in the divisions of his neighbours, whatever their character might be; saving, indeed, the
chieftains of rank, who walked gloomily apart, pondering their
plans for the approaching battle. The laughter and confusion in
the place, were at their height, when the sounds of wild singing, in the distance, arose even over the noise and tumult of the
assembly before the Temple.

Instantly, the dancers paused in their evolutions, the old
men started from their seats, the lovers hurried from their hiding places, the bathers forsook the water, the mothers and children emerged from their sports in the shade, and the surf-
swimmers, who were just setting out for their dangerous diver-
sion, turned and made for the shore. Oldest and youngest, grav-
est and gayest, as if by one common impulse, arose and hurried
in the direction of the wild, unruly voices.

In another moment, leaping and raging onwards like mani-
acs or daemons, the mysterious Areoi fraternity (the wandering

players of Polynesia) emerged from the avenues; and, driving back again the impatient crowd until they halted on the lower part of the green sward, prepared for their wild representation.

This band of libertines, had more the appearance of evil spirits, than of humanity. Their bodies, were daubed over, in the most grotesque and, at the same time, the most revolting manner, with charcoal. Their faces, were disfigured by a bright, scarlet dye; and their heads and waists, were ornamented with wreaths of beautiful yellow and scarlet leaves. To the evil influence and example of these purveyors of popular amusement, may be attributed all the worst features of the Polynesian character. Revered as sacred and the direct descendants of gods, their worst crimes and exactions, passed unchecked and unavenged. Their lives one unbroken round of indolence and iniquity, they wandered from district to district, exhibiting their strange performances, as the privileged panders to the worst vices of human nature. On this occasion, the present, was their farewell visit; for, the extraordinary preliminary ceremonies that harbingered their representations, were already preparing, in another and a distant portion of the island.

Loud was the laughter of the reckless populace, as one of the band, commenced the entertainment, by a speech of the most vehement eloquence, ridiculing the approaching war and its principal actors on both sides. Satire on public events and public people, was the most darling of their privileges, and on the present occasion, they used it with an unsparing hand. The address, was followed by a sort of chorus chanted with extraordinary rapidity and animation by all the members of the troop; and that ended, they arose and commenced their final dance.

Whirling round and round, in the most intricate evolutions, their motions, gross though they were, were hardly revolting, from the wild, picturesque grace of every movement. Ever startling, ever varying, the most refined profligacy of civilised countries, could invent no luxury, more dangerously fascinating to the general eye, or more fatally destructive to the general character, than the mazes of the Areoi dance. Fatigue, seemed to be as unknown to the performers, as satiety, to the audience. Old and young-men, women and children, crowded round the band, watching with noisy delight, the half grotesque, half fearful exhibition, before them. Wilder and wilder, grew the movements of the dancers; shriller and shriller, rung their discordant music on the air; and louder and louder, still, rose the applause of the beholders. Hard to be imagined, and harder to be described, was the tumult of the scene, at this moment. Furious as the mirth had now become, its desperate character, seemed but little likely to retrograde, notwithstanding the amazing protraction of the amusement. The orgy, indeed, might have continued almost without interruption, until far into the night, but for the appearance, at this moment, of one of the inferior Priests on the Pyramid of the Temple, whose presence, without, at that period of the day, seemed the earnest of a speedy delivery of the answer of the oracle. Accordingly, the volatile crowd, the instant they perceived him, immediately quitted their mad entertainment, and hurried with strangely altered demeanours, towards the scene of the more important ceremony.

Saving, when a low murmur occasionally rose from their ranks, the assembly were now completely hushed. After another interval of expectation, the patience of the populace was at last rewarded by the appearance of Ioláni, upon the sacred pinnacle.

To the utter astonishment of the multitude, his demeanour was distinguished by a calm solemnity, strangely at variance with the accustomed raving fits of the Priests, upon delivering the commands of the oracle. There was something in his motionless, commanding attitude, and his elevated and solitary position, that awed the bold and terrified the faint-hearted, among the audience assembled beneath him; and many a tradition of priestly power and priestly oppression, arose on their memories, as little by little, they reverently fell back from the immediate precincts of the sacred place, and silently awaited the address of the greatest among the ministers, of their tyrannic and mysterious religion.

For the first few minutes, Ioláni directed a penetrating and angry eye over the crowd beneath him. Then, advancing a few steps, in sorrowful and solemn tones, he spoke to the assembly thus: —

"Mowin, people of the land, your homes and your possessions; your happiness and your honor; your wives and all they that ye have loved; for, still is Oro unappeased, still is the altar vacant, still is your native earth, unhallowed by the blood of the sacrifice"!

"I stretch forth mine eyes: and lo! the men of valour, who have trodden the mountain labyrinths from their youth, but are weary of tracing them now. I look down upon the concourse of the people: and behold! by twos and threes assembled, they who have boasted in the camp of their cunning, who have proclaimed their penetration in the councils of the wise; but, where are their wiles in the hour of need? Are they left to Idía, in her hiding-place among the mountains? Are they departed at the voice of the sorcerer? Or lodged with the women and the little children of the land"?

"Seek her! Seek her! Is there no encouragement in the victory in the woods? Is there no incitement to obedience to Oro, in that success, so unhoped for, and yet so complete? Will ye forsake your god, ye that are devout, when he has battled for ye unpropitiated? Will ye be foiled by a woman, yet, ye that are brave—that are terrible among the warriors of the land"?

"Who is there among ye that fears not death, if shame write the epitaph on your tomb? Which of ye desires life, if dishonour darkens your house and derision haunts ye, wherever ye go"?

"Yet so shall it chance with ye all, if Oro is unsatisfied. Think not, that because ye have conquered in the skirmish, in the great battle to come, ye shall conqueror as well. The god has encouraged ye at the first, that ye might the better obey at the last. Not as an earnest of victory, was the fight in the wood; but, as a command of submission to the will of the Spirit of War".

"For, behold, Mahíné is cunning, and the hearts of his warriors, are athirst for the contention even now. The first tree that ye fell in the forest, doth it vanquish the stubborn resistance of the rest? The first rank of the rebels that ye have slain, hath their destruction exterminated the power of the mighty army behind? In the great and terrible battle to come, shall ye need no inspiration but your hatred? No aid but your weapons of War"?

"I turn mine eyes towards the waste of ocean; and lo! arising still and stealthy from its surface, the morning wind streams over all the earth! The flowers, in their beauty, bow to its victorious approach! The leaves of the forest, in their multitude, are moved and scattered by its swift advance. Over the noble mountain tops and down in the secret corners of the vallies and rocks, it wends ever onwards. It passes over all. It is turned backward by nothing on the earth; and so, rejoicing in its might, it vanquishes the obstacles of the land, and behold it forth once again upon the wilderness of waters beyond"!

"So, from their far district, arise stealthily the hosts of the enemy. So, (the War-god unappeased) shall your women, in their beauty, yield to the will of the oppressor. So, shall your warriors, in their multitude, be dispersed at the advance of Mahíné's victorious band; and so, prevailing through your coasts, shall they reach again their homes in security and triumph"!

"Despair not, weary not, then, in the search. Alive, or dead, hunt but the victim down and all will yet be well. Produce her before the Temple walls, and the enemy shall fly before ye. The fairest of their women and the best of their possessions, shall fall into your hands; and the proudest of the rebel chiefs, shall surely be humbled at your feet; for in a vision of the night that is past, the War-god hath promised me thus"!

Here the Priest paused for a short time, to watch the effect of his harangue upon the multitude beneath him. Saving, however, when the lamentations of the women, or the low wail of some terrified child, rose occasionally on the air, the utterest silence reigned over the auditory. The men, in groups apart, either crouched silently on the earth, or paced sullenly round the outer-most circle of the crowd. Ioláni's address seemed to have taught them, rather to prepare for the defeat, than to ensure the victory; and the same ominous and dogged despair, was expressed in the demeanours of all.

In a few minutes (and now in fiery and agitated tones) the Priest again spoke.

"Do the warriors despond"? cried he. "Is determination departed from the brave? Arise once again! Pursue and despair not; and the victory shall yet be yours"!

"For *I*—even *I* the beloved of Oro! The companion of the god! will head ye in the search. Led by the spirits of your fathers, guarded by the Arbiter of the battle-field, cunning has no power to baffle, nor danger to weary *me*! Let the young men arise and come forth! Let the aged and the feeble, remain and supplicate here. Tomorrow's sun—by the glory of Oro I swear it!—shall rise over the altar, to illumine the sacrifice at last"!

The effect of these words was electrical. The men with one accord started up and crowded round the pinnacle, from which, Ioláni had addressed them. To be headed by *him*, was an earnest of success to all, and a proof of enthusiasm for the cause of the god, never vouchsafed by a dignitary of the land, before. Wonderful, as an example of the iron tyranny of superstition over the heart, was this man's influence over his people. Not a word fell from his lips, but was regarded as a direct inspiration from another and a nobler world; and while the despondency characterizing the first portion of his harangue, had sunk his audience to the lowest depths of misery and despair, the energetic boasting of the latter, had, strange to say, the power of effecting in their feelings, a revolution, the most instantaneous and the most complete.

Nothing could at this moment, equal the enthusiasm of the assembly now. In an astonishingly short space of time, the fighting men and spies were mustered, the sentinels placed, the women and children driven from the ground, and three distinct bands of pursuers organised; the most numerous and disciplined of which, was instantly headed and led by the wily Ioláni, in the direction of Vahíria.

The sun, that night, went down in thick, angry clouds; and, as the concourse separated and sought their homes, the old and the experienced, foretold an approaching storm.

CHAPTER III

The Pursuit

If ever Ioláni tasked his energies to the utmost, it was upon this occasion. This, was his last chance for vengeance on Idía and for the preservation of his credit as oracle of the War-god. Upon his success in the pursuit, he had now staked his all; and he determined that the struggle should be tremendous, before he lost. Every responsibility, now rested upon him alone. The little power of action natural to the King, had deserted him at this important crisis in the affairs of the state. The great chieftains would advise in nothing, aid in nothing, while the favor of Oro was still unobtained. He was without help, or companion, in his difficulties, until the sacrifice was secured. Succeed in his enterprise, and his glory was at its height; fail in it, and his downfall was irrevocable and complete.

There was no time now for delay. On they went through the little villages in the vallies, along the smooth turf pathways of the wood-covered hills, and up the deep ravines in the mountain sides, until they passed the inhabited regions and gained, as the sun set, the forest fastnesses of Vahíria.

The distance between the Temple and the Lake, when uninterruptedly pursued, was but from two to three hours journey. It occupied the Priest and his followers, however, a considerably longer period; for, they were under the necessity of separating to examine every suspected lurking place, in their way. Hence, the singular lateness of their arrival at the great scene of their exertions, which was indicated by their crafty leader, to be that side of the lake, where the water-god[']s Temple stood. As they wended onwards, they had comforted themselves with the prospect of a moonlight night for the pursuit; for, they were then in the wilds of the forest and the canopy of leaves overhead, almost completely shut out the firmament and its threatening aspect from their eyes.

But, now, they had arrived at an extremity of one of the masses of forest; and hurrying out upon the barren, rocky ground, they obtained an uninterrupted view of the lake and the western heaven.

The sun had just gone down and there was a cold, autumnal wind abroad. The dusky waters of the lake were already ruffled in an unusual degree, and the darkness, was fast creeping up the mountain precipices beyond. Dull, leaden-coloured clouds, were sailing fast over the brightness left by the departed sun, and there was a terrible and ominous silence in the atmosphere, that the distant moaning of the wind, rather aided than interrupted. The Priest scowled as he cast his eyes toward the sky, and his followers whispered anxiously among themselves, as they watched his sullen expression. They were hardy, experienced men; it was not the storm they feared, but the place where they were doomed to encounter it.

Their halt was of short duration; for, by the order of Ioláni, they again entered the forest and occupied themselves in selecting the dry reeds, so plentiful at this particular spot, to be used as torches—should they be required in the night.

"I purposed", said the Priest, "to search, by moonlight, through the caverns in the rocks below; for many a hiding-place, have I, myself, explored among them; but behold! how the anger of Oro has broken forth in the clouding of the sky! and listen—already, his voice of terror is heard among the mountains"!

As he spoke, the low, mournful sound of the rising thunder was heard in the distance; and the fall of the heavy rain-drops, was audible on the leaves above.

"For those who have set out", continued the Priest, "to range the island on either side of us, a shelter among their fellow-men, will offer at every step; for, the eastern and western districts are plenteously peopled; but for us, we are desolate and afar from the habitations of man, and our hiding-places in the storm, must be in the solitary caverns of the earth. The water-god's Temple stands not afar off, but its walls are ruinous and weak, and the tempest that is approaching, is overwhelming and very terrible. In the depths of this forest, are many caves and hollow places, wherein we may be hidden until the storm is past. Fire then, the torches in haste, for the fury of the god is at hand. In the hours of darkness, the victim may be secure; but the morning that visits her tomorrow—by the glory of Oro I have sworn it—shall be her last"!

Again, there was a longer and more anxious whispering among the men; and one, stepping up to the Priest, intimated to him for the first time, that a body of warriors had departed to scour the shores of the lake, before the delivery of the oracle's second answer. These, he urged, might at that very moment be within hail, and he entreated permission for his companions, at all events, to try the experiment. The more they were, the securer should they feel. They dreaded not the storm, but they feared exceedingly, the wild-men who were reported to lurk in the forests of Vahíria, in great numbers.

"Call as loudly as ye will"! shouted the Priest furiously, "but the torches—cowards! triflers! the torches"!

The storm was now up, and the scene both to eye and ear, was awful. The terrific loudness of the thunder-claps, unimaginable to inhabitants of northern lands, echoed sublimely among the mountains afar-off; the lightening, flashed out with a sharp, wizzing sound, most fearful to listen to; and in the intervals of the war in the firmament, were heard the fierce crashing of the boughs overhead, and the yells of despair and terror from the human beings beneath them. The flashes of the electric fluid, following one upon another, with inconceivable swiftness, showed the ruin that was running riot over the beauties of the place, in its most appalling colours. The trunks of the great trees, glanced, livid and indistinct, in the ghastly radiance that illumined them; and the slender wild-plants and creepers, writhed about in the fury of the blasts, in the most horrible and fantastic shapes. The thick darkness seemed filled with angry voices and peopled with spectral forms. Now, the wind dirged in the distance, its fitful and melancholy symphony. Now, it rushed in quick, furious gusts, through the trees that were near at hand. Destruction rode triumphant on the storm. The face of Nature, was altered and deformed. The majestic repose of the forest was gone; and, over the fallen beauty of the earth, there seemed to have arisen, in the hours of the night, the tumult and confusion of a Hell.

The position of the pursuers, was now critical in the extreme. To retrace their steps was impossible. They had unwittingly, penetrated deeper and deeper into the wilds of the forest. Their torches had been extinguished by the rain; and, although he confessed it not, it was evident to the warriors that their leader knew as little of the almost interminable natural labyrinths around them, as themselves. When to these sources of disquietude then, is added their belief, that the tempest was a plain manifestation of the fury of Oro at their delay in providing his victim, their agony of apprehension, on that fearful night, is fully accounted.

On they dashed! To keep motionless with such peril overhead, was impossible. On! On! Past the torn masses of brushwood, down among the swampy hollows, round about the scathed and dripping tree-trunks, with fresh bewilderment at every step in advance. The storm was at its height, the thunder was roaring its loudest, the boughs were crashing and the rain was beating down among them, faster and faster, when a loud exclamation, from one of the men who had straggled a short distance from his companions, brought the whole party to an abrupt halt —

"The wild man! The wild man"! muttered the savage, staggering up towards the Priest, and falling immediately afterwards insensible at this feet.

Villain as he was, Ioláni was a man of dauntless courage. While his followers huddled together on the ground, motionless with fear, he deliberately groped his way in the dreaded direction. Had he been ever so abject a trembler, he must at this moment, have risen superior to fear; for, in that action, lay the fulfilment of his destiny on earth.

He had nothing to guide him, but the glare of the lightening; yet, as if led by an infatuation, he paused at the right place, just as the darkness resumed its rule over the scene; and waited for the next flash.

One—and he beheld an open space among the trees and therein a mound of stones. Two—a solitary man, watching intently the speck of angry heaven above him. Three—his position and his features. And then, the thunder roared louder and louder, and down sunk the thick darkness again, over the earth.

He retraced his steps. He no longer stood out a superior being to the rest of his companions. He was as silent and awestruck—as hurried and headlong in his onward flight—as careless of blows and falls in the gloom, as they. He was as rejoiced and as eager as the faintest-hearted among them, when, after half an hour of that desperate journey, he felt rock beneath his feet, and heard the distant surging of the waves of the lake, and saw (by the lightening again) that they were once more on the verge of the forest, and that a cavern and a shelter lay yet before them.

It was a damp, rugged, miserable place, but they crept joyfully into the darkest of its noisome recesses; and thus they watched the weary hours out, until the storm began to lessen, and the morning was at hand once more.

The Priest never divulged, and his followers never enquired, what he had seen. The man, especially, who had discovered the solitary tenant of the woods, crouched the farthest from Iolâni, who as carefully avoided *him*. A mutual dread of each other, possessed both. A fear oppressed them, that one might communicate to the other a fresh horror—a better observation of the sight they had both beheld. It is an inferior—a common alarm only, that generates companionship, even amongst enemies. A fellow trembler, is the worst aggravation of suffering, which the victim of a deep overwhelming terror, can undergo.

As the dawn crept up on the firmament, the Priest walked forth alone upon a terrace of rock that overlooked the lake, to mature his plans for the day; and found, to his astonishment, that it was the self-same spot whence they had beheld the sunset, on the evening before. The thunder still sounded its hollow retreat in the distance, and the rain drops still pattered faintly, on the torn, dripping leaves of the forest. The waters of the lake, had changed in the night, to a monotonous dun colour, and still heaved wearily about, though the violence of the tempest was over and past. The tops of the mountains were hidden in deep mists, and the thick, black clouds of a few hours since, had amalgamated into great masses of a grey hue, cold and indistinct to look upon, yet promising, in the eastern heaven, a bright and beautiful day.

Scarcely had the Priest raised his eyes towards the prospect before him, when he detected, at some distance, a little com-

pany of people winding their toilsome way among the rocks
round the margin of the Lake, towards a far extremity of the
forest he had wandered in with his followers, throughout the
night. Without a moment[']s hesitation, hoping and fearing all
things, he turned again towards the wilds behind him—his
dread of the journey, overpowered by the motive that prompted
it—and made for a track that he knew they must pass on their
homeward route.

It was a toilsome and uncertain way, made doubly irksome
by the feverish impatience that now possessed him. But, he
reached the halting place before them, and heard as he paused,
the sound of their voices and the noise of their footsteps as they
crushed in their onward march, the small branches strown in
their path, by the violence of the midnight storm.

On they came—nearer and nearer yet. He hurried breath-
lessly forward to meet them. Joy for the oppressor! Misery for
the wronged! [T]he fugitive had been taken in the night!

There she was! guarded in front, by two warriors, and followed by the other members of the band, with her child and the
weeping and affrighted Aimáta. The instant they perceived the
Priest, the party halted; and Ioláni and his victim stood face to
face.

It was a strange sight to behold, but Idía was the calmest of
the group. Mingled expressions of triumph and ferocity, lit the
countenances of the warriors; grief and despair, spoke eloquently in Aimáta's demeanour; fiendish malignity, lowered
over the features of the Priest; but, the victim seemed swayed
by no emotion, agitated by no terror. Her dim and sunken eye,
bore no expression now; and the pale, pinched lips, neither
curled in disdain, nor quivered in fear. For, alas! when its
spring-time has passed away for ever, the heart grows the
meeker in its demands, in proportion to the smallness of its
heritage; and even sorrow and suffering, then, become a custom, with a facility melancholy to behold!

The Priest whispered a few words in the ear of one of the men, who instantly started off in the direction of the cavern that harboured his followers. This done, he commanded the removal of Aimáta and the child to the rear; and its darkest and worst expression, began to arise upon his countenance, as he spoke.

This movement, escaped not the observation of Idía. In an instant, she aroused herself from her abstraction and made an effort to regain her offspring, which was as immediately, restrained by the guards; and the woman, so lofty, so superior to the rest, but a few minutes since, now fell at the feet of her persecutors, and entreated with an agony of tears, to *be* restored to her child.

A few minutes after, and the infant was snatched from Aimáta's arms by one of the men, and by him, passed to the Priest. The despairing supplications of the women for its restoration, were of no avail. They were still dragged in advance, while Iolani bore his offspring onward in the rear.

He continued, gradually, to fall farther and farther back, until he became the hindermost of the troop and was hidden from the captives, by the people before him. The guards pressed rapidly forward with their prisoners for some time, until they gained some rising ground at the extremity of the forest. Here, they halted for an instant, and looked backward.

The Priest and the child were gone.

CHAPTER IV

Father and Son

Quickly about it Ioláni! The woman and the girl are both in thy power now. Despatch the child, and thy vengeance is complete, and thy pride is satisfied!

He was alone! The vacillation of purpose that had seized him in the early morning, now, that the day was advanced and the victim secured, seemed to have left him forever. All things, as usual, apparently contributed to aid his guilty purpose. He was too far from his troop to hear the shouts of the warriors, or the shrieks of the agonised women; and there was nothing near him, to interrupt the awful stillness of the forest atmosphere. But this, in anticipation, a benefit; soon became to him, in experience, a great and a bitter evil. And now; when not a leaf stirred on the trees, nor a flower on the earth beneath; when the doomed child, lay silent and motionless in his arms; when the same utter absence of sound reigned everywhere—*now*, he would have given worlds for a breath of wind; he would have bartered half his vengeance, for the fall of a withered bough— for anything to interrupt the ominous and mysterious stillness; yet nothing moved in the ancient and solitary place, but himself.

Gradually, there arose a strange spell for him in that silence. It influenced him slowly, he knew not how. He stopped unconsciously in his onward path. He drew his breath more softly and cautiously than was his wont. The child's weight, at that moment, wearied his arm; but, he dared not change its position, from the fear, that the action might occasion a noise. It was very fearful. He had begun by hoping, for the very thing that he most dreaded now—a sound.

He looked down upon his living burden. The infant's watchful, dilated eyes, were gazing up with a mechanical, unchanging expression of dread upon his face. It was the very counterpart of the mother's first look at him, when he had tempted her to its destruction. The more he contemplated the countenance of the child, the more strange and frightful was the resemblance. He seemed even to hear the mother's voice calling to him through the desolate silence—Ioláni! Ioláni!

His heart beat loudly in his bosom and he shrunk upon the ground. A shivering ran through his flesh. The damp dew of agony broke out upon his brow. He closed his eyes. He called upon his gods—*he* the unbeliever and the cheat! *He* the hypocrite, the lecher, the villain! Even *he* sought a refuge in the worship he defiled. Like Christian—like Pagan, even *he*, must acknowledge his religion, only to aid his sin. He knelt—he implored. An instant's cessation from this overpowering terror, was all he desired—an instant's—an instant's only!

An instant[,] Priest? That important, glorious, immortal instant, of the fortitude of the good, for the trials of the bad, is the treasure they dig for in Hell—the only boon that thy master Satan can never bestow!

How should he act? What refuge was left for him now? He never hated the child so much, as at this, the moment when he feared it most. He never more ardently desired the mother's death, than now, when the sacrifice awaited him and yet he was unable to move. Already, the victim was guarded in the Temple; the time of the ceremony drew nearer and nearer; the impatient warriors awaited his approach; the enemy were preparing for the fight—Vengenance, Duty, Success, whispered to him in

still, stern accents, from within—Ioláni dost thou tarry? and
should he delay—should he madly procrastinate still?

There, too, was the child—the accursed fruit of an accursed
love—still gazing into his face, still looking him into madness,
still living on, in spite of him. One moment[']s determination,
one moment's return of his former self, and he was rid of it
forever. A few yards before him, lay one of the deep, natural
dells of the forest. It seemed the place of all others fitted for the
accomplishment of the deed. His limbs trembled convulsively
and he tottered and staggered in his gait as he approached it;
but, he gained the edge of the bank at last and looked down.

It was a noisome and desolate place, whose sides—steep and
rugged—were, here, formed by masses of discoloured rock;
there, by patches of soft turf and decayed heaps of leaves.
Round its bottom, lay a dark, weedy marsh; in the deepest part
of which, the rain of the preceding night, had formed a pool of
dull, stagnant water, whereon there rested lazily a few withered
leaves, basking in the pestiferous vapour that floated sullenly
and slowly around. Nor sun-light, nor warmth intruded here;
for, of all parts of the forest, this was the thickest in trees and
the least explored by human footstep. It was known among the
natives, by the name of "Wild man's Dell"; one of those outcasts
of humanity, having been seen, some years since, to haunt its
melancholy precincts, by travellers who had occasionally
chanced to pass the place.

The Priest approached nearer to the brink and turning his
face from the eyes of the child, he strove to nerve himself to his
bloody purpose. Not the slighest dread of the place affected
him. His own present terror, was too real and intense, for aught
so dreamy and indefinite as superstition, to companion it for an
instant. At this moment, he felt no pity—no remorse; and yet,
to cast the child down, was a task he was unable to achieve.
What withheld him he knew not. What actual horror affected

him he could not divine—but there he stood immoveable; gazing down upon the pool of water, as if in a dream.

Erelong, by some mysterious link, the dell began to connect itself in his mind with the midnight scene he had witnessed in the forest. Soon, the dull water he was looking upon, seemed to reflect that hollow place among the trees and its outcast and fearful inhabitant. More and more vivid grew the ghastly repetition of the scene. A darkness gathered over his eyes, and again, in his imagination, did the thunder howl forth, the lightening flash and the thick, fierce rain pour around him. It was too terrible to be borne; he groped his way out of the shade, towards some streams of sunlight gleaming through a distant opening among the trees; and then, the impresssion of the storm faded from his mind; but, the vivid remembrance of the outcast, lowered before it still.

It seemed as if the thousand imaginary fears—the many assaults of irresolution, that had been spared him during the commission of former crimes, had arisen, at the signal of his present iniquity, to heap on him, in one short hour, the torments of years on years; and then to resolve themselves—after having laid waste the region of his heart—into a single recollection—a simple remembrance of a terrible and unwelcome sight. But even in this, lay a mystery mortal penetration could not fathom. It was a memory unlike other memories. It seized the attention and fascinated and wearied it at the same time. It became a still, slow, familiar torment, at once—a misery, whose stubborn vitality, nothing could injure or destroy.

In this recollection, lay for him, a retribution for past and a punishment for future offences; for it was the destined companion of his thoughts, till the hour of his death. It was to destroy what little of the gentler emotions he had once possessed. It was to blunt his wretched enjoyment of the successes of wickedness; but, to leave his appetite for them, untouched. It was not to interrupt his service to iniquity; but, to snatch away for ever from him, its rewards. Not as the torment, was it, that wearies only to reform; but, as the voice of a past crime, calling to him incessantly, for justice and atonement, and in an unknown tongue.

Neither its purpose, nor its nature, was known to the Priest; yet he strove instinctively, to shake it off; for he felt already, that at this moment, it mastered him in his actions, though it strove not with his thoughts. On and on went the inexorable moments; and still the child drew breath, still the woman struggled to plot its preservation, still the girl lived unpolluted by his arms. To remain indecisive longer, was impossible. There was no combatting the strange spell that was over him. There was no defying the supernatural protection, that seemed to hover over the child. He must sacrifice his vengeance in one point, if he would not lose it, in all. He must abandon his intentions for the son, if he would prosecute his purpose against the parent and her beloved.

Determining thus, the miserable wretch—his whole frame trembling as if with mortal agony, and his eyes averted in horror from his own offspring—suffered the child to crawl from his arms upon a smooth turf bank at his side. For one instant, he stood watching it with a malignant scowl and devoting it with the most hide[ous] execrations, to famine and death. Then, he slowly stole off, ever and anon, turning to look back upon it, and to heap fresh curses on its head. As its low wailing struck upon his ear, he quickened his pace, and his eye (sullen and expressionless, now,) wandered vacantly over the landscape before him. At length, he gained the track that led to the town; and then, he sped rapidly onwards, for the sunlight already began to fade from the forest openings around.

CHAPTER V

The last interview

The report was soon spread through the villages, by the scouts in advance, that the victim was secured; and the few people that the exigences of the impending battle had spared to their homes, now ran out by twos and threes, to catch a sight of the prisoners. Fearfully had their aspect changed since the halt in the forest with the Priest. Idia was born along by her guards, on a rude sort of litter of branches and spears, so pale and motionless to look upon, that the beholders began to imagine that the pomp and glory of the sacrifice had been already destroyed by Death. By her side and clasping her hand, walked the weary and still faithful Aimáta, her young countenance most lovely with the melancholy beauties of patience and resignation. Though the tears rose in her eyes, when the women and the little children who still loved and pitied her, came forth—some, with words of consolation and sympathy; others, with their simple offering of flowers—only to be scornfully repulsed by the guards around her, she uttered no complaint—discovered no despair. Beautiful and impressive was such virtue, in one so forlorn and so young! The Gentle Denizen of Heaven, might have wept as he watched it from on high; and remembered his own days of bitter persecution, among the warriors of Superstition and Crime!

Onward wended the troop. As they drew nearer to the Temple, their numbers were swelled by fresh bands of fighting-men

and fresh multitudes of the general populace; and amidst the
yells and shouts of the people, and the harsh, monotonous
sound, of the war drums, the concourse halted before the
shrine of their warrior-god.

The chiefs had received the commands of Ioláni for the disposal of their prisoners. Aimáta, he had directed to be confined
and guarded, in a lonely hut in the neighborhood of the Temple, charging them, at the same time, to treat her with the utmost consideration and care. With reference to Idía, she, as the
victim of the god, was to be watched by two Priests in his own
habitation, immediately adjoining the sacred place, until his arrival in the town, which he assured them he would effect, in
time to commence the sacrifice by sunset. It now wanted about
two hours of period.

As they led the woman away, Aimáta made a final effort to
gain from her a last farewell. But, still she remained insensible
to all outward objects; still, she awoke not from her deep stupor
of grief. And they hurried her roughly onward to the Temple;
and she spoke no word, she made no sign, even then.

While liberty frees the body, capitivity loosens the soul. It is
when the body is in bonds, that the spirit most experiences its
perilous privelege of freedom. Then is it, that the divine companion of our mortality, effects its longest flights—its safest de-
sertions from our side. Then is it, that it is most uncontrolla-
ble—most jealous of its mysterious and infinite immunities.
Little thought the Priests, as they watched their prisoner in her
dark, dismal confinement, how ardently and how truly their
wretched victim longed, that they who had confined her body,
could imprison her spirit too. Little did they imagine how poor
would be the harvest of the finest tortures they could inflict
upon her, after the field had been reaped and rifled beforehand,
by miseries, that even *their* ruthlessness could never invent.

Since the disappearance of her child, not a word had escaped the ill-fated Idía—not even to the girl she had watched over and loved, so long. Saving, in its unnatural paleness, there was no sign on her countenance of the storm that was raging at her heart. With the same terrible and ominous calmness that had characterized her demeanour on her journey, did she enter her prison and behold her inexorable guards. They gave her a little water to moisten her lips and they placed a few withered, flavourless fruits, by her side; and then, sat down as far from her as the limits of the place would allow, and watched her in utter silence.

Soon, however, the merciful confusion that had until now clouded her faculties, began to wear off, and her mind wandered strangely towards the days, that for ever, were past and gone. Vivid remembrances—for years inexperienced—of the simple pleasures of her childhood; of the bright, beautiful spots of earth, that she had once looked on and loved; of stranger children, who had cared for her when she was lonely and who had rejoiced with her when she was glad, rose softly and sadly over her heart; to delude with the promise of healing, but never, alas, to heal! For, ere the memory of the Past, could soften, or soothe, the experience of the Present, stood forth, to harrow and to grieve afresh; and the faster those visions appeared, the more surely were they destroyed, when their form was most apparent; and darkened, when their brightness was most alluring and divine.

And then, her thoughts—returning to their old occupation—fixed once more upon her child. Its infantine endearments, once noticed only to be forgotten, stole to her heart again, with a poignant influence they had never in reality possessed. The slightest charms, the most evanescent peculiarities of her lost offspring, one by one, passed vividly over her mind; and its last murmurs, its last attempts at speech, seemed to ring—how sadly musical, how deeply eloquent to *her*!—upon her ears, again. All that the child had been, all that the child might be, she felt within her now—now, when the utmost she could hope, was that its grave might never be touched, that its cold—cold body, might never be desecrated nor disturbed. Throughout its brief, sorrow-darkened life, it had been unto her as a fellow sufferer and as a comforter—Oh! Even as the gods of their people were to others, such had been the infant to her! —

And now, how was its soft cheek pillowed? When should it awaken again? —

Up! Up! watchers of her captivity! Look to *your* safety and *her's* in the hour of need! For see! her thoughts have worn out, at last, the sufferance of her mind. Her lips are parting with a strange and unearthly smile; and her eyes are gleaming, with a wild, sudden fire. Let her but rend those bonds she tears at so fiercely now, and ye will be even yet spoiled of your triumph and your sacrifice. Ha! they loosen[,] they bend! Do they snap?—No!—They resist her efforts, she staggers, she sinks again to the ground! Water—more water, for her parched lip and burning brow. The raving fit passes, and the exhaustion, the half death, is forth on her once again.

Look out from the Temple walls! The slow—slow hours, are drawing to their end. The sun is waining towards the bosom of the sea. The master-fiend is near at hand. The scattered warriors are gathering themselves together. The silent and awe-stricken multitude, are already on the sacred ground. Hark! The signal is given at the door. Her time is come! Wake her from her long, deep trance! Arouse her that she die!

🙚 🙙

Years and years after the period of our narrative, the Polynesian peasant, was used to describe to his affrighted children and his curious neigbours, the altered and horrible aspect of Iolâni, the Priest, when he returned to the Temple. What had occasioned this alteration never was known. The popular supersitition, however, soon ascribed it to an encounter with the wood-daemons and ghosts, that were supposed to haunt the shores of the dreaded and desolate lake; and in after seasons, among the wild songs of the land, was numbered as the people's favourite legend "the night battle of the Priest".

They thought he would have dropped to the ground, so unsteady were his steps, so utter was his exhaustion, as he neared the end of his journey. But he reached it at last—when, just as he was about to enter the sacred place, a scout—breathless and travel-worn—stopped him, with the information, that the enemy were marching over the frontier.

The chieftains were called together; and one and all, agreed in discrediting the man's information. He bore a suspicious character among them; and that was great reason for distrusting him. His answers, when they questioned him, were vague and contradictory in the extreme. He had seen the body of men that had aroused his fears, at so great a distance, and for so short a time, that it was considered doubtful, whether he could by any chance be certain that they were not a detachment of his own people, on their way to head quarters. Then, the shortness of the time that had elapsed since the skirmish in the woods, seemed to render impossible, the re-animating and re-organising of the rebel army, so completely, as to fit them for the great crisis of their lawless attempt. Added to which, it appeared inconceivable, that Mahíné should venture a battle, without a fresh performance of the ceremonies of war, which line of conduct, he must however have adopted, if the scout's intelligence were correct. In short after much deliberation and confusion of plans, it was at last determined, to send out trustworthier spies, to confine the suspected man, (betrayer

they deemed him *now*) and to proceed, at all hazards, with the
sacrifice, at once.

There were some, among the subordinate warriors, who remonstrated against so blind and dangerous a security; but, their
opposition was of no avail. The strange infatuation of Ioláni,
upon the subject of the sacrifice, seemed to have extended to
his political colleagues; and their desires, and not their reason,
induced them to make light of any obstacles that militated
against its immediate perpetration. So, the populace, discon-
certed and dispirited by all they had latterly heard and seen;
and the fighting-men, some doubtful, and some disaffected, repaired to their former stations. There was a spirit of melancholy
foreboding in the hearts of all. The captive women, were, now,
not the only mourners among the people. From the great actor,
in this great scene, down to the very children that wandered
about the multitude, the same dull, heavy disquietude, possessed every one; and an audible murmur of dread and discon-
tent arose from the assembly, as the Priest, turning from the
council, entered impatiently, the precints of the sacred palace.

He stepped into his dwelling at once, and it was remarked by
the two watchers who awaited him there, that he seemed unconscious, alike, of their presence and their charge. His eyes
wandered incessantly from place to place, and he appeared incapable of restraining them, for an instant, on any one fixed
point, even when they greeted him reverentially as was their
wont. They turned towards the woman; for, they had loosened
her bonds in the fear that her insensibility was the approach of
death, and that the torment inflicted by them, was the cause of
that omnious and dreaded trance. She arose as they looked, and
tottering towards the Priest, fiercely seized his right hand.

"Blood"! she muttered in a hoarse and horribly unfeminine
voice. "Blood there again"?

And she fell to tracing every line in his hand, with her trembling fingers, and looking it over and over again, with her wild, vacant eye, as if it could speak that one, last, important truth to her heart, that she despaired of hearing from his lips. Then, she whispered, mechanically, old words of endearment that had passed between them once, tearing the while at his apparel, as if to force him to listen to her. But he gave her no answer. For a few moments he seemed lost in thought. Then, suddenly turning towards the attendant Priests, he ordered them to look to the preparations, without; and on their departure, prepared to move nearer to the door, himself. But, at his first step towards the entrance the woman sprung up and wound her arms round his neck moaning it in his ear again—"Dead"?—

With a fierce execration he thrust her from him; and, pressing backward against the wall, gazed upon her face, as if the despair and anguish expressed in its every lineament, ministered delight to his heart. "Dying! Dying!" muttered he, in tones of savage triumph. "Hard by the Temple track, is the Wild Man's Dell. It is an accursed and solitary place. There, does the living infant moan, as the cold wind withers it, hour by hour. The offspring that thou hast dishonored me with, behold it is forsaken there! None shall be near to help—none shall hear and answer to its cry! For Famine hast thou preserved thy child! Dost thou glory now that thou hast thwarted me when I said to thee—obey? Wilt thou scorn me to my face, in thy prison, as thou didst in the cavern in the rocks? Thou evil spirit! The hour of triumph is now mine own! Thou wretched one among the people! The season of thy submission is come, and the signal for thy death, is sounding, already, from without!"

As he spoke, the roar of the martial music, denoting the King's approach, was heard from the altar. The miserable woman sunk upon the ground, and hid her face in her mantle, as if to shut out all mortal objects from her eyes, when the

Priest drew back the door, and signed to the servitors to enter the prison-house. His attendants seized on the victim, and led her to the appointed place. The procession formed; and [he] took his post firmly and proudly, as ever. It was his last triumph over the tyranny within him, and it was a triumph worthy of the man. They moved toward the altar; and just as they reached it, the sun went down —

Chapter VI

The Battle

It will be necessary, to pause an instant here, to describe that particularly to the reader, which has hitherto been but generally hinted at—the plain before the Temple; for, upon this spot, hinges a main point of interest, in the present narrative.

Unlike most of the sacred buildings in the Island, the Temple of Oro stood upon a site, but partially shaded by trees—those becoming guardians of its sister shrines. On two sides, the smooth, beautiful turf, stretched away for a mile, or more, before the level of its surface was broken, either by the forest, or the habitation of man. On the third, however, (the direction of the enemy's frontier) the ground was rocky and uneven, and thickly studded with trees, almost to the Temple walls. At this spot, stood the altar on which it had been determined, in the present instance, to offer the victim to the god. Here, from the sacred character of the situation, not a single hut had been erected; and the lone and shady avenues, wound onward, unprofaned by the labour of the husbandman, into the vast, inland forest, arising beyond. By this way, was the nearest and most difficult approach, to the hostile district. In many parts, innumerable dells and caverns, and not a single footway to guide him, awaited the traveller. From the multitude of hiding places thus presented, to fortify the immediate neighbourhood of the Temple, with any chance of success was impossible for the rude warriors of the land. Their chief security against attack

from this quarter, lay, only, in the almost utter impracticability
of penetrating the natural labyrinth around, in anything like
martial order or regularity. On this occasion, Ioláni and the
war-chiefs, had simply had recourse, to placing scouts at the
different outlets of the forest, more as a measure of wholesome
security, than of absolute necessity; their intention, being
rather to attack, than to defend. They believed that they were in
a more forward state of martial preparation, than the enemy;
and they determined to seize the immense adavantage, in such
warfare as their's, of removing the scene of battle, from their
own district, to that of the hostile party.

The disposition of the assembly, at the moment preceding
the sacifice, was impressive in the extreme. A little apart from
the rest, and nearest to the wood, were Ioláni and the victim;
the latter, bound to the altar, and awaiting her death, without
the slightest sign of emotion, or evidence of fear. Next to the
two principal actors in the scene, were the inferior Priests, the
warriors of distinction, and some guards, supporting the apparently lifeless Aimáta; who, by order of Ioláni, had been in-
cluded in the procession. Beyond these, came the great body of
the fighting-men, stretched out for several hundred yards, in
one dense, dark mass; and further yet, the useless old men, and
the women, and the children. Not a sound broke the deep stillness of the atmosphere, but the hollow roaring of the main
ocean in the distance, over the coral reefs, as the Priest—whose
features were now fearfully distorted—raised his weapon to
strike. Suddenly, however, to the astonishment of the multitude, he let it again fall towards the ground; and turning to the
defiles behind him, listened intently.

He had heard, or thought he had heard, from the post of the
scouts, a faint cry. The slightest alarm unnerved him, now. He
strained his eyes over the deep gloom before him; but, nothing
appeared. He listened with the utmost caution and care; but, no

further sound, from the dreaded quarter, struck upon his ear. This, was no time for vacillation; the task was set by himself, and must be achieved by himself alone; and again he turned towards the victim.

The club was firmly clasped; his body, was thrown back to give deadly force to the blow; his other hand, was wreathed in the woman's hair; the weapon was half raised, again; when an arrow from the wood behind, struck him on the right shoulder; and another, immediately afterwards, lodged in his thigh. He fell to the earth; and the next instant, the battle had begun over the prostrate body of the Priest.

On they poured—the men of blood and massacre! The soldiers of rebellion and crime! with their rebel-chieftain fighting at their head. At the first onset, the warriors of Iolâni fell back, dragging their wounded prophet with them, on the main body below. And here—upon the smooth turf, and under the holy moonlight—the terrible and deadly fight, began in earnest, at last.

Meanwhile, the men who had disabled the Priest, (after having suddenly surprised and murdered his scouts) had seized the girl Aimâta, and loosened from the altar, the war-god's intended victim. In this daring proceedure, they were headed by Mahíné. Not an instant was lost by the warriors. A few passionate kisses for the still swooning girl; a few hurried words to his followers; one look after the women, as they were dragged off into the woods; and the rebel-hero, was shouting the war-song of his tribe, in the midst of the fray.

Neither side hoped, nor gave quarter. Pillage and revenge, animated the one army; and despair and determination, the other. Wilder and wilder, grew the shrieks of the bewildered women and children of the attacked; louder and louder, through the still night air, rang the furious imprecations of the Prophets of War; and shriller and shriller, rose the crash of

weapons from the midst of the fearful conflict. No chances of
fortune or security were here. It was a hand to hand fight—a
duel of thousands—a war of extermination. Hark! That cry of
triumph from Mahíné's hosts! They have slain and captured the
first man. They bear his writhing body aloft, upon the spears.
They hurry to the Temple, and cast it down before the war-god.
They bathe it in blood. They burn it to ashes. It is the first fruit
of the battle; and offered by the rebels, to the spirit-arbiter of
the strife. "Victory for Mahíné! An omen for Mahíné!" cry the
Prophets of War, as they smear their bodies with the blood of
the offering, and waving their banners, hurry where the carnage is thickest and the fighting is most fearful.

Hark! Hark! Their voices are raging above the confusion of
the field! "Mahíné! Mahíné! Thou goest forth to glory! Thy
warriors shall conquer! The King of the land shall bow before
thee! Strike and spare not! Though they weep to thee, pity not!
Thou[gh] they grovel and moan before thee, never forgive! As
the hailstone, among the flowers, destroy the multitude of thy
foes! As the rocks of the ocean, be thou when they attack! As
the whirlwind among still waters, when thou fallest on them in
thy turn! Thou shalt pile up their dead, till they reach the tree-
tops! Thou shalt slaughter their flying, till the rivers run blood!
The spirit of battles is fighting with thee! Thou goest forth to
glory! Mahíné Mahíné"! —

And, on the other side, the Prophets keep no silence.
"Arouse—arouse ye warriors of the land! Remember your fathers, how they fought—your ancestors, how they triumphed!
Despair not of the victory! Ioláni is living to commune with the
god! For *his* cause do ye struggle—he shall not desert ye! Remember your women and your possessions!—your Prophet
and your King! and spare not the rebels! They are dogs before
Oro! Spare not! Spare not! Though the morning rise on the battle, weary not of the carnage and the strife"!

And now, dark clouds began to float up over the face of the moon; and the torches were lit, and borne on high by each party, to light them to their murderous work. The battle had by this time lasted more than an hour. The smooth, delicate turf, was polluted and withered by blood. The beauty of the flower-gardens, was mangled and destroyed, by slaughterers and slaughtered. The voices began to fail, and the clanguor of weapons to increase; and yet, the battle was still undecided! For, the fewer the combatants, the more deadly was the strife.

Both armies, had gradually swerved toward the borders of the sea. Already, warriors from each side, might be seen fighting, even in the water, for the possession of the King's fleet; in the event of the struggle concluding on the ocean. But, at this instant, the Priest Ioláni, supported and surrounded by a strong guard, appeared on the field. The King's party rallied at the sight of him, and drove the rebels back, until the contest raged once more, beneath the Temple walls.

At this moment, as if to shorten the work of carnage, the moon again shone out; and it was then, evident, to the combatants on each side, that an extermination, or the end of the battle, was come.

Here, the fierce struggle yet raged unchecked; where, striding over the dead bodies at their feet, the warriors still plied the work of carnage. There—exhausted at last—two hostile ranks, watched each other in utter silence, awaiting but the breathing time, to recommence the struggle, with the dread and fiend-like ferocity, that had marked its outset. On one side, crouching afar off, the slinger still studied, by the moonlight, his deadly aim. On the other, the wounded, upheld by the unhurt, staggered back to the fight, to vent the fury of their torments, in a last attack. While, at the outskirts of the one army, were to be seen:—the aged man, weeping in his desolate dwelling, for the fall of his kindred; the woman, draggging the dead warrior from

the field; the old and the helpless, with trembling hands, dig-
ging the grave that was to secure from mutilation and dishonour, the body of a chief; the solitary child, screaming in terror, by the corpse of its father; and the famished wild-dog,
watching from among the trees, the departure of the living, to
feast upon the dead. Then, on the other portion of the plain,
there were:—the dying warriors, moaning out with their last
breath, encouragement to their fellows in the fight; the grim,
cold corpses, stretched forth in the moonbeams; and the
wounded, tottering back to avenge their slain, and expiring ere
they reached the field. While sounding yet, there rose, above
even the din of the conflict, the battle-song of Mahíné, and the
ravings of the Prophets of War!

A third of the rebels, and the half of the King's party, were
now slain and wounded; and it became evident, at last, that victory was siding with Mahíné and his band! Slowly—inch by
inch, blow by blow, death by death—they drove back their op-
ponents, upon the villages where the images of their gods, their
great Priest, their women, their children, and their possessions,
were all enshrined. The vanquished, had determined, man by
man, to die at this post; the enemy, had prepared to win it over
their bodies, when a command was delivered, from Ioláni and
the King, that the wreck of their party should abandon the
struggle and make for the mountain fastnesses, under cover of
the night.

Racked by pain of body and agony of mind, the Priest[']s
powers had deserted him from the beginning of the battle; and
he was now, as incapable of action, as the King himself. The
emergency of the moment, wrung from him the command for
the retreat; and that was his last act of decision, his last evidence of skill. He was borne off by the women, in a litter, his
helpless brother bewailing with the old men and the children,
at his side. The last onset, was made by a desperate and devoted

few; under cover of which, the remnant of the conquered, betook themselves to flight; to be pursued, erelong, by the ruthless conquerors, to the death. Yet a few moments more, and where the moon had risen on the living and the proud; it now shone down, alone, upon the silent and the dead!

CHAPTER VII

The Retreat

Pursued and pursuers, were now set out upon their night march through the forest, in the opposite direction to the rebel camp. Not the slightest attempt at order, or regularity, was made by the conquered party. They had nothing to guide them towards their refuge, but the fitful glimpses of moonlight, that now and then, passed through the gaps in the thick foliage, above—nothing to warn them of the whereabouts of the enemy, but the groans of the wounded wretches, whom they sacrificed to their resentment, as they passed them by, or the glimmering of their torches through the dusky trees, as they, ever and anon, gained upon them, in their flight. Indeed, so considerably did Mahíné's bloodthirsty warriors soon decrease the distance, between their victims and themselves, that it became evident, erelong, that the only chance left for the unhurt and the slightly wounded, was the abandoment of all consideration for the more helpless among the companions of their retreat. Their sole dependance now, lay in the principal chieftain of Ioláni's hosts, who wounded and heart-broken as he was, still held the reins of command. From this man, emanated the first instructions to abandon the wounded; and with tears rolling down his cheeks, the aged warrior set the example to the rest, by leaving his dying son, to fall into the enemy's hands.

But among the warm-hearted, though erring, people of the land, there were many who refused to emulate the stoical ex-

ample of their chief; and from the very midst of the human hatred around, evidences of human affection, yet arose, on that
fatal night.

There was one man, sorely and mortally wounded, whose
wife and brother, had hitherto dragged him on in the rear, in
spite of every obstacle. Farther and farther behind, had they
unconsciously lagged. Their tribe had called to them to quit
their charge, if they would be saved. One moment, they hesitated; and the next, they had halted in the woods, and were
ready for their martyrdom whenever it should come. The
woman and the young man, looked on each other, for a few
minutes, in expressive silence; and then the wife supported the
husband's head, as calmly, as when she was wont to comfort
him, in the days of peace; and the brother, raised his weapon,
and stood over them: and there, they waited for their fate. The
lights gleamed brighter through the trees. The yells of triumph
and the groans of misery swelled louder and louder. The
branches snapped and parted. There was a crash of weapons—
one piercing shriek—and the next instant, the lights were again
dim, the cries were again faint, and all that moved, now, in the
desolate place, was a lock of the woman[']s hair, as the wind
stirred it from her face, and a withered leaf, that fell unnoticed,
upon the rigid features, of the noble and devoted three.

Then, there was an old man, who had been left to expire by
the rest, and to whom, a solitary child had remained, who had
resisted his entreaties, and was determined to stay with him, to
the last. As the enemy approached, the doomed warrior
crouched behind a tree, and covered his companion with his
body; so that, haply, the little one, at least, might escape. They
came on. They discovered him by their torches. They dragged
away the child, speared it and left the old man behind, to
mourn over the corpse. He pulled a handful of leaves and earth
from the ground; and in striving to hide the body in the insuffi-

cient cavity that he had made, and in cleansing from the face of the boy, the drops of blood that trickled there from his own breast; he, too, was gathered to the dead, that peopled the wood that night.

Turn we now, from the silent and the cold, to those that are left, to suffer and to fly; for, the hours have worn on, and the little band of the escaped, are within reach of the place of refuge.

The ground now occupied by the fugitives, was rocky and mountainous, and without pathway, or beacon of any kind, to guide the steps of a stranger. The moon had gone down; and assisted by the darkness and a superior knowledge of the place, they had gradually increased the distance between the enemy and themselves, on quitting the low-ground. The litter had, at this point, been discarded; and, supported by his brother and the more hardy among the attendants, the Priest wound his toilsome way, on-foot, after the main body of the conquered. A few women and children, were still among their number; but these, were now well-nigh exhausted, and had, already, begun to entreat that they might be left behind, to die in peace. The war-chieftain, had once or twice attempted to communicate with Ioláni; but, the faculties of the Priest, seemed ruined for ever, so vague and witless had his answers now become. His brother had stiven to soothe him from his strange mood & the women, comforted and mourned with him. But, no change was wrought in his demeanour as yet; for, no change had come over him, within. The agitation of the moment of sacrifice, the surprise of the ambuscade, the confusion of the battle, the misery of the retreat, had all left the vitality of the forest remembrance, untouched. It lay on his spirit now, as bitter, as mysterious a burden, as at the first moment, when it rose to haunt him in the presence of the child.

Though journeying onward slower and slower, the vanquished still continued the ascent of the mountain; the young men, ever and anon, watching from the exposed points, the progress of the conquerors, as with dauntless patience and perseverance, they tracked the steps of the fugitives, from the vallies below. At last, the remnant of the saved, gained a deep and precipitous ravine, over which, a rude bridge of tree-trunks had been thrown. This means of passage, the instant it had been used by all, was destroyed; and on the farther side, the wreck of the King's party halted with one accord.

At this spot, almost on the brink of the ravine, was erected a kind of stage of immense strength, formed almost entirely of wood. Passing under this, the fugitives gained an enclosed space of considerable extent, three sides of which, were guarded by a stone wall, twelve feet in height; the fourth, being protected by the platform already mentioned. The ground at the farthest extremity from the ravine, sloped gently downwards, and at a short distance from the fortress, was plentifully wooded. This approach to the enclosure, was considered the most dangerous of all; and the wall, here, was, of great thickness and strength; its top, being paved like a terrace, for the convenience of the guards, whose watch-tower in time of trouble, was that eminence. The interior of this place of refuge, was occupied by a few rude huts, a grove of plantains and bread fruit trees, and an rivulet of spring water. On the top of the platform, were several masses of rock, heaps of stones, and other projectiles, to be used, should the enemy attempt the capture of the place, by scaling the sides of the ravine, immediately below. This refuge, belonged to no distinct party, but was the possession, for the time being, of whoever might reach it the first. To reduce it by force, was considered an impossibility. Against famine, its inhabitants were well provided. All they had to fear, was the chance (terrible at such a time as the present) of surprise.

At the instant of entry, every individual among the fugitives, was employed in preparing for the expected assault. Of the stronger, some, proceeded to the woods around for extra supplies of provision; and others, commenced blocking up the passage under the platform, with great stones. Of the weaker, some arranged the weapons; and some, tended the wounded. Thus, in an inconceivably short space of time, the refuge was put in a state of thorough defence; and, their immediate labours achieved, the King's party awaited, almost in utter silence, the enemy's approach.

In the principal tenement, were assembled, the King, the women, the children, and the severely wounded; and on the ramparts, were placed the guards. All herded together, save the chieftain and the Priest; and of these two; the one, stood alone upon the top of the platform; and the other, crouched apart, under the shelter of one of the stone walls.

Day now began to break; and those who had met it but to rejoice, on the morning before, watched it in silence and in sorrow, today.

The King, who but a few hours since, had moved among thousands, now looked round, upon hundreds alone. Of the richness of his possessions, there was left but a bundle of weapons. Of the number of his councillors, there remained but a disabled and disheartened man. He was the first of his line, whose reign had been sullied by defeat so entire, as this. Nor guide, nor comforter, had he longer in the Priest. His Queen, had been slain at the threshold of his dwelling. He was deserted of his gods, and deprived of the flower of his army. The dishonour of flight, he had suffered already; there remained for him, now, but the last two ordeals—captivity and death.

As, in bitterness of spirit, he thus thought over his adversities, the ill-fated ruler turned once more, towards, the silent and solitary Priest. But Ioláni had no word, no greeting for him.

The fall of a dynasty and the massacre of an army, were contemplations, too nobly sorrowful, for such a heart as his. He could think of the victim's escape, and of Aimáta's preservation; for, there was cause here, for blaspheming his gods. He could brood over his abandonment of the child; for, in that act, there was a nourishment, even yet, for his hatred of the mother. He could recal[l], deed by deed, the iniquities of his past existence; for in that employment—terrible as it was—lay his only chance of penetrating the mystery of his forest remembrance, destroying its eternal connection with his thoughts, and averting its fatal and continual influence over the actions of his life. But, to think with his fellow creatures, to plot with others, for others advantage, was, at such a time as this, an impossibility. What cared he now, for the duties of his office, or the celebrity of his name? Give him back but his vengeance, release him from the torment of a memory and a heart; and King and country, honour and liberty, he would lose for ever, without a tear, or a complaint.

As the sun arose over the platform, the fugitives watched in silence for the first intimation of the enemy's approach; and the King, unable any longer to endure the misery of suspense, mounted to the post that the old chieftain still held alone.

The warrior's face was turned towards the sun. He leant, heavily on his club, and gasped for air, though the mountain breezes were now arising plentifully, from the earth beneath him. A deadly paleness and a stern rigidity of feature, distorted his countenance. Suddenly, however, the dull, death-like glare of his eye, was lightened by a wild, fierce look; his whole frame trembled violently, he made an effort to speak, tottered towards his master, and pointing to the woodlands below, sunk at his feet. The first ranks of the enemy, were approaching the ravine!

The King groaned in despair; and lifting the old man in his arms, spoke to him in a gentle and sorrowful voice. The dying warrior, turned his eyes upon his lord, and attempted to kiss his hand. The King tore the armour from his breast, and raised him to the air; but, the fixed and rigid expression of his face, now changed no more. Alas, for the safety of the monarch and the hopes of the garrison, the chieftain's last battle, has been fought upon the plains below!

CHAPTER VIII

The fate of the child

Scarcely had the Priest lost sight of his offspring, before the bushes from behind the dell, parted slowly and from the opening, there stole out, softly, a solitary man.

Keeping studiously out of sight of the child, this figure, approached as close to it as was compatible with perfect concealment; and crouching down, regarded the little unfortunate, with a long and patient investigation.

The only clothing of the man, was a torn piece of cloth, wound round his middle, with fibres of the cocoa nut tree. His long, ragged hair, reached to his waist; and, like his beard, was of a dusky, brown colour; being, apparently, scorched to that hue, by long and constant exposure to the burning of the sun. The skin of his face, was parched and discoloured; across his forehead, was a deep, revolting scar; and, over his under lip, his front teeth protruded, like tusks. His form, had natually been of great height, but was, now, so crooked and deformed, that his stature was far from imposing; and his gaunt, bony arms, appeared, in consequence, of most disproportionate size and strength when compared with the rest of his body. About his flesh, were thorn scratches and contusions; and he limped in his gait, as if severely injured in one of his limbs. Though the first emotion excited by the sight of him, might have been terror; the second, must assuredly, in most hearts, have been pity alone; so complete an air of forlorness and suffering was there, in his whole demeanour. There was nothing in him to evidence the grandeur of man—nothing to assert his outward equality with humanity; but the aspect of his eyes; and, even these, in their extraordinary expressiveness; in their sudden, perfect eloquence, were almost unearthly to look on. If thoughts he had, they must pass like hurricanes over his mind. If he possessed feelings, they must rise on his heart, only, to find no resting place there; for, every mortal emotion, seemed to have an interpreter, the most instantaneous and the most evanescent, in this, the sole feature, in which, the beauty of humanity was discoverable in him, still. Now, those impressive eyes, darkened in sadness; now, they brightened in joy; now, they gleamed in ferocity; now, they softened in kindness. Mysterious—almost awful, were they to behold; so painfully were they at variance with the rest of his appearance; so completely had they defied the deformity, that had, elsewhere ravaged his form.

Erelong, as he watched from his concealment, the cry of the forlorn and forsaken child struck upon his ear. At first, he trembled; as if the sound had nothing but horror for him. Then, he hid his face in his lank, shapeless fingers; and then—as if fired by a sudden idea—he disappeared; almost immediately returning, with some fruits and a shell of water in his hand.

He approached the child with a kind of dread, hiding his features, by holding his hair over them like a veil; and placed his little supply of provision by its side, kneeling and humbling himself to the ground, the while, as if before a being, that could annihilate him at a word.

There was something, at this moment, impressive and fearful in the scene. The dark, majestic trees, arching overhead; the dim, dull light, over the place; the streaks of sunbeam, falling fantastically over the two figues; the position and appearance of the man; the frantic terror expressed in the countenance of the child; the gloomy sameness of the distant prospect of trees—all was in keeping with the supernatural reputation of the place; all was in strict harmony with the characteristics of its miserable inhabitant.

Cradled, as he was, in danger, and cherished in terror; surrounded, as he had been, from the first dawn of his infantine perceptions, by the wildest, the most ferocious of the people of the land; it was the suddenness of the man's approach, rather than the deformity of his appearance, that terrified the child. His separation from his mother and his seizure and subsequent abandoment by the Priest, had almost exhausted the very endurance of his faculties for fear; and erelong, the tears again coursed down his cheeks; and, as he gazed once more, on the crouching figure of the outcast, his expression, gradually became one more of wonder, than of dismay.

Then, after an interval, the man ventured (his hair still falling over his countenance) to take the child's hand in his, and to fondle and caress it softly. The little creature started at the action, and shrunk back, as if contact with the hard, horny skin of his preserver, pained his delicate flesh; but, no fresh tears appeared on his cheeks, no fresh cries came from his lips. Gradually and carefully, the outcast increased the familiarity thus begun (the child shrinking at each new advance, but, still, never attempting to repel it) until he fairly held the object of his care, within his arms. Then, he took the bread fruit, and softened it in the water, and fed the child with the studious consideration—the affectionate, enthusiastic care, of a woman. Lastly, he placed it gently on its former resting place, and set himself to gather the brightest and most delicate of the wild flowers that grew around, weaving them into rude garlands and fantastic shapes, and scattering them before the child, to destroy, or to fondle, at its infantine pleasure. In the hurry and abstraction of this employment, his hair was discomposed, and his face became partly visible; but, the forsaken one, still continued his pleasant amusement, without a gesture of fear, or an expression of distrust. Erelong, the smile returned to his lips; he murmured his low, imperfect attempts at speech; and, soon, he even quitted the flowers, and wreathed his fingers in the long, tangled beard, of the outcast, as he bent over him; examining with infantine wonder, its length and appearance, and never shrinking from, nor trembling before him, now.

Suddenly, however, a change came over the face of the man. His eyes flashed and dilated, and his whole frame trembled convulsively. He drew back from the child, tottered to a little distance, out of its sight; hesitated, returned a few steps; and then, as if by a last and superhuman effort, disappeared among the woods.

Now, he sped rapidly onward, heedless of obstacles, and moaning and muttering to himself, fearfully. Now, as if utterly exhausted, he sunk to the ground, tearing at the earth with his hands and teeth; the foam gathering round his lips, his eyes glaring fiercely about, and his limbs quivering, as if in the extremest agony. At one time, he half raised himself from the earth, looking piteously upon the solitude around him, and murmuring in a broken voice, a few simple terms of endearment, or calling sorrowfullly, upon a certain name. At another, he peered around him with an expression of the extremest dread; and, then, drawing himself back, he fiercely raised his hand, as if to strike a sudden and determined blow. At this action, the raving fit would seize and torment him again. It was a fearful madness, while it was over him; but, it lasted not long. An exhaustion soon appeared in his form, a ghastly paleness overspread his face, and he lay motionless and silent upon the earth; save, when a sudden shivering ran through his limbs, or a low, deep sigh, occasionally escaped his lips.

Then, in a little while, he arose; and, removing from his face and person, the consequences of his sudden visitation of suffering, he slowly retraced his steps, towards the child. Saving, in a casual and transient return of its wildest expression to his eye, there was, now, no outward evidence of the torment he had so lately undergone; and his demeanour towards his infantine charge, was as patient, as gentle, as submissive, as before. His sudden delirium, seemed to have been anticipated and suffered, as a familiar visitation—as a misery, so often experienced, that it had become a custom at last.

He set himself again to his task of humouring and diverting his companion; and his attempts were met by the child, with the same welcome and delight, as before. And thus, the two, watched out the hours patiently, in their solitary resting place, until the sunset was near—the memorable sunset, that marked the mother's worst danger, and the son's happiest preservation—and then, the man, taking the child in his arms once more, disappeared slowly with it, past the lonely dell, and through the brushwood, from which he had emerged on the departure of the infamous Priest.

He wended onward, through the thickest part of the forest, (passing the open space and the mound of stones, on which he had been seen by Ioláni) until he gained one of the wildest of the woodland recesses; where, the ground was rocky and uneven, and rendered apparently impassable, by the closeness of the trees, and the quantities of wild plants and brushwood that grew between them. Forcing his way through these obstacles, and taking the utmost care, at the same time, that the obstructions in his path should work no harm to the child, he arrived—after descending for a little distance—at a range of basalt rocks; and entered one of the deepest and largest, of the many cavities, that yawned around.

From this place, although the thickess of the trees, and a rising in the ground, hid it from view, you could hear, on a stormy night, the surging of the waves of the great Lake. The appearance of the cavern, within, was vast and gloomy. In one corner of it, lay a quantity of dry moss and withered leaves. In another, a tattered remnant of female wearing apparel, carefully concealed in a fissure in the rock. The open space before the mouth of the cave, was worn into a little pathway; on one side of which, flourished a patch of small and exquisitely beautiful flowers, which was shielded from injury, by a strong palisade of iron-wood stakes. There was an air of utter, unbroken solitude, about the place, most melancholy to behold. It was one of those retirements—hermit-like and lonely—where the slightest evidence of a human presence, has an absorbing interest for the most careless eye—where the humblest achievement of human art, wears a romance, painfully mysterious, to the most volatile mind.

The first action of the outcast, was to grope his way, through the gloom of the inner portion of the cavern, to the spot where the piece of woman's dress was hidden; apparently, with the view of ascertaining, whether it had been, since his absence, perfectly unnoticed and untouched. After feeling it carefully all over with his hands, he returned towards the outer division of the cave and began to scatter his provision of dry moss, in a little recess in the wall; and, on the couch thus simply and speedily arranged, he gently placed the infant; seating himself by its side, to watch it until it slept.

But, as the cold night air began to penetrate the place, a shivering passed over the child's frame, and he began to weep. The outcast involuntarily turned towards the piece of wearing apparel, concealed behind him. He half advanced to it. Then, as if lacking the courage to disturb it, he only gathered some more of the moss, and covered with it the body of his charge. But the restlessness of the child, soon made this protection of no avail; and after another instant's hesitation, he drew his strange treasure from its hiding-place, and wrapped it round the body of the infant; the use to which he had put his possession, seeming to oppress him with a suspicion of its safety, for he kept his hand over it, until the object of his care sunk at last, into a deep and quiet slumber.

Then, he left the cavern, and walked backwards and forwards over his little pathway; stopping at last, as if by an irresistible impulse, by the bed of flowers. These, seemed to arouse in him the faculty of memory; for, his eyes softened (in other days they might have filled with tears!) as he looked on them; and, as he stooped down; and plucked away a few withered leaves that had fallen over his enclosure, he muttered, mechanically, the same few terms of endearment, and the same name, that had escaped him in his raving fit, but a few hours before. Erelong, however, he again returned to the cavern, and sat down once more, by the sleeping child. And, thus peacefully passed the night of battle and slaughter, with the forest habitants. Thus was the forsaken and defenceless infant, preserved and cared for, while the powerful tyrant who had plotted its destruction, was hurled from the pinnacle of his might; and the warriors of the land, were overthrown in their glory, and humbled in their resolution and pride! —

CHAPTER IX

Mahíné's revenge

The night of the battle, was the signal for the return of its wonted tranquillity to the rebel village. On the spot, where the pomp of sacrifice and the bustle of martial preparation, so lately had reigned; the moonlight now shone, in uninterrupted brilliancy; and, where but a day before, groans and laughter—cursing and jesting—sounded in the utterest confusion, and with the wildest uproar; the gentle music of the breezes among the rocks by the shore, and the rustling of the leaves of the grove round the dwelling of the chief, were heard alone. Some of the houses, appeared quite deserted; while, at the doors of others, were to be seen, only, a few women and children, or a solitary old man, quietly enjoying the beauty and stillness of the night. One by one, even these vanished; and the pathways and gardens were all deserted, as the escort of warriors conducted the rescued women towards Mahíné's abode.

These men, on the setting out of the army, had received their full directions from the chief; and, thus far, had obeyed them with the utmost precision. They had stolen upon the Priest's scouts; murdered them, with but one exception, without noise; had released the women and brought them to the rebel village; and now, prepared to follow Mahíné's commands, regarding their treatment there. Both their charges were to be lodged, if possible until his return, in the chieftain's dwelling. But, should Idía insist upon her enlargement, they were to permit her to be at liberty, taking the utmost care, however, that Aimáta should, under all circumstances, be subject to their own especial guardianship. Old and experienced men, had been selected by Mahíné for his service, in this instance; and they proved worthy of his confidence, from first to last.

The sojourn of the women, was in the loveliest part of the Island; and they had all the simple luxuries of the land at their command; but, these benefits, came at a time, when neither, had the heart to notice, nor the inclination to use them. The scenes of terror through which she had passed, had thoroughly subdued the youthful elasticity of Amiáta's mind; and she had now, the further misery to undergo, of uncertainty as to the fate of her young warrior. But, even yet, the girl's patience and fortitude did not entirely fail her; and many as were her own woes, she applied herself as industriously as ever, to aid the recovery of the ill-fated Idía.

There is no more wonderful proof of the intimate connexion between man's corporeal and spiritual formation, than the resemblance of the ruler, by which the powers of endurance, are regulated in each. If pain has the privilege to assail, after it has lost the power, in the body; grief, has the same valueless immunity conceded to it, in the mind; and, not more surely does the insensibility, but herald the finer sense of feeling, in the one; than, in the other. Of mental lethargy, a forcible example was shown, at this period, (as well as on the previous occasion of the journey to the Temple) by the condition of Idía. No tears, rolled down her cheeks. No quivering, appeared on her lip. Not a sigh, nor a gesture of grief, escaped her. And yet, perhaps of all the seasons of her trial, the worst was now arrived. She looked at the girl as she knelt by her side, and seemed to recognize her with ease; but, she never spoke to her, as had been her wont, in the days of sorrow, before. Fearing, that she had escaped one death, only to fall a sacrifice, to another; Aimáta redoubled her efforts to relieve. For that night, they were still in vain; but, on the next, a change arose.

A strange restlessness now seized her. She hurried from place to place, with a half troubled, half vacant air, as if striving to recall some word, or event, that had latterly vanished from her memory. Then, she would draw Aimáta to her side, and repeat to her, over and over again, the minutest circumstances, connected with the birth and subsequent preservation of the child; with simple pathos, dwelling upon the slighest details, as if, this self-laceration, were a comfort to her, in her distress. And then—after a long interval of silent and painful thoughtfulness, a flash of bright, unnatural exultation, passed over her countenance; and she hastily and affecionately embraced the girl, telling her that the hour of her departure was come—that she had a journey to make into the woods, and must about it, straight.

In the utmost astonishment and dismay, Aimáta questioned her upon her purpose; and, she at last confessed that the sole object of her contemplated pilgrimage, was to attempt a discovery of the body of the abandoned child—that she had, after much painful effort, retraced to herself, the result of her prison interview with the Priest—that he had, discovered to her the scene of his crime—and that she nourished a hope—the part of the forest where the deed had been committed, being desolate and lonely—that the corpse of the infant, might yet be lying undisturbed, in the place of its miserable death. She would involve no one, in the peril and uncertainty of the search; and, she, therefore, prayed earnestly, that none would be so cruel as to oppose her in her attempt. Successful, or unsuccessful, a very short time was all that was required for the execution of her project. Her absence would be of consequence to none, and she entreated to be allowed to depart, without interference, or debate.

All this, was spoken without a word of lamentation, or a tear of sorrow. The slight prospect—even thus miserably—of being re-connected, once more, with her child, assumed to have spread a transient and deceitful calmness over her heart; and there was a mingled expression of anxious, fearful hope, and of deep, latent misery, in her eye, as she looked on the girl, most melancholy to behold. Aimáta's determination, as Idía ceased speaking, was taken in an instant. Forgetful of all the dangers, in this time of war, encompassing the land; and, more especially, in its lonely places; she, at once, announced to the woman her determination of aiding her in the mournful search; only, to be immediately opposed in the execution of her generous purpose, by the mandate of the guards.

Her utmost entreaties, failed to influence them in the least. Their orders were positive; the woman might depart, but the girl must remain. Under such circumstances as these, the peril of Idía's attempt, occurred forcibly to Aimáta's mind. She promised acquiescence in the will of the men, in every particular; if, one even among them, would but protect the woman, on her way. This request, also, was refused. They were commanded to hold their post until the chief's return, and could not disobey so peremptory a requisition. The dangers of Idía's journey, were in their eyes, so few, that they considered that others of her sex, might guard her as safely as they; and, such protection as this, they would accord; but, no other.

Feeling, that companionsip for Idía, however inefficient, would mitigate her anxiety on her behalf, Aimáta closed with the proposal of the guards; but, the realisation of their project, was attended with much difficulty. The women, one and all, feared exposing themselves at such a period, in such a place as Vahíria, and resisted with much obstinacy, the duty imposed upon them. Under any other circumstances, the warriors might have used no further attempts at persuasion; but, in this instance, they knew, that to indulge Aimáta in her present detention, was to secure the favour of the chief; so, they perservered in exacting the performance of their promise; and, after some delay, two, among the females of the place, were selected as the woman's escort. With the servile obedience, customary in Polynesia, from the weaker, to the stonger sex; the women, with visible fear and reluctance, armed themselves, and submitted to the decree of the guards. And thus; the mother, started in silence for the forest; and the maiden remained in tears, in the dwelling of the chief.

CHAPTER X

The besieged

For a few moments, heeding neither the rapid approach of the enemy, nor the habitants of the enclosure below; the King gazed upon the dead body of the old warrior, in sorrowful silence. His last remaining servant of renown and capacity, was snatched from him. He had no councillor, no companion left. Never did he feel his power, so utterly lost, as at this moment. Never did the misery of his forlorness assail him so poignantly, as now. He raised the corpse, and descended with it in his arms, among the people. A dogged despair, possessed their numbers. Death and captivity, seemed to have lost their terrors for them; and they waited their destruction, the same cold, insensible tranquillity, appearing in the demeanour of all.

More afflicted, by nature, with indolence, than with imbecility of disposition, the King was now roused to action, by the necessity of the moment. He hurried to the platform again, calling upon the wreck of his warriors to follow him. The enemy, had by this time, felled some large trees, had constructed with them, a new bridge across the ravine, and were preparing to pass. The arrows of the beleaguered party, were instantly employed to oppose their advance; at first, with some success; for, five or six of the hostile warriors, were slain in crossing their bridge. The assistance of the King's fighting-men, was, however, of short duration. Showers of missiles from the main body of the rebel army, soon compelled them to abandon their exposed position; and the besiegers ultimately passed over to the fortress, unmolested by the besieged.

The King and his party watched them, from behind their defences, in painful suspense. Since the battle, their numbers seemed to have been increased; and, as they trooped gallantly past the solitary fortress, they made a goodly and a martial show, with their banners, their instruments of music, and their War-Priests, shouting the song of victory, at their head. They encamped at a short distance from the place of refuge; and immediately after the halt had been effected, an ambassador, bearing a flag of peace, approached the walls of the enclosure.

He was received by the King. The purport of his message from Mahíné was, that the chieftain, willing to be merciful, advised him for the first and last time, to yield; if he would save his own life, and the lives of those about him. It was, moreover, set forth in the harangue, that the insurgents had already been reinforced, and were, then, in expectation of farther help; and, that the King being now destitute of allies and defenders, it became, therefore, evident, that his only choice left, was life on Mahíné's terms, or death on his own.

As the man concluded his address, the unfortunate ruler looked despondingly round upon his little handful of wounded and weary fugitives. With the dogged valour of their calling and nation, the battle-worn warriors, awaited without a gesture of agitation, the command that was to doom them either to captivity, or death. Their unhappy monarch, gazed on them fixedly for a few moments. An instant's look of fury and hesitation appeared in his face; to be replaced, however, immediately, by an expresssion of the deepest misery and despair. He turned again towards the herald; his head sunk on his breast, and he groaned, rather than spoke, those two melancholy words—"I yield".

The messenger had no sooner conveyed this intelligence to

the camp, than Mahíné and his principal chiefs, escorted by a strong guard, approached the walls. The defences of the ende doorway, were immediately removed; and the besieged, in sad array, passed out, between the lines of their conquerors.

First, came the King and his brother, the Priest. The appearance of Ioláni, seemed to strike the *utterest* astonishment, into Mahíné's ranks. Whatever the enemy's plans might be, they had evidently been formed under the supposition, that the Priest had perished in the retreat; and, the instant he was seen, the chieftain, was addressed by many of his coadjutors, in taunting and angry tones. This disagreement, however, was soon silenced; and the wreck of the royal army, followed by the few women and children who had escaped the horrors of the battle, passed onwards, unnoticed and unmolested, to the rebel camp.

The council of war, convened by Mahíné and his chieftains, was attended solely by Ioláni and the King. Before detailing, however, the result of their conference, it may be necessary to observe, that the offer of peace, had been made by the rebel commander without the concurrence of his experienced warriors; whose council, had been to avoid departure from the sanguinary rule, usual on such occasions as the present, of exterminating the vanquished. This advice, Mahíné had positively refused to follow. The heat of the battle and the fury of the pursuit once past, his ruthlessness departed with them. His connexion with the the gentle Aimáta, had done more to soften and to humanize his nature, than his bloodthirsty councillors were able to conceive; and nothing could shake the merciful determination, that he put into effect, in the manner already detailed.

The conference was of short duration; for, where the power was all in the hands of one party, it was likely to be but little interrupted by discussion. The terms on which Mahíné consented to waive further hostilities, were:—first, the abdication of the throne, in his favour, by the King; and, secondly, the immediate removal of the deposed ruler, his brother, and the companions of their flight, to a lonely and distant island; the return of any one of them to the shores of Tahíti, being an offence, to be visited by instant death. Such, was the daring and ambitious use that the chieftain made of his hard won victory. His terms were accepted with the callousness of utter despair, by the wretched monarch and his spirit-stricken brother. The white and red band, allegorical of peace, was immediately brought forth; and, as if in bitter mockery, the dethroned and helpless King, was forced to take the usual oath, never to rend it in war, while such a casualty, could by any means, be avoided. This observance concluded, the whole body of the warriors and the people, moved again in the direction of the coast. The chieftain, to bear the news of his victory to his beloved; and the rest, to prepare for the remaining ceremonies of peace, at the Temple of Oro.

It was remarked at the conference, by Mahíné's warriors, that what few words Ioláni had spoken during their debate, had been of the most vague and contradictory description; and that his reputed energy and boldness, seemed to have entirely deserted him. They watched him curiously, as he passed slowly by them. There was a fixed, savage glare, in his eye; and a wild, unnatural smile, on his lips that made them tremble, as they looked upon him. He seemed to be incessantly in strange and stern commune with himself. No outward object, or action, appeared to affect him in the slighest degree; and, as he still wended onward, muttering at intevals to himself, they whispered to each other, that he was suffering a dread and secret punishment from the gods—a spiritual penalty, without either remission or repeal.

CHAPTER XI

Mother and son

Heavy were the hearts of Idía's companions, as they sullenly followed their guide, into the recesses of the forest. Many and many a glance did they turn backwards, towards the happy homes they were doomed to leave; and, many and many a look of distrust and discomfort, did they cast after the woman, as she led them, deeper and deeper, into the solitary woodlands. The further they journeyed, the more dilatory and uncertain became Idía's guidance. She strayed from one path to another, apparently without the slightest cause for such voluntary enlargement of the journey, at so early a stage of their undertaking. When they remonstrated with her, upon their unnecessarily wasting their powers of endurance, she neither noticed, nor answered them. Erelong, they began to feel suspicion of her motives, and offence at her reserve; and they whispered anxiously to one another, from time to time. A little further on, and they would be unable to find their way back—should retreat be necessary. At the point they had now reached, that resource was still within their power; and, after a little hesitation, they determined to use it, whatever might be the consequences of such a proceeding, to themselves.

In furtherance of this selfish purpose, the eldest of the women, now called to Idía to halt; and, in sullen and determined tones, spoke to her thus:

"We have born with thee the weariness of the way thus far;

but, we will bear it with thee, now, no more. Behold, thou leadest us ever onward, we know not whither, for a purpose the most dangerous and the most vain. If *thou* hast thy little one to seek for, that is dead; *we* also, have our offspring to look to, that are alive. Pursue then thy search alone, for we fear to follow thee further, into such a solemn and dreary loneliness, as this. Against our desire, were we driven forth to journey with thee. Of our own will, do we purpose, even now, to brave the fury of the fighting-men and to turn back. Better is it to suffer the anger of those that we know, than to risk encounter with the strangers and wanderers, who make their desolate sojourn here. Therefore, be the hazard what it may, while there is yet light, we will bestir us and return".

The unfortunate and deserted woman, fixed on them one long, woful look, of reproach; but attempted no reply, spoke no farewell, as they left her to her fate. She watched them with a sad and mechanical attention, as they disappeared through the trees; and then, with a bitter sigh, she addressed herself to her journey again.

Now and then, she halted and looked carefully round her; partly, as if from fatigue; partly, as if from an irresistible impulse; but, with the exception only of such occasional delay as this, she held still upon her solitary way. If once she could reach the shores of the great Lake at any side, she felt assured, that she could find the scene of the child's abandonment, without difficulty. But, her ignorance of the bearings of the forest, involved her discovery of Vahíria in great uncertainty. Ever and anon, she stopped to listen, if perchance the rippling of waters were audible from any part; but, the same utter and solemn silence, was all that rewarded each attempt. Her heart burdened with misery, and her limbs tottering with fatigue, she still continued to press slowly forward, until at last, completely worn out, she gained a spring in the forest, from which, ran a small stream of the clearest water. After having halted here, to recruit her energies, she followed the course of the rivulet. Its banks, soon began to widen; and erelong, she felt rocky and uneven ground beneath her feet. As she still wended, onward, the multitude of the trees began to lessen; and she gained at last, one of the outlets of the forest; beneath which, lay the ruined Temple of the Water-god, and the waters of the desolate Lake.

By this time—so long had she wandered in the woods behind—the sun was past his meridian; and the lonely woman, after a brief glance at the scene of all her happiness and all her woe, struck into the track, where she had been first met on her capture, by the relentless Priest.

Her demeanour became now characterised, by an agitation fearful to behold. At every step, as she hurried forwards, she looked widely around her, until she gained the turf bank, where Ioláni had abandoned the child. In an instant, she observed the fragments of garlands scattered over the place; and— crouching on the ground to examine them—she discovered marks of footsteps, on the soft, porous earth. With an hysterical cry of exultation, she traced these tracks, past the lonely dell, and into the thicket beyond. Here, she lost all sight of them; but, she still pressed forwards—the briars and thorns, opposing her passage in vain—until she gained (every limb bleeding from laceration) the open ground before the outcast[']s cavern. At this place, the footmarks again appeared. Without an instant's hesitation, she followed them. At the mouth of one of the caves they stopped; and there, striding forth to meet her, with uplifted club and eye of fury, was a solitary and hideous man!

And on his arm, clasped to his bosom, what saw she? A child! It moved, observed her, uttered a well-remembered cry, and strove to escape; stretching towards her its little arms. A child! It was *her* child! It was alive! It was happy! It had escaped! It was beautiful still!—Her hapless one! Her own!

What recked she now, of the club, or of him wielded it? She flew to the man, clasping her hands, and kissing in entreaty, the

mantle that was wrapped round the child. The little one, redoubled its cries and its efforts to escape. The man's arm gave way,
he dropped the uplifted weapon; and, the next instant, she had
it on her bosom—the living, moving infant, for the cold corpse,
she had wandered so far to inter!

Over and over again, did she gaze distractedly upon the
child's form; and still, she could not persuade herself that she
had recovered it, uninjured. Minute after minute, utte[r]ly unconscious of her situation, did she consume in fondling her restored offspring, and in heaping on it, every term of endearment, that her language possessed. Erelong, however, she
looked up; staggered towards the very outermost portion of the
mouth of the cavern; and pressing the infant convulsively to
her breast, gazed round again, with an expression of the wildest
astonishment and dismay.

The outcast's eyes were fixed on her, in deep and eloquent
melancholy. His club lay beside him unnoticed; and he held in
his hand only, the mantle that had wrapped the child's form
while in his arms, which he had snatched from it, when the
mother had obtained possession of his charge. His lips half
parted, and moved as though he would have spoken; but, not
an audible word escaped him; and, after an interval, he turned
towards the resting place he had arranged for the child, and
taking from it a garland of flowers, bent his steps towards the
innermost portion of the cavern.

At this moment, Idía's escape might have been effected with
impunity; but, she stood rooted to the spot. Her eyes, had
turned insensibly, towards the bed, from which, the outcast
had just removed the garland; and, on which, the child had evidently lain. She marked the industrious, affectionate care, that
had fashioned and arranged that couch; she thought on the
charity, that had cherished and preserved the forsaken child;
and, such a strong and sudden gratitude overspread her heart,

as merged all suspicion of the preserver, into thankfulness for the preservation. Acting, therefore, under her first generous impulse, she advanced half way into the cavern, and, in tones of the utmost gentleness, addressed its miserable inhabitant.

He was occupied in folding and arranging the garland he had taken from the bed, within the remnant of wearing apparel; delaying the task, as though he loved to dwell on it. At the first words that fell from the woman's lips, he started up, and depositing his strange treasure in its accustomed hiding place, led the way abruptly and in silence, to the mouth of the cavern.

As they gained the open ground, Idía perceived that the tears were rolling plentifully down the outcast's wan, furrowed cheek. She attempted to address him, again, in some simple expressions of solace and gratitude; but, he only murmured a few broken and almost unintelligible words of entreaty, and motioned her to leave him.

She departed instantly; for, she dared not dispute his will. Yet, ere the foliage could hide him from her view, she turned and looked back, in the hope that he might yet sign to her to return. But, he was lost to all outward contemplations, now; and the last that she saw of him, he was sitting by his little plantation of flowers, as silent and motionless, as the rocks of his solitary sojourn.

Her purpose was soon fixed. Near as it was to evening, she determined to attempt to return, rather than to risk so dreary a night refuge, as the forests of Vahíria. In her present mood of ecstasy, she dreaded no fatigue—anticipated no mischance; so, she set forth, in haste, for her homeward journey. It was a weary way; but—though ever and anon she unconsciously wandered from the direct path,—she trod it in returning, with a facility unknown to her, in her setting out, arriving uninjured, to dissipate the alarms of the faithful Aimáta, and to hear of the downfall of the infamous Priest. To the invitation of the chieftain, to attend with his beloved and himself, the ceremonies of Peace, she returned a grateful, but a firm refusal. As she had mourned over the child, (said she) so would she rejoice over it—alone. And they left her at the sea-side village, and departed hurriedly, for the Temple of the battle-god.

And here—ere we proceed farther—it may be necessary to pause for an instant's investigation, of the history of the extraordinary being, whose preservation of the child, and whose mysterious connexion with the fortunes of the Priest, render him an object of some interest and consequence, in the present narrative.

This unfortunate, was one of the *many*, who had been appointed to swell the list of victims, to the Paganism of the Pacific Islands; and one of the *few*, who had escaped the horrors of the death by sacrifice! In his happier days, he had been a person of rank and consideration, in the Island of Eimeó. While on a visit to the adjacent territory of Tahíti, in the pride and fulness of his heart, he had spoken so boastingly to Ioláni of the extent of his possessions in his native place, that the Priest's curiosity induced him, for a short period, to become the guest of the man of plenty. On the first day of his arrival in Eimeó, he became enamoured of the wife of his host—a beautiful, but most evil-hearted woman, who yielded to his passion, at the utterance of its very first entreaties. To possess himself securely of his worthless prize, was, now, the next labour of Ioláni. He persuaded his paramour, without difficulty, to impeach her husband to the King, as disaffected to his person and rule. The iniquitous stratagem, succeeded but too well. The usual consequences of his offence, immediately fell upon the suspected person. He was marked, by command of the government and the Priest, as the next human victim, to be offered up at the altars of the deities of the land.

The miserable man thus doomed to death, was, accordingly,

captured and led out to be sacrificed on the appointed evening. The infamous intentions of Iolâni were, however, fated to be frustrated, at the very moment of their apparent success. By dint of great personal strength and activity, and by taking advantage at the right time, of an instant of heedlessness on the part of his guards, the victim escaped, and fled for his life; pursued by a host of warriors, whose numbers were headed by the guilty and infamous Priest.

His flight began, over a level and extensive plain, at the extremity of which, he arrived in an incredibly short space of time, having distanced all his pursuers, with the solitary exception of Iolâni. As the fugitive gained the forests, the dim Twilight gave place to a cloudy night; and he trusted that, in the darkness, he might bewilder his last enemy and escape. But, whenever he halted for an instant, he still heard behind him, the footstep of the wily Priest. In vain did he attempt every artifice that cunning could suggest, or activity perform; his pursuer kept so close upon his track, that his only hope, lay in continued and straightforward flight. By the time he had gained the solitary dell, mentioned some pages back, he felt that his senses were becoming bewildered, and that Iolâni was gaining upon him. Goaded to desperation, as he reached the brink of the cavity, he turned—unarmed as he was—to defend his life. The Priest, who was nearer to him than he supposed, attacked him, unprepared, and dealt him, in the darkness, a blow upon the forehead, that rendered him insensible. He fell back into the dell, as if stricken to the death; but, in such a position and place, that Iolâni's utmost efforts to find him that night, were unavailing. His pursuer, however, soon gave up the attempt to possess himself of his body, believing that he was slain outright, and purposing to renew the search, when the light of morning, should crown it unfailingly, with success. But, ere the dawn appeared, the miserable victim of the Priest's iniquity, recovered from his swoon. His wound, severe as it was, was not fatal; and he had strength to drag himself to so secure a hiding place, as enabled him to baffle the utmost efforts of his enemies to discover him, when the morning came.

From that time, to the period of his introduction to the reader, his existence had been one unbroken round of solitude and grief. The terrible inroads, soon made by loneliness and suffering, on his person, guaranteed his security from capture; and the few wayfarers by whom he was occasionally seen, instead of hunting down the *sacrifice*, fled from the *wild man*, in astonishment and dismay.

In the first few months of his seclusion, half maddened by his loneliness, and unwilling in the plenitude of his affection—though with every proof before him—to believe in his wife's share, in the foul conspiracy, that had exiled him from his kind, he ventured, under cover of the night, to steal to the scene of his escape; only to be heart-broken, by the discovery of the fullest evidence, of his faithless partner's connivance with Iolâni, in the perpetration of his wrongs. He watched her out of her abode, possessed himself, in her absence, of part of her bridal garments, and returned to his seclusion, to cultivate a little bed of the flowers she had most loved to weave into garlands, in the days of his happiness, and to brood over the relic of her wearing apparel, in unrelieved and unnoticed sorrow.

The strange perversity that led him to nourish a grief so unworthy of his heart, paved the way for other evils, yet in store for him. The awful loneliness of his position, soon began to work fatally, upon a mind, whose energies were already so prostrated, as to offer no resistance to its ominous and evil influence; and, among his other misfortunes, occasional fits of insanity, now came to play their part, in tormenting the hapless wanderer of the wilds of Vahíria.

To analyze the nature of this unfortunate man's feelings, as they kept pace with the deformity that gradually overspread his form, is a task too gloomy and too extended for the present narrative. Suffice it to say, that his first natural yearnings after his kind, began, gradually, to turn to a directly contrary emotion—to a horror and distrust of humanity, but too natural, to the continuance of his isolated and melancholy situation. This growing misanthrophy, his connexion with the child had the power, for a season, to check within him. There is a vitality about the better feelings of humanity, that few suspect. They slumber within us often, but they rarely die. And thus it proved, with the outcast of Home and Happiness. He witnessed the abandonment of the child, although too late, to face and discover the perpetrator of the crime. The better influences of human nature, had the power to work within him still; and, from preserving the forsaken one for its own sake, at first; he soon grew to watch it, from the more selfish and natural motive, of securing some companionship in his loneliness and affliction. How soon, this last hope of consolation, was banished from him, for ever, the reader is already aware. An instant's observation, showed him, but too clearly, the right of the woman to the child; and, an instant's reflexion, nerved him to bow patiently to this fate. This struggle was his last. The thwarting of this final expectation, snapped the only bond, that still bound him to humanity. From this moment, his fits of insanity became more and more frequent. In a brief period, spite of his struggles to avert the calamity, every association connected with his flower bed and his relic of wearing apparel, faded from his heart; and, erelong, of the once gentle and happy Islander, a confirmed an[d] dangerous madmen, was all that remained!

CHAPTER XII

The mourners among the people

The march of the conquerors and the conquered, on their return from the fortress, presented a singular contrast to their rate of journeying, on setting out for the place of refuge. Among his other acts of clemency, the chieftain had conceded to the vanquished party, the privilege of burying all those of their dead, who had fallen in the retreat, reserving to himself, the right of disposal, as regarded the slain on the field of battle. This act of unusual indulgence, was hailed by the exiles, with gratitude and delight; and they now lingered sadly and slowly on the paths, over which, they had so rapidly hurried, on the night before.

It was a melancholy sight, even on those spots where the corpses were comparatively few, to see with what heroic patience, the survivors of the fight, ministered to the last necessities, of those who had loved and cared for them once. The roughest expedients that the conquering party could invent, were powerless to goad them faster to their journey's end. They knew, that the privilege conceded to them by Mahíné, in the wood, must cease, upon the battle-field; and they determined to use it to the utmost, as long as it was their's. Here, you might see a group, animated by the melancholy triumph, of having discovered that all whom they honored and loved, had been slain in the retreat, and could, therefore, be secured from mutilation and dishonor. There, on the contrary, lingered a few

wretches, who had found none among the corpses that they
could claim as their own; and who envied their companions,
the dead that had escaped the fray, to be sacrificed in the flight.
Ever since their sentence of exile, a finer order of sympathies
seemed to have sprung up in the hearts of the banished. The
silent and the cold, at such a time as this, were not wont to
claim so much of their care. A strange and sudden alteration of
feeling, had arisen among them now. And still, they lingered,
longer and longer, on those dismal paths. Still, at the very outskirts of the forest, they continued to use that privilege, so
hardly earned, and so eagerly enjoyed.

And, when they arrived at the plain, at last—when the
homes, hallowed to them, by their loves and their amusements,
met them, at their final return, as black and mouldering
ruins—when, the fields and the gardens they had rejoiced in,
from morning to evening, showed grim and ghastly, with the
burden of their dead—when, in bitter mockery, the ocean that
was to bear them to their banishment, rippled with its accustomed melody on the blood-polluted beach, and shone far off,
by the coral reefs, with its accustomed brightness—*then*, did
they bewail them in their misery; *then*, did they bow them to
the ground, in their comfortless and utter despair.

At first, among the numbers forming the party of the deposed King, a few were to be seen wandering sadly, among the
dead that they dared not touch; or, idling, in vacant, almost
idiotic sorrow, about their pillaged and ruined homesteads.
But, gradually, even these, as if dreading the comparative loneliness, imposed upon them by their temporary separation from
each other, joined the main body of the sufferers, congregated
about the person of the prisoner King; and watched, like their
fellows, with gloomy and mechanical attention, the dismal
preparations, for the concluding ceremonies of Peace.

And, now, was heard, as the sun began to sink in the cold,

calm waters, the song of victory, from the Prophets of War; their voices, now sinking into a deep and hollow cadence; now, rising fierce and loud upon the air, as the theme, or measure, varied for a time. While the strain proceeded, the warriors of Mahíné, were seen in all directions, dragging the bodies of the slain to the Temple, and piling them, in grisly and shapeless heaps, against the walls, as an offering to the greatness of the battle-god. For a considerable period, this horrible labour, was continued with the utmost regularity and dispatch; saving, when a chief, paused for an instant, to possess himself of the skull of an illustrious enemy, to be converted into a drinking vessel and trophy of war, at the feast of victory. At last, this revolting task was completed, and the warriors formed in one dense, dusky looking mass, opposite the living victims of their martial prowess, to await the arrival of the chieftain-King.

Nothing, at this moment, could be wilder, or more supernatural, than the scene. The moon was just rising, and illuminated the calm waters of the Pacific, and the torn, bloodstained earth of the island of Tahíti, with a southern softness, most beautiful to behold. The tops of the trees, on each side of the plain; the ranks of the reposing warriors; and the confused heap of captives, crouching on the ground, were, here and there, partially and picturesquely shown forth, by the same lovely and brilliant light. While, the innermost portions of the rocks, that girded at each extremity, the shore, and the Temple walls, with the dead around them, shrouded in deep obscurity, contrasted grandly with the moon-brightened scenery just described. Then, there were the islets, far out on the reefs, glowing unshadowed, in the splendour of the night atmosphere; and the forests and mountains, far away in the inland distance, here dimly lightened, there reposing in a soft and uninterrupted darkness. And, yet, though thus impressive the night, by the watchers on the plain, its beauties were unnoticed and unfelt; for, to hearts hardened

by ferocious triumph, and to eyes dimmed by misery and
shame, the charms of nature, possess, neither the eloquence
that affects, nor the loveliness, that astonishes and delights.

Erelong, the sound of solemn music, was heard from the
woods behind the Temple; and Mahíné and Aimáta, followed
by a long train of people from the different districts of Tahíti
and the neighbouring islands, entered upon the scene. In the
morning, the general anticipation had been, that the performance of the ceremonies of Peace, instead of commencing only
when the night-time had arrived, would have been concluded
by sunset, at the latest. Many causes, however, combined to effect so unexpected a delay as had now occurred. For, in addition to the hours on hours, wasted by the conquered party, in
burying those of their slain, who had died on the retreat, much
precious time was consumed, on the part of Mahíné, in arranging his departure from his native village—partly, from the difficulty of collecting and arranging his followers; and, partly,
from Aimáta's extreme unwillingness to accompany him to the
scene of the battle. Indeed, on gaining the appointed place, the
chieftain repented that he had insisted on her obedience to his
will; for, no sooner had she beheld the dismal prospect before
her, than the poor girl's artificial fortitude completely deserted
her, and she entreated, piteously, for permission to await the
conclusion of the ceremonial, where the horrors of the battle-
field and the misery of the captives, might be hidden from her
eyes. As she preferred, with tears, her request, a momentary
shade passed over the brow of the young warrior. But, the dictates of love, are stronger even than the iron promptings of custom, in their influence over the heart. Its wrathful expression,
soon passed from Mahíné's countenance; and the girl's entreaty was granted, without reservation, or delay.

The ceremonies then began, by Mahíné's wise men and
councillors, advancing to a certain place, and (being met by the

deposed King and the wreck of his warriors) addressing an ora-
tion to the vanquished, which set forth the great and unusual
clemency of the victorious chieftain towards his enemies; the
terms of their banishment; the penalties of revolt; and, lastly,
the virtuous determination of the new ruler, for a long and last-
ing peace. The answer of the ruined monarch, contained, simply, an excuse for the non-attendance of his brother the Priest,
in consequence of his wounds, and a protestation of implicit
obedience, on *his* part, to the will of the new ruler. He had proceeded, however, but a brief space in his harangue, when his
emotions of shame and sorrow, utterly overpowered him. He
stopped abruptly, and to hide his grief from the eyes of his conquerors, occupied himself in preparing the young branches,
that were to be entwined with others, supplied by the opposite
party, into the sacred wreath, that was the emblem of Peace.
This ceremony concluded, the appointed animals were offered
up to the gods, and the Priests, by divination, declared the
length of time, that the truce was likely to continue. Then, the
final mystery—the "heiva" or grand dance, was commenced by
the men and women of Mahíné's tribe, to the inspiring music of
the drums and flutes. The most extraordinary feature in this
performance, was the attempt of each dancer, in his turn, to
surprise the guards who stood round their newly-elected King,
and to approach his person, so nearly, as to kiss his hand, or to
touch the folds of his royal garments. These attempts, at ex-
pressing the utmost devotion to the cause of the monarch,
seemed to excite the most intense interest and curiosity, and
every successful effort, on the part of the performers in the
dance, was rewarded by the bystanders, with loud and long-
continued shouts. Upon the conclusion of this strange ceremonial, proclamation was made, concerning the morrow's solemn
feast, and the installation of the new ruler; and, the assembly
then separated. The main body of the warriors, remained en-

camped upon the ground, to watch the vanquished, until the morning's dawn, should close the preparations for their banishment; while, Mahíné and his principal chieftains and councillors, wended their way, towards their temporary refuge for the night, at a short distance from the field of battle. The triumphant warrior, stopped on his way, to visit the hut, where his beloved was guarded and lodged; but, no welcome awaited his entry; for, the young Aimáta was preparing for her repose, not in smiles and happiness; but, in silence and tears.

And, when the weary hours of the night had worn to their end, and the first flush of dawn had appeared in the eastern heaven, the desolate plain, was alive again, for a brief space, with the bustle of preparation. The fleet of war-canoes, was drawn up in order, at the water-side; the warriors and the populace, were ranged in their appointed places; and the wounded, the sorrowful, and the conquered, were brought forth, for their long, bitter banishment. The dethroned King, preserving a stoical patience and calmness, unusual to such a disposition as his, led the way. The fallen Ioláni, glancing around him with an expression of impotent anger and scorn followed his brother; and, after him, came the main body of the exiles—the wounded warrior, the heart-broken woman, and the terrified child—a weary and a woe-worn company!

They entered their barks; the guards pushed off from land; and, sadly and slowy, they floated from the homes they had lived in, and the shores they had loved. Then, as the little fleet gradually lessened to the sight, the multitude on the beach, obeyed the signal of their chiefs, and departed through the woods, for the home of their rebel King.

The breezes arose fresher and purer from their mighty wilderness of waters; the dim, grey clouds, warmed instant by instant, into a soft and glowing hue; and the bright sun arose over the plains of the Temple, to rejoice, no more, the hearts of a happy populace; but, to mock the deformity of grim, cold corpses, and to heighten the desolation of ruined and deserted homes!

The End of Book II

Book III

"The web is woven—
the work is done"

Gray

CHAPTER I

Mahíné's Bridal

The autumn sun never shone more brightly on Tahíti, than on the days that were dedicated, to the marriage and accession, of the new King. Never was contrast more extraordinary, than, that now offered, by the present appearance of the inhabitants, as compared with, the past. Now, the Priest wandered, pensively, about the quiet precincts of the Temple; and the warrior basked him[self] in the morning sun, bereft of his arms, and shorn of his apparel of war. Now, old men and the children, mixed, confidently, in the ranks of the sturdy husbandmen; and the women, fondled their infants, unrebuked, in the deserted recesses of the camp. The same aspect of peace, reigned everywhere; and the same indolent and simple cheerfulness, appeared in the demeanour of all. On the sea coast, were, now, to be seen—as the cool eventide approached—fleets of canoes discharging their freight of happy visitors from the neighbouring islands. In the shady pathways of the village, were little groups of the peasantry, in their holiday attire, dancing to the soft, luxurious music, of the native flute; and, in the distant woodlands, there lingered lazily onward, the young man wooing his beloved; the old warrior bearing his weapons to their place of rest; and the child, gathering a fresher and fairer flower at every step, to add to the store of festal garlands, already hoarded at home. Not a desolating remembrance connected with the late war, seemed to influence a single heart among the populace. Their words, their looks, and their actions, were all of joy. And as light was the song, and as merry was the music, of that happy people; as if, tumult were unknown on their shores, and sorrow and bereavement, unremembered in their dwellings.

As the marriage day dawned, the feasting began. But as yet, there was no indiscriminate mixture of the sexes, and the scene was, therefore, rather curious and impressive, than enlivening and picturesque. Every simple dainty that the island could afford, was strewed over the soft, green turf, before the privileged and stronger sex; and, in the distance, for the better gratification of every sense, the dancing girls and the musicians, practised, indefatigably, their luxurious arts. Hour after hour, was the revel sustained, without a word of anger, or a symptom of weariness, to harm its unflagging continuance, until the music of the drums and flutes, gave signal, from the forest glades, of the commencement of the festival games; and then, the feasting was abandoned, at last, and the whole population crowded eagerly to the sports.

The place dedicated, on this occasion, to the island amusements, was a smooth, grassy plain, of some extent, bounded on all sides, by magnificent trees, and sloping, from each extremity, towards the middle, almost in the form of a natural amphitheatre. In a short space of time, this spot, at first only occupied by the attendants on the games, was filled down to the very barriers, that indicated the appointed locality of the performers in the sports, by the joyous and impatient multitude. No variety could be more beautiful, than that, presented by the apparel and positions of the spectators, as each, gradually, arranged himself at his favorite point of view. The lustrous white, yellow, and scarlet hues, of the dresses; here, brightened by the sunlight; there, softened by the mellow darkness of the shade, contrasted beautifully, in their gay intermixture, with the quiet,

monotonous colour, of the verdure around. Here, were no carefully arranged seats, to spread an unnatural air of order and
propriety over the positions of the assembly. Some, stood erect,
impatient for the sports. Others, careless and easy-tempered,
reclined listlessly, on the ground. One group, pressed forward
to the barriers. Another, slowly retired, to join the hindermost
of the audience, at the outskirts of the wood. Now, a company
of young men, climbed the trees, the better to view the games;
and ensconced themselves, gaily, among the cool, shady
branches; and now, an ambitious urchin, struggled to win his
way through the barriers, and gain the best and nearest place of
all. The same continual confusion and movement, pervaded
every rank of spectators; and the laugh and the jest passed from
mouth to mouth, until the old forest rung again with the
sound. At last, after some delay, the moment of excitement arrived. A wrestler of Tahíti and a wrestler of Eiméo, entered the
lists to prepare for the struggle; and the silence of intense expectation, now pervaded the festive assembly.

The men were both naked, with the exception of their linen
girdles. The champion of Eiméo, had slightly the advantage of
his adversary, in height and build; but, the native wrestler, was
far his superior, as a specimen of manly beauty and grace. Each,
was the most celebrated in his island, for personal prowess; and
the present contention, was generally looked to, as finally deci-
sive of their respective claims to the supremacy of the field.

For the first few minutes, the antagonists kept their distance;
each watching, cautiously, the movements of the other; for, the
practice of wrestling in the Pacific Islands, allowed artifice of
any description to be used, when one, or other, of the combatants, felt doubtful of achieving success, by personal strength
alone. At last—as if impatient of longer delay—the champion
of Eiméo rushed in, and closed with his man; grappling him by
the shoulders, and trusting to his superior height and weight,

to cast him to the ground. The Tahíti wrestler acted wholly upon the defensive, until he felt that the brunt of the other's assault was over. Then, suddenly, quitting his hold of his adversary's shoulder, and, thereby, for an instant, shaking his footing, he seized the man of Eiméo round the waist, lifted him into the air, and hurled him violently to the Earth.

The moment after, the air was rent by the shouts of the beholders, and the discordant music of the war-drums. The barriers were taken by storm, and men, women, and children, like frantic creatures, danced in triumph, round the body of the prostrate man. Hundreds of voices, sung in wild chorus, then different songs of victory; and yelled forth, their wildest expressions, of triumph and defiance. Higher and higher, rose the tumult; as the party of the fallen wrestler, answered the rejoicers, by the most vociferous declamations on the prowess of the conquered; and the most savage predictions of his rival's approaching downfall. A scene of fiercer clamour and confusion, could scarcely be imagined; and, yet, when the tumult raged at its very highest, the appearance of a fresh set of wrestlers, was sufficient to calm it, almost instantaneously. The people retreated to their places, as suddenly as they had left them; and the sports began again, only to end in the same extraordinary demonstrations of enthusiasm and delight, on each occasion, until the provided number of combatants was exhausted, and a different series of amusements, appeared, to occupy the attention of the joyous multitude.

The same peculiarities marked the celebration of the succeeding games, that had characterized the wrestling match; sham fights, dancing, and throwing the javelin, constituting these fresh sources of entertainment. As the evening approached, the festivities were concluded for that day, by the performances of the Areoi society, which were of the same description, as those previously mentioned, in the former part of the present narrative. This last exhibition concluded, the music again sounded; but, now, in a solemn and measured strain; and the assembly, anxiously whispering among each other, directed their steps towards the avenues that led to the Temple of Peace; posting themselves along the sides of the pathways, to watch for the bridal procession that was now expected to appear.

The patience of the crowd was, on this occasion, but little taxed; for, scarcely had they taken up their positions aright, before the distant warblings of the flute, were heard from the recesses of the forest; and, erelong, winding slowly up the long and shady avenues, the marriage procession—simple yet imposing—appeared in sight.

First, came the Priests in their sacred garments, followed by a body of musicians, arrayed in yellow robes, the patterns, on which were traced in red, and represented the different orders of flowers which the island produced. At some distance after these, marched a chosen band of the most illustrious of Mahíné's chieftains, their loose under dresses of white, setting off, to the greatest advantage, the ample shawls of rich, dark red, that were wrapped round the upper part of their persons. Then, came, simply and tastefully habited, in snowy robes, a company of the youngest and most beautiful women in the Island. Then, followed the bride and bridegroom; and, behind all, walked the relations of the King, and Idía and her infant child.

If ever the girl's soft, happy countenance, looked beautiful, it was at this moment, when every variety of pleasurable emotion, that the heart can contain, was struggling for its share of eloquent expression, in her face. Nothing could be more exquisitely tasteful and becoming than her bridal costume, from the turban-formed braidings of hair, and the triple wreath of white, red, and yellow flowers, that adorned her head; to the scarlet-bordered robe, that fell over her feet. Nothing could be more natural and seductive than her attitude and appearance, as she

stood in the solemn and subdued light of the inner portion of
the Temple, trembling, between her mixed feelings of pleasure,
at the passionate admiration of the King; and her awe at the
near approach, of the commencement of the sacred ceremony.

And, now, arrayed in the most imposing habiliments of his
order, the chief Priest came forward, and addressed a solemn
admonition to future constancy, both to husband and wife;
concluding his harangue, by the eloquent and pathetic prayer,
usual on such occasions, for the future happiness of the married pair. Then, a large piece of white cloth, typical of the sa-
credness and purity of the ceremonial, was brought forth; and,
Aimáta and the King, clasped each other in silence by the hand;
the skulls of Mahíné's ancestors, having been previously taken
from the tomb of his family, and placed by his side. For, it was
the bold and beautiful superstition of this, poetically-minded
people, that the spirits of the loved and honoured dead, were,
thus, lured to the guardianship of their posterity, on earth. The
most perfect reverence, now appeared in the demeanour of all
present, at this, the most important period, in the nuptial ceremony; when, the spirits of his fathers, were lingering round
Mahíné's form, to hallow his vows, and to prosper him in the
days of his future existence. For a considerable period, the silence continued, unbroken; each attendant at the Temple, remaining fixed and motionless in his position, as the walls
around him. At length, at a given signal from the chief Priest,
the bride and bridegroom, fell back into their former places, the
skulls were carefully removed, and the final ceremony was prepared for, by Idía and the parents of the King.

Having first taken between them, a piece of white cloth, Idía
and the mother of Mahíné, inflicted several wounds, with a
sharp instrument, in various parts of their bodies; so severe, as
to cause the blood to flow freely, upon the linen that was held
by each. This, when perfectly saturated, was born by the two

women, to the feet of the King and his bride, who affectionately embraced, in return—the one, his aged mother; and, the other, her generous protector and friend. This strange proceeding, was not dissimilar, in intention, to the preceding ceremony. As, in that, the skulls of the dead, were typical of the favouring presence of departed spirits; so, in this, the blood-stained cloth, was suggestive, of the truth and vitality, of the affection of those, dearest, to the principal worshippers at the altar. Thus touchingly and poetically, was the form of marriage con-stituted, in the Pacific Islands! And, yet, no ceremony was so temporary in its effects, and so little reverenced, or regarded, when it was once over. Indeed, it may truly be said of the wed-ding contract, in this land of luxury, that it was framed with intelligence and care; only, to be broken at will, by frivolity and caprice.

With this ceremony, the nuptials concluded; and, led by the chief Priest, the bridal party again appeared in the Temple ave-nue. Instead, however, of returning to the village, they struck off, into a path in the woods, that conducted to a little hut, standing in a retired valley; surrounded, and almost concealed from view, by its stately protection of trees. Here, the proces-sion halted. The young couple were placed upon a grassy bark; and, while the great chieftains and councillors, did homage, in turn, to their newly-elected King; the women of the party, made their simple presents of flowers, fruits, and gaily-tinted wearing apparel, to the young Aimáta. These duties performed, the parting embraces were exchanged; and the different assis-tants at the bridal, prepared to depart; for, the sun was now fast sinking, in the western ocean.

The hum of voices from the avenues had already ceased; the crowd had dispersed; and the paths of the forest, were solitary for the night. The Priests, wended their way towards the Tem-ple. The chieftains and councillors, repaired to the palace of the

King. Idía departed with her child, to her lonely habitation. And Mahíné and Aimáta, as they lingered in the brief Twilight, at the door of the seclusion, were left alone, in the solitude of the Temple woodlands.

CHAPTER II

The hunt for the outcast

Two months, had now passed quietly onward, since the celebration of the wedding of the King; and, in the exercise of their accustomed avocations, the people of the village, had already half forgotten the days of feasting and merriment that were past. In the first glow and selfishness of his love; Mahíné, scorning the advice of his warriors, had retreated, with Aimáta, to one of the islets near Tahíti. Here, in joyous indolence, he and his beloved, passed the last pleasant days of autumn, with their singers, their players, and their dancers—now, reposing in the shade of the cool, cocoa nut groves; now gliding by moonlight, in their canoes, over the quiet surface of the midnight ocean. This indifference as to the necessity of strengthening his newly-acquired government, was received with considerable scorn and apprehension, by the older and the more experienced of Mahíné's councillors. Resolved to awaken the King to the peril of his ill-timed inactivity, they visited him, a second time, in his seclusion; only to be again received, with the same contemptuous indifference, that had marked his reception of the petitioners, on the previous occasion.

The immediate consequences, of this ill-omened disagreement between the King and his ministers, may be easily imagined; to the more remote, we shall not at present advert.

While Love, was thus battling it gallantly, on the islet, against the obstinate incursions of Duty; the lonely Idía still

remained, unmolested, in her village home. Peace, seemed, at
last, to have returned to her life; but, the happiness that had
companioned it, in the days that were past, still delayed to follow its advent. The various and deep emotions, whose violence
she had suffered so long, left the trace of their existence, in the
profound and habitual melancholy, that, at this period, settled
upon her heart. Spite of herself, she still yearned towards the
fatal days of her first connexcion with the Priest. All that she
had suffered from Iolâni's ruthlessness seemed but the melancholy index, to all that she had enjoyed of Iolâni's affection.
Degrading as she felt this weakness to be; to overcome it, was
beyond her capacity; and, saving, when at certain moments, the
very presence of her child, was of itself, a stern and sorrowful
rebuke to the uselessness of her musings, her thoughts still
wandered, mechanically, to the passionate lover of Vahíria;
rather, than, to the inexorable tyrant of the Temple and the
Field—For, alas! though we rouse the affections, by the caprice
of an instant; it is, often, only to be doomed to quell them, by
the labour of a life!

Her existence, now, was one, sorrowful monotony; increased, rather than broken, by the insufficient companionship
of the child. Her single consolation in her loneliness, was to sit,
evening after evening, when the infant was hushed to rest, occupied with her thoughts, and gazing out, upon the bright, luxurious landscape, as it gradually softened and grew dark, at the
approach of night. Hitherto, she had followed this peaceful employment, without accident or interruption; on the evening,
however, which the present chapter commemorates, she was
destined to experience a serious hindrance, in her innocent occupation of her lonely hours.

As was her wont, she watched, on this occasion, by the
child's side, until it had fallen asleep; and, then, repairing to the

door of her hut, she took up her usual position, and fell, erelong, into her usual reverie.

As the Twilight faded off, and the moon rose, the restlessness
of her mental, infected her bodily, faculties; and, quitting her
seat, she paced for some time, up an down before the door of
her dwelling; now, gazing upon the star-bright heaven, above;
now, upon the still, dusky ocean, beneath. As she lingered, for
an instant, at one extremity of her garden path, she saw, or
thought she saw, a figure creeping along, under the shelter of
the walls of the hut. For the first few moments, her agony of
terror was so great, that she stood rooted to the spot. Every
ominous, or unexpected occurrence, was now connected in her
mind, with the machinations of the Priest; and, not withstand-
ing her certainty of his banishment, the wily Ioláni, was the
intruder she expected to meet, as, with desperate resolution,
she approached the door of her dwelling, at last.

One brief instant, she hesitated ere she entered; and the
whole series of her sufferings at the hands of the Priest, rushed,
like a whirlwind, over her mind. The next moment, her resolution again came to her aid, and she gained the interior.

The moonbeams that stole through the open doorway, fell
full upon the couch of the child. Its slumbers, were not more
undisturbed, when its mother had watched it last, than, now,
when her place was occupied by the outcast and madman of the
Lake Vahíria.

There he sat! his deformity made more ghastly and terrible
than ever, by the pale, cold light, that illumined it now. His
eyes were fixed dreamily and sadly, upon the infant's countenance; and, from time to time, he scattered over its bed, a handful of flowers; as though, he believed himself still in the cavern,
where he had accomplished the preservation of the object of his
care. In the first surprise and terror of the moment, Idía uttered
a loud shriek. The outcast instantly started up, seized the child

in his arms; and, with the strange cunning of insanity, retreated to the darkest corner of the hut, with the intention of accomplishing the removal of the woman from the doorway, either by luring her within, to rescue her offspring; or, by driving her without, to seek for assistance. He was not, however, destined to escape with such impunity. The woman's screams for assistance, brought to the hut, a party of husbandmen, homeward bound from the fields. The instant their footsteps were audible, the madman rushed from his concealment—for the frantic fit was forth upon him now—dragged Idía from the doorway, hurled her to the ground, and confronted the party who were approaching to the rescue, at the extremity of the garden path.

He attempted to burst his way through them; but, one of the men, rushed at his throat; and another, snatched the child from his grasp, and flew with it, into the hut. The next moment, ere the remaining three of the husbandmen, had gained a hold upon him, he had caught the peasant who had first closed, and was still struggling with him, up in his arms, like an infant, and had dashed headlong, into the thicket before him.

There was nothing to guide the horrified peasants, as they hurried after their companion, but his cries for help, and the wild laughter of the madman, as it startled the still night air. Soon, the cries ceased entirely, and the laughter was all that was heard, as it, gradually, sounded distant and more distant. They still followed, however. It was a fearful chase, and attempted at a fearful time; but, while the slightest hope remained, they determined to rescue their ill-fated comrade, be the peril whatever it might.

But, he was past their help already. His strength, was weakness, in the madman's grip. With his left arm clutched fiercely round his victim, and the fingers of his right hand, pressed upon his throat, the outcast strangled him, like a child. He was a dead man, in the first few minutes, of that terrible flight.

Merrily! Merrily! now; over the moon-brightened plain, through the pathways of the deserted woods, and out upon the smooth white sands, of the ocean beyond! While the stars glitter forth! While the dead man's face is livid to look on! While the curses of the pursuers, are echoing in the forest behind!—there is food for exultation—there is enchantment in flight! The wind whistles low! The waves moan sadly, on the lonely shore! Merrily onward, madman! Merrily onward!

They pursued him to the beach. He turned, one instant, as they called to him to yield. Then, redoubling his exertions, he made for the high rocks that girded the shore; and set himself to climb their rugged and precipitous sides. And, now, the husbandmen gained upon him; for, he was encumbered with the burden of his horrible prize, and lost ground, at every step in the ascent. They saw that their only chance of arresting his progress, was in the passage of the rocks, and they redoubled their efforts. But, to thread the precipices, became, now, no easy task, under the uncertain light of the moon; and, erelong, fruitful as they were, in the requisites for the prosecution of their dangerous attempt, they came to a dead stop, on the brink of an abyss.

The place was fearful enough to look on, at such a time. The chasm, though extremely narrow, was deep and dark; its further side, being the highest, and the most precipitous. How the outcast, burdened as he was, could have crossed such a gulph, it was impossible to conceive; but, there he stood, on the topmost pinnacle of rock, full in the moonlight, glaring down at his baffled pursuers, with the dead body, still clasped in his arms. At this moment, they discovered for the first time, that their comrade's life had been sacrificed by the madman. To rescue his corpse from dishonor, was, now, their only hope. They threatened—they entreated. In their agony of anxiety and impatience, they groped about the smooth surface of the rock, for missiles, to accomplish by Force, what Stratagem was unable to perform; but, all in vain. At length, one of the party, who had ventured to crawl a considerable way up the cliff, called out to his companions, that he had discovered a means of passage, across. They had prepared to obey the summons, when that terrible laugh of derision, again struck upon their ears. They looked up. The madman, at the same instant, raised the corpse above his head, cast it fiercely down into the gulph, and disappeared from their sight.

They heard the body strike once, or twice, against the projections of rock—then, there was a moment's silence—then, a soft still splash, among the deep waters at the bottom. He was gone!

The outcast's steps were, now, again directed towards the beach. He sped rapidly onward, until he reached a little creek in the shore where the forest took the place of the rocks and reached almost to the water's edge. At this place, the outlawed wretch halted, overcome at last with fatigue. Erelong, however, he changed his first position of listless repose, for one of intensive attention, as if some unusual sound, had struck upon his ear. After listening for a few minutes, he cautiously crept—keeping out of the moonlight—to a ruined hut, that stood, half hidden by trees, at an extremity of the creek, and peered through one of the numerous rents, in its half shattered walls.

He had scarcely occupied his post of observation for an instant, before the vacant expression, left his eye, and was succeeded by such a look of ferocious triumph and intelligence, as had never beamed in it before. While all that was savage, in his peculiar form of insanity, remained; all that was idiotic, seemed to be suddenly removed. The longer he looked, the more undivided was his attention, the more absorbed his demeanour. His arms were clasped convulsively over his breast, as if he feared to allow them the slightest liberty of motion. He had all the air, of a man who feels that his passion is passing the boundaries, that his cunning has raised to oppose it; and, who determines to prolong his resistance to himself, to the very last.

If ever the return of his reason, could have benefitted the outcast, it was at this moment. For, of the two men, whose secret consultation, he heard, but could not comprehend; the one, was Otahára, the most celebrated sorcerer of the Pacific Islands; and the other, was Ioláni, the Priest.

CHAPTER III

Ioláni's Escape

Ere we proceed further, it will be necessary to pause in the progress of our narrative, to account for the strange re-appearance
of the Priest, on the shores that he had dishonoured, and
among the people whom he had wronged.

The island to which the defeated party had been conveyed by
Mahíné's commands, was distant, about thirty English miles,
from Tahíti. The inhabitants were few; the soil was barren and
unpromising, as compared with that of the larger islands; and
the mountains and forests, were inaccessible and wild. To clear
the woods, to cultivate and improve the natural vegetation, and
to assist in the erection of new dwelling houses, were the tasks
imposed upon the dethroned King and his banished companions. The new ruler had contracted an unaccountable fondness,
for this unpromising spot; and had formally announced his intention, when the different improvements were completed, of
making a summer residence of the place.

The exiles had no resource—watched as they were by their
guards—but to submit without complaint, to the labour imposed on them; and, to the astonishment of every one, the most
obedient and diligent of their number, was the once proud and
inexorable Priest. Two reasons actuated this man, in his present
course of proceeding. The one, was the hope that incessant
bodily toil, might lighten the torment within him. The other,
was the necessity of lulling all suspicion of him, among his

task-masters, in order to effect the accomplishment of his first grand object—escape.

He was still, at heart, as great a villain as ever; but, the recollection of past, and the planning of future iniquities, had lost, for him, their former fascination; and were now become a toil—a trouble, that his nature still urged him to undertake, but refused to sweeten to him more. The one, incessant, remembrance, that had saddened the days of his glory, still remained within him, to embitter the season of his downfall. With the exception of the most general incidents, every thing besides, connected with the harangue from the Temple and the night in the forest, had faded from his mind. He had forgotten the number—even the names of the men, who had accompanied him in that ill-omened pursuit. He had forgotten the once well-known localities of the forest, and the aspect of the different hiding places, they had searched on their journey to the desolate Lake. But, the remembrance of the mere glimpse, of the outcast— prominent alone, among the host of incidents that had happened during the night of storm—lived within him, with a vividness unclouded by Suffering, and a vitality uninjured by Time. All former events, once clear in his recollection, seemed to have vanished and past away, as if to leave the space of his memory clear, for the extension and growth, of that one remembrance, whose mystery there was no penetrating, and from whose tyranny, there was no relief. Over and over again, had he attempted to recall to himself, such actions, of his past life, as might enable him to identify with some original, the phantom that incessantly haunted his slumbers by night, and his thoughts by day; but, in vain. Its increasing existence within him, must, erelong, have tormented him into insanity, but for the presence, of another subject for reflexion, in his mind, that repressed its power, while it fostered its vitality; and, that consisted, in the incessant consideration of some means of accomplishing the vengeance, that he had desired so long, and that he seemed destined never to achieve. To the continuance of his malignity towards Idía, and to the rise of a sudden suspicion, within him, concerning the cause of his sufferings and downfall, was wholly attributable, his intense anxiety to escape.

As a Prophet of the War-god, and an obedient and industrious exile, he was permitted to worship, unobserved, by any one, but the native Priest, in the little Temple of the island. The serviceable canoes, were all under the constant superintendance of the guards; and the companion of his devotions, was universally considered, as a warm adherent to the cause of the newly elected King; so, that, this privilege, conceded to him of necessity, was considered as safe an exercise of mercy, as they could by any possibility, adopt.

The hopes of Iolāni, centered in the habitant of the Island Temple. He was a man of thoroughly Polynesian simplicity and indolence of character, and his wily companion was not long in taking advantage of peculiarities, so admirably adapted to his designs. Day by day, did the consummate villain worm himself into the confidence of the warm-hearted priest; until, his influence over his victim became complete. The plan of escape, was then matured by Iolāni, and its immediate execution, was left to his unfortunate companion.

Upon an unfrequented part of the island, they had observed a worn-out canoe, abandoned by its owners, as utterly useless for any purpose whatever. This frail bark, the native priest—by the direction of Iolāni—dragged, in the night-time, into the inner and sacred portion of the Temple, as the only place left then, for its secure concealment. Here, at all spare hours, the unsuspecting islander worked at repairing the canoe. Dazzled by a profusion of promises, and pleased by the most artful flattery, the poor wretch had already conceived an attachment and reverence for his unscrupulous comrade, that disposed him to the most implicit secrecy, and inspired him with the most generous enthusiasm for the cause of the exile. In a few weeks, his labours were completed, and he showed the sea-worthy vessel to this confederate, with a child-like triumph and delight, that might well have touched even the pitiless heart of Ioláni, the Priest.

They waited several days longer, ere they ventured upon their departure. At last, one evening, the sun went down amidst dark and murky clouds; and this night, they fixed on for their attempt.

The exiles were lodged in a large hut, the door of which, was scrupulously guarded at all hours. Ioláni waited, until his fellow-prisoners were all composed for the night; and then, climbing to the roof of the building, he removed enough of the roof, to allow him to pass to the outside. The thatch had been previously loosened in the day time, by the Island priest, or he could scarcely have disarranged it, without causing a disturbance, that might have led to a discovery. Having gained the top of the hut, he cautiously replaced the thatch, and dropped to the ground at the back of the dwelling; the pattering of the rain, that now began to fall; and the surging of the waves, securing him from the peril of being heard by the guards, at the front of the hut.

He threaded his way, cautiously, through the darkness, until he arrived at the Temple, where his trembling companion awaited him. Saving, that he occasionally sternly chided him for his fears, Ioláni observed a strict silence towards his companion, as he assisted him in conveying the vessel, to the appointed place of embarkation.

The islander instinctively shuddered and drew back, as he looked upon the dark, angry ocean, and the stormy sky-above.

But, it was now too late to repent. The canoe was launched, he was dragged in by the Priest, and the next instant, the two were forth upon their perilous and lonely voyage.

As long as they were within the reefs, the canoe lived well in the sea; but, they had made little way on the main ocean, before it became obvious to both, that the vessel was too heavily laden for her strength. The fastenings of the planks, soon became slightly loosened, and through the chinks thus made, the water began occasionally to ooze in, in small quantities. The islander, terrified at the sight, entreated to be allowed to put back; but Ioláni snatched the paddle from his hand, and directing him, in an angry voice, to bale out the water, whenever it appeared, he still held the canoe on her outward course.

The rain poured down faster and faster; the fierce, angry wind, came rushing over the ocean in sudden and severe gusts, and the farther they voyaged, the more did the water gain on them. Neither of the men, now, exchanged a word; but, as the moon, for an instant shone forth from behind a cloud, both glanced back upon the sea. Their mutual, but unexpressed suspicions, were fearfully verified. The sharks were already in their wake!

It now became evident, that the canoe must be lightened, or that the two who guided it, must fall a prey to the sea monsters. Ever and anon, the eyes of the islander were cast up upon Ioláni, as he silently continued his labours, with a strange expression of despair and dread. For a few minutes yet, the poor wretch continued to bale out the water, as before. Then a shudder passed over his frame, he ceased his efforts, and grasped, mechanically, at the sides of the frail bark; crawling to the stern, and peering tremblingly, through the thick darkness upon the waves behind. During this period, Ioláni's eye was never off him; though, he continued to labour, as if absorbed only in conducting the vessel. Suddenly, however, he paused—

uttered a savage execration—and, as his victim turned at the sound of his voice, struck him on the head with the paddle. The islander fell back stunned; and the next instant, the villain had flung him into the sea.

Once more, the moon shone out for a brief period. Ioláni looked forth. There was an instant's tinge of dark, upon the momentary brilliancy of the waters. Then, the clouds flew onward; and the solitary tenant of the bark, returned to his labour again.

Now, however, the canoe floated higher upon the ocean, and the loosened planks, gaped less widely, as she rose with the swell of the waves. But the Priest had bought his security, more dearly than he thought. Though its cruelty had not departed from his heart, its insensibility had vanished for ever. An abject fear for his safety,—a cowardly, unrepentant horror, at the crime he had just committed now assailed him. In every billow, he saw a death of torment and a grave of dishonor. In the monotonous dirging of the ocean, he heard but the voices of accusing spirits. His hand shook, as he grasped the paddle. His frame trembled, as he bent him, despairingly, to his labour. Ever and anon, he looked anxiously behind him; his disordered imagination, picturing his wretched companion, as still holding his post, and dooming him to destruction, even yet. Land, wherever and whatever it was, was the centre of all his hopes. He could suffer torture and death on the blessed earth, rather than his lonely voyaging upon the midnight sea. Onward and onward, he urged his course. While terror pursued him on the waters, fatigue could overcome him, only on the land. Onward! Onward! There was no rest—no peace for him, until the morning dawned, and the mountain tops of Tahíti, appeared with the day.

While, night upon the earth, comes as a companion, night upon the sea, approaches as a stranger, to the heart of man. The mortal associations connected with the one, are never united to the other. The moonbeam, has a luxurious softness, while it lingers upon the mountain-tops that we have trodden; and the darkness, has a refreshing gloom, while it hovers over the vallies that we have lived in and loved. But, there is melancholy in the brightness; and terror, in the obscurity of the night, when both fall, alike, upon an undiversified space—on a monotonous wilderness, where nothing ever remains to be remembered, or appears to attach. It was thus gloomily, that midnight upon the ocean, appeared to the hardened heart of Ioláni the Priest. Look where he would now, there were no outward objects, to relieve him from the torment, within. The most fearful superstitions of his nation—once neither experienced by him, nor believed— assailed him in myriad shapes, in his loneliness and danger. But even now there was no remorse, no repentance in him. Terror might overpower and Irresolution might cloud his heart; but, it was only for the moment; for Revenge and Ruthlessness, enduring as ever, lay graven beneath them still. He could tremble like the devils; and like them, he could not repent.

At last—oh how long and how weary was the delay!—the gloomy firmament brightened in the East, and there were the welcome mountain tops! There was the safe and solitary haven in the shore! He was saved from his peril! There was triumph and vengeance for him, yet!

CHAPTER IV

The Sorcery prepared

The prevalence of the belief and practice of sorcery, among so superstitious and imaginative a people, as the Islanders of the Pacific, can be a matter of but little wonder. Their Mythology, peopled sun, moon, and stars; valley, mountain and forest, each, with their separate race of spirit habitants. No wilderness, however sublime—no nook, however humble, but was haunted, in the native belief, by its attendant sylphs or daemons—viewless to mortal eye, yet all-powerful over mortal heart. Of these deities, all were approachable by invocation, to the chosen Priests, and Prophets of the land. From those whose earthly mission was for good, were supposed to have issued, to men, the first revelations of the beauties and benefits of the Polynesian heaven. From those whose privilege was for evil, had arisen over the people, the gloomy dawnings of sorcery and witchcraft.

The belief—strengthened daily by experience—in the fatal powers of the wizard, was shared, without exception, by the whole mass of the inhabitants of the Pacific Islands. From motives of revenge or apprehension, numbers, from year to year, were subjected by the sorcerers, either to lives of mental and bodily misery; or, to a sudden and violent death; often, without the slightest warning of their approaching doom. In those cases, where suspicion hinted to the victim, the quarter whence his persecution arose, counter spells were employed—to fail or to succeed, precisely as the sufferer[']s apprehensions, might ultimately prove to be fallacious or correct. The dark secrets of the science, were known but to few; and were handed down as an omnipotent and hereditary inheritance, from father to son. To this day, the true and natural causes, of the effects ostensibly produced by the wizard's incantations, have, of necessity, been but superficially investigated. It is simply known, that the sorcerers were in possession of a practical knowledge of herbal poisons, wonderful to contemplate, in a race, in many respects, so little cultivated. But the nature of their fatal concoctions, and the secret of their action upon the human frame, the utmost researches of the travellers of the North, have never been competent to divulge.

From the period of the battle and the defeat, a dark suspicion had arisen in Ioláni's mind, that the mysterious visitation he had suffered under since the night of the pursuit, was the work of sorcery, employed on him, in revenge, by the wretched woman, whom he had abandoned and wronged. His whole faculties, had now become concentrated upon the possibility of effecting her destruction, by the very means that he imagined she had used for his torment, herself. This method of satisfying his vengeance, he had feared to use, in the season of his glory and repute; for, betrayal and discovery, would, then, have been fatal to the preservation of his holy character in the land; and he scorned, moreover, in those days of his pride, to be indebted for the furtherance of his revenge, to any but himself. *Now*, however, his determinations were all changed. He was a ruined man—a wanderer, for the future of his existence, on the face of the earth. In sorcery, lay his last chance of triumph over the object of his implacable hate. He had all to venture, and nothing to lose; and he was determined that his last effort in iniquity, should be worthy of his ancient self.

How he escaped his banishment, is already known. He de-

layed not an instant, on reaching the shore; but hurried to the
ruined hut, mentioned a few pages back. It was perfectly empty,
when he entered; save, that the trunk of a young plantain tree,
covered with strange devices, rested against the wall; its top,
pointing in the direction of the wood behind.

The apparently accidental disposition, of this solitary piece
of furniture in the dwelling, seemed full of instruction to the
Priest. He looked steadfastly on it for a few minutes, and then,
quitting the hut, he proceeded inland.

Cautiously, yet swiftly, he sped onward through the forest
paths, until he gained a spot, wild and gloomy in appearance, in
the centre of which, stood an old tree. Here, another plantain
was placed; but, this time, with its point on the ground. He
examined it with the same care that had marked his observation of the first sign, and then, penetrated abruptly into a dark
thicket at his left.

At every step, the ground now became more rocky; and, here
and there, there appeared deep, dark caverns, or rather pits, in
the earth. At the mouth of one of these, lay a third plantain,
with a torch and the materials for lighting it. Making immediate use of these necessary preparations for his subterranean expedition, the Priest, with some appearance of hesitation, entered the cavity.

For some distance, the ground sloped downward; and Ioláni
was obliged to crawl upon his hands and knees, until the de-
scent was concluded. When, however, he had reached the level
portion of the cavern, ample room was afforded him to stand
upright; and no further obstructions cramped the freedom of
his movements. It was a strange and secret place. The natural
labyrinths—apparently interminable—branched out, in several
directions, on each side; and threading their mazes unguided,
seemed at first sight, a work of the utmost danger and impossibility. The Priest, for a few minutes, halted and looked round

him in bewilderment. Then, as if he had suddenly perceived some secret sign, of the same nature as those examined by him before, he made, straight, for the largest of the passages in the cavern.

Every now and then, he paused and listened; but, as yet, nothing struck upon his ear, save the monotonous splash of dripping water, and the crackling of the burning torch that he carried in his hand. He stole a little farther onward. And now, he felt a cold wind blowing upon his face; and, ever and anon, a wreath of smoke swept suddenly past him, and was lost in the labyrinths behind. Still a little farther, and he could distinguish the sound of a human voice. At this point, he halted, and called in a loud tone—"Otahára! Master! It is I—Ioláni, the Priest"!

For the first few moments, there was no reply. Then, he heard pronounced, in a hoarse hollow voice, the following words:—

"Call upon thy god, that he preserve thee; for, Heva and his evil spirits are thronging round thee, here! Oro is powerful; cry unto him, if thou woulds't approach and live"!

A little onward, there was an abrupt turn in the subterranean passage. The Priest followed it undaunted, and, the next instant, beheld the sorcerer before him.

At this point, the cavern ended in a wide recess; unarched save by the branches that, full fifty feet above, stretched over the place. The rocks that formed its sides, were broken into the wildest forms—now overhanging the ground, now stretching backward, until lost to sight, in the gloomy thickets of the forest aloft. In various, beautiful, and fantastic shapes, long creepers sprung from their tops, floating backwards and forwards with the wind, in their dusky prison house. Here, where there was a cavity in the pit-side, the water oozed forth, and dripped lazily down, upon the stones beneath. There, where there was a prominence, a few patches of moss—damp and rotten—

checquered the dark surface of the rock. Part of the ground, below, was occupied by a smouldering fire; part, by the remnant of a huge tree trunk; on which, stood a solitary man, of great age, glaring down upon the dark, red embers, at his feet. With one hand, he clasped to this breast a profusion of dried herbs and flowers. With the other, he supported himself against the sides of his desolate hermitage. A large white robe covered his form, and around his head, was woven a chaplet of withered leaves. His limbs trembled, and his lips were half parted, with an expression of mingled agony and triumph. Now, as he flung his handful of herbs on to the fire, and watched the smoke, in strange and mysterious shapes, curling upwards to the trees overhead, his eyes flashed over the scene, with the fitful brightness of insanity. Now, as the offering was consumed, and the thick vapour faded and was lost, they wandered vacantly and mournfully to the red embers again; and, then, his lips moved, and in a deep and hollow voice, he murmured his spirit-invocation—sometimes, to the vaults that yawned around; sometimes, to the desolate forest, whose majesty encompassed them from above.

Neither by word, nor action, did Iolàni attempt to offer interruption to this strange ceremonial. At its conclusion, however, he endeavoured to address the Sorcerer; but, Otahára angrily and hastily signed to him, to keep silence, and led the way out of the caverns, in the same direction, as that by which, Iolàni had effected his entrance. Not a word, even yet, was spoken by either. The wizard still preceded the Priest, pausing, only to alter the disposition of the plantains at the different points of the forest, until they gained the deserted hut; and, then, the Sorcerer spoke.

"Was *that* a place" cried he "for mortal converse"?—"Was it fit, that we that are men, should lift up the voice yonder, saving in supplication? Has reverence deserted thee, that thou hast profaned with thy feet the paths of the spirits of darkness? Why was the plantain set in its appointed place, but to warn thee from the caves? If thou woulds't speak, say on, now. In thy haste, thou hast grievously offended; but, in thy repentance, thou shalt yet have hope"!

This rebuke, was heard with the utmost patience and humility, by the Priest. After a short interval of silence, and apparent contrition, he drew nearer to the Sorcerer; and in low earnest tones the two began to converse together.

In the first portion of the consultation, as the Priest dwelt upon his wrongs, his sufferings, and his escape, the stern calmness of expression on Otahára's countenance, remained undisturbed. But, in the second, as the conspiracy for vengeance was gradually divulged, a look of satanic malignity and delight, appeared in the Sorcerer's sunken and sinister eye. He bent forward, and listened with the utmost attention to Ioláni's discourse; at the first pause in it, intimating assent to whatever entreaty was addressed to him.

But, in the excitement and agitation of the moment, the Priest seemed to have missed the answer to his address. He fell on his knees before the Sorcerer, and grasped his hand in supplication.

"Is my brother silent"? cried he. "Is thy servant's anger awakened without a cause? Have I lied, when I swore to thee that I had suffered? Have I cursed without reason the worker of my woes? Who lured me from my glory and my possessions?—Who bore me a child to dishonor me?—And preserved it to defy me?—Who leagued with mine enemy, and kindled the war, whose end, was defeat and banishment?—She!—Otahára! Brother!—It was She!—Why am I bereft of my possessions and my power? Why am I tormented through day and night, and sunshine and tempest, and heat and cold, by a misery that none have suffered before?—Through HER! Shall a woman's

sorcery do this, while thou art in the land? For all this, shall
no vengeance be mine?—Dost thou doubt me that I am firm?
I have murdered! Otahára, I have murdered on the midnight
sea! I have shed blood, where the warriors of the land had
spared it, even in the fight! I will shed more for thee! I will slay
at thy command! I will bear blows and curses from thee, so
thou revengest me!—Behold, I am kneeling to thee—I, that
was proud! I am supplicating at thy feet; I, that was master
once! Give me my vengeance! Otahára! My vengeance! My
vengeance!"

"It is thine"! cried the sorcerer furiously. "Up and make
ready! It is for *her*, to rave; and for *thee*, to rejoice"!

Ioláni had every reason to believe in the sincerity of the wizard's compliance with his wishes. Fellowship in old iniquities,
is the only tie that villains can and must acknowledge, and it
was their's. A few moments more, matured the plan. The Sorcerer departed to his spells, and the Priest awaited him, until
night-time, in the lonely hut.

Weariness was heavy on him, and he laid him down on the
ground, and endeavoured to repose; for, now that he was on
the land, that he had gained over the wizard, and that he had
ensured his revenge; in his miserable confidence, he imagined
that his torments were removed. But, sleep was not farther from
him on the stormy ocean, than, now, on the sunbright and
peaceful earth. The same terrors assailed him in the day, as in
the night; and the fearful and undying remembrance, still tortured him as was its wont. Since his last iniquity, another
change had been wrought within him. Loneliness, anywhere,
was now become to him, a great and a terrible torment. Follow
the Sorcerer he dared not. To wait on—to watch through the
weary—weary hours, in fear and misery, was his lot, till the
night arrived that signalled the beginning of his revenge. And,
there he crouched—muttering and moaning to himself—the

dauntless and inexorable tyrant of a whole nation, by the very multitude of his iniquities alone, fallen to a miserable falterer, between the extremes, of a villain's lowest malignity, and a coward's veriest indecision and dread.

The sun had set, the darkness had come on, and the moon had risen about an hour, when Otahára returned. As the Priest hurried eagerly toward him, on his approach, the malignant smile again appeared on the Sorcerer's face; and, with the words—"It is done"—he held forth to Ioláni's eyes, a lock of dark, soft hair. The Priest gazed in utter bewilderment, at the sign, thus produced. Ere, however, he could audibly express astonishment, Otahára again spoke.

"Behold"! cried he. "I have neither tarried nor slept. It is *her* hair, that thou beholdest, now; and through it, shall the daemon enter, that causes the charm to work. The sun was low in the heaven, as I reached the thickets, that encompassed the hut. Before the door, there walked a guardian, a husbandman of Mahíné's tribe. I watched and waited on. And, so, the Twilight arose and past away, and the darkness of the night, began to steal upon the earth. Then, as weariness overcame him, the peasant lay down before the threshold of the dwelling. I looked a little while—— and lo! he slept. Yet a little more delay, and I crept, in silence, towards the entry. Sometimes, there was a muttering of voices from within. Sometimes—from without—the husbandman stirred in his repose; for, his slumbers were already startled, by the dreams of night. Shielded by the darkness round the walls of the hut, I stole yet farther in. One only stream of moonlight, penetrated the place. Its brightness was on the woman, as she sat by the child. And, she kissed it, and mourned over it. My hand was ready; and when she flung back her hair over her shoulders (for the infant wailed, whenever it drooped on his face,) I gained the prize, unsuspected and unseen. Behold, it is here! Rejoice brother! Rejoice! A little season of supplication more, and vengeance is thine"!

And, again he held it forth to the Priest. *Her* hair—alas! alas!—the hair, that had once floated over his breast! The hair, that his own hand had adorned with flowers. The hair, that his own lips had praised for its luxuriance and beauty! And, now, he could abandon it to the foul incantation—to the polluting possession of the sorcerer, without a throb of pity at his heart, or a flush of shame upon his brow!— Alas! Alas!

Clutching the ill-gotten treasure in his hand again, Otahára moved towards the door. At that action, its expression of ferocious triumph forsook the countenance of the Priest. He grasped, convulsively, at the Sorcerer's robe; and detained him, in his hasty departure.

"No more loneliness" he muttered savagely. "It is very terrible to be alone! I will follow thee, wherever thou goest! Even into the caverns, themselves, I will track thy footsteps! There is no sun, no light, no beauty, for me, when I am alone! The curse is uppermost, when none are near"!

A sneer of contempt passed over the Sorcerer's stern features. But, ere he could reply, (in trembling and supplicating tones, now,) Ioláni again spoke.

"I murdered him—Oh, Otahára! Brother!—I murdered him, upon the midnight sea! Yet, I could suffer that, for my hands are red, with other blood, than his. But the wild man! The effigy! The evil spirit that is within me, for ever!—There is the torment that I cannot suffer alone! Have mercy on me! Leave me not to myself! Have mercy! Have mercy"!

"Remember that thou art silent in the caverns"! returned Otahára, sternly. And without another word, he led the Priest towards the woods.

It was this interview—from beginning, to end—that the outcast witnessed, as already described, from the outer wall of the hut. Though, his shattered reason, rendered it impossible for him to comprehend a single word of the preceding dialogue, he had marked and recognised—mad as he was—the person of the Priest. All other impressions of the time when he had mingled with humanity, had faded from his mind, but this. Insanity, had veiled, but had never yet destroyed, his remembrance of his enemy's outward form. On all other points, he was a madman. On this, he was still a thinking and a reasoning being. At the moment, when the Sorcerer was about to abandon his wretched confederate, he started suddenly to his feet; but, as Otahára returned, he again resumed his crouching position of observation, until the two departed together for the forest; and, then, he stealthily arose, and tracked their footsteps, from as great a distance as he could.

He followed them, until at the spot where the old tree stood; they suddenly disappeared from his eyes. After wandering about this place, for some time, in the vain attempt to recover their track, he returned to the locality, where he had last beheld them, and hid himself, behind the trunk of the withered tree.

He laughed and muttered, incessantly, to himself, as he kept his lonely watch; ever and anon, peering, cautiously, into the dense darkness around; and then, again, crouching more closely still, in his hiding-place. With the peculiar cunning of his miserable race, he appeared to imagine, that the Priest and his companion, had seen him, and were attempting to conceal themselves, in the same manner as himself, in the thickets around. The morning dawned, and found him still on his watch; the same ferocity in his expression, and the same caution in his demeanour, as in the night.

The brightness, heralding the rising of the sun, had just appeared in the heavens, when a rustling was audible in the brushwood, and the next instant, the Priest, followed by the Sorcerer, again appeared on the place. At the first sight of

Ioláni, the outcast half sprung from his hiding place; but, the instant Otahára was visible, he checked himself, and waiting, until they had well past him, he set himself to follow them, with the same caution, as before.

Whatever, had happened in the incantation of the past night, it had worked with fearful power, on the heart of the Priest. His countenance was, now, almost livid in hue; and his eyes wandered, incessantly, backwards and forwards, with an expression of perpetual fear. At the slightest word, or action, of the sorcerer, he started with terror; and, as he tottered onwards at his side, he murmured to himself, almost without intermission— "The vengeance is mine"! "The vengeance is mine"!

In their way toward Mahíné's village, they took those paths, that were most circuitous, and least frequented by the populace of the island. At length, they gained the thicket, before Idía's abode; and, here, they halted and watched the entrance to the hut.

Erelong, they saw the woman come forth with her child. The traces of tears, were wet upon her cheek; and, ever and anon, she started, involuntarily, as if afflicted with a constant and causeless dread. They saw her disappear among the woods; and then, they cautiously entered the dwelling.

A basket of baked bread fruit, was standing within. The Sorcerer, muttering some words so rapidly that they were unintelligible, drew from his bosom, a handful of herbs; and pressed the juice out of them, upon the food. Then, stepping up to the woman's couch, he concealed the lock of hair under her pillow; and then—an expression of savage triumph, again irradiating his features—he drew his companion back, into the hiding place in the thicket. The Sorcery was prepared!

A long, weary interval, elapsed, before the woman's return. At last, they perceived her in the distance. She entered the dwelling, and appearing, outside, immediately afterwards, with the fatal basket, sat down before the door, and proffered to the infant, a part of the contents.

But, the child was fretful and ailing, and refused to touch the nourishment; so, the portion that she had destined for its share, she was fain to eat herself. The deadly meal was soon ended; for, the continued weeping of the little creature in her arms, seemed to take from her all enjoyment of the repast. She endeavoured, by every simple attempt in her power, to calm the wailing of the infant; but, in vain; and she sighed bitterly, as she pressed it to her bosom, and re-entered the hut.

The object was achieved! The Sorcery was prepared! But, the triumph he had hoped for, from the accomplishment of his vengeance, was as far as ever, from the heart of the infamous Priest. Vague forebodings, now oppressed him for the first time, of the chances of counter spells, and of the possibility of failure, or treachery, on the part of Otahára. The demeanour of the Sorcerer had, latterly, inclined him to doubt his sincerity— to suspect, even, that he, himself, was the real victim of his art. But, not a single suspicion of the many that haunted him, did he venture to divulge, as he still pressed onward by his wizard's side. And, so, the two turned again rapidly, towards their solitary haunt; and, the outcast, like a living shadow, yet followed in the rear.

CHAPTER V

The Island—seclusion

By courting the luxuries of retirement and indolence, in opposition to the twice urged entreaties, of the very men, to whose attachment, he ought to have looked, as the safeguard of the stability of his throne, Mahíné, at the height of his triumph, committed his most irreparable error. Among those now around him, there were none to awaken him to his duty, or to shame him from his inglorious ease. The few warriors, who, as his personal attendants, had followed him to the island, were mere youths, whose natural predilections, the festivity of their ruler's court, exactly fulfilled. The derisive sentiments entertained by the King, for the dismal predictions of his councillors, were all echoed and applauded, by these careless revellers; and the murmuring of the flute, and the cadence of the song, sounded on, among the groves of the islet, as constantly and as merrily as ever.

In truth, Mahíné was perfectly spell-bound, by his passion for Aimáta. This union had been a new existence for him—a novelty in the pleasures of love, that he had never imagined before. The girl's influence over him, that might have been exerted for good, was, unconsciously, used for evil, alone. Young, tender, and light-hearted, she had the same reckless enjoyment of the present, and the same fatal indifference to the future, as her lord; and, when every natural luxury, that the island could produce—every artificial enjoyment, that the inhabitants could invent, crowded, in prodigal profusion, to brighten their happy affection, it was little wonder, that the rebukes of ascetic councillors, and the murmurings of veteran warriors, fell powerless on the ears of Aimáta and her chieftain-King.

Meanwhile, on the main island, to the experienced eye, matters began, even now, to wear an ominous aspect. The greater part of Mahíné's army, being levies from distant districts, and desperadoes from other islands, had fought under his banner, not from attachment to the chief, but from the love of battle, and the hope of spoil. From these men, the first serious murmurings were heard. At the commencement of the war, they had been given to understand, that the reduction of Tahíti, was to be, but the prelude, to a series of victories over the rulers of the neighbouring islands; which, as fast as they were conquered, were to be placed under the dominion of appointed chieftains, from the great body of recruits. This promise, on his marriage and accession, the King had, at first, pretended to forget; but, on finding that the claims of his petitioners were not to be thus easily disposed of, he, suddenly changed his plan, and flatly denied, that his word had ever been given, as represented by the stranger warriors. In vain, did the more attached of his followers entreat him to ward off, for a time, the approach of the storm thus excited, by reiterating his promise, though ever so determined in his own mind, to resist its performance; until, some means should be discovered, for satisfying, in another way, the exactions of the mercenary troops. He treated their counsel, with the same indifference as ever. An infatuation seemed to possess him. He appeared obstinately bent upon securing his private enjoyment, at the expense of his public character—upon sacrificing, without care, or consideration, the absolute necessities of Duty, to the unimportant exigencies of Love. All that was active and ambitious in his character, was temporarily lost, in all that was indolent and luxurious; and the attached and enthusiastic among his followers, gradually gave up all hope of working his conversion; and awaited the result of their leader's infatuation, in dogged and gloomy despair.

So, the days passed on, until another month had nearly elapsed; and, then, were to be seen, on the island, the preparations, for the departure of Aimáta and the King.

Though inattentive to the call of Duty, to the voice of Affection, the heart of the girl, was as open as ever. Not all the enchantments of her sojourn, had erased, for an instant, from her memory, the grateful remembrance of the friend and companion of her season of suffering and peril. In the latter days of her seclusion, she began to feel, that her happiness, supreme as it was, was yet imperfect, apart from Idia, and her infant child; and she pressed for the return to Tahíti, and to the little village, where the woman still dwelt.

Ere she had concluded her entreaty, Mahíné's command had been given to his followers, to look to the arrangements for the homeward voyage. The revellers abandoned their haunts; the flower-garlands were scattered on the ground; and the sounds of music and laughter, were hushed in the woodlands. The preparations were soon completed; and the faint breeze arose from the sea; and the waves of the broad, bright ocean, glittered in the glorious sunbeams, as if to hallow the return of the children of Luxury and Love.

But yet—even yet, that all-important departure was delayed, for Aimáta and her young chieftain, lingered to the last moment, with natural attachment, over the beauties of their island-sojourn. And, while their attendants were awaiting their arrival on the shore, they were still wandering—irresolute even now—amid the scenes of their past happiness.

They roamed on, through solitary places, delighting to all eyes; but, to their's—how consecrated by affection, how beautified by enthusiasm and youth! Here, where the long, green pathways, wound onward and onward, under their archway of trees—there, where the flower-gardens were displayed in all their loveliness, at the clear water-side, they lingered in utter silence, to gaze their last, at the simple treasures, that each had so long looked on and loved! It is in such sorrowful farewells as these, that the undue and painful sensitiveness of the heart, which teaches us to forbode without cause, and to regret without resignation, is oftenest experienced; and, for this reason, the girl was in tears, and the chieftain's brow, wore the first melancholy expression that had saddened it, since the day of his nuptial feast. Positive ills, neither the one, nor the other, could be said to fear. Aimáta's heart-sinking, was not a presentiment, that sorrow was destined, again, to darken the dwelling of her friend; nor Mahíné's depression, the apprehension that danger was to welcome him, on the shores whose government he had usurped. Both, in their youthful confidence and elasticity of spirit, could only imagine, that whether on the great, or the little island, the same lot of happiness, must await them. And, yet, both, while wandering over the beauties of their sojourn, felt a sorrow that the nature of their departure could not authorise, and that their anticipations of the future, could not explain.

A little interval more—and the canoes, were at last afloat for Tahíti. The voyage, with so calm a sea and so propitious a wind as now favoured them, was easily and speedily accomplished. They passed the coral reefs—the surf—swimmers already sporting around them—and touched the strand of their island home.

As they entered the village, Aimáta felt the King's hand tremble within her own; and, as she looked in his face, she saw that it wore an expression of mingled astonishment and anger, that she had never observed on it before. Ere, however, she could address a word to him, the veteran chief of the army, had withdrawn him from her side, and was whispering anxiously and hurriedly, in his ear.

Although, to the inexperienced girl, the sudden emotion observable in the demeanour of the King, was a matter of the utmost surprise; to one, skilled in the character of the people of Polynesia, the aspect of the village, at this moment, was fully sufficient to warrant the sudden agitation of Mahíné, on his return to the seat of government.

The husbandmen, fishers, and others of the labouring portion of the populace, instead of being dispersed at their daily tasks, were assembled together, here and there, in small groups; the same sullen indolence, appearing in the deportment of each member of the different circles thus formed. Such portions of the now disbanded army, as were visible in the village, were disposed in the same suspicious manner; but, these last, appeared to be conversing vehemently and incessantly, and were more restless and agitated in their movements, than their humbler neighbours. The women and children, too, looked frightened and sorrowful; and lingered about the men, as if in expectation of an outbreak, or calamity, of some description. Neither by word, nor action, did any one testify the slightest pleasure or surprise, at the return of the King. The same appearance of ominous depression, was observable in the demeanour of the entire multitude. Among a people, who—simple and affectionate as they generally were—were yet to be excited, in an instant, to either of the extremes of obedience or revolt, such signs as these, were sufficiently alarming, to anyone; and to none more so, on this occasion, than to the newly-elected King. The conference between Mahíné and the chieftain, brief as it was, was an angry one; and they separated immediately, on its conclusion; the warrior, returning to the camp; and, the truant ruler—after scowling fiercely on his refractory subjects—accompanying his beloved, in the direction of the dwelling, of Idía.

They quitted their attendants, at the village, and proceeded unaccompanied, along the little footpath, that led to the solitary hut. As they neared the door, Aimáta called to its inmate, with her old expression of welcome; but, no answer was returned to the salutation. Giving way to her impatience and curiosity, the girl broke from Mahíné's side, and leaving him to follow her, entered the dwelling, alone.

CHAPTER VI

The Sorcery successful

The King followed his beloved, with feelings of bitter disappointment and anger, still in his heart. The sight, however, that presented itself to his eyes, on his gaining the interior of the hut, turned the current of his thoughts, into a different channel, at once.

The brilliant sunlight, streaming in, through the open door, illumined the rude apartment of the dwelling throughout; and cast a vivid, cheerful brightness—strangely at variance with the spirit of their occupation—over the different persons assembled there. At the foot of one of the sleeping mats of the island, crouched two women, from the neighbouring village; their faces hidden in their mantles, and their deep emotion, only visible by the convulsive tremors, that occasionally, agitated their frames. A few withered flowers and remnants of bread fruit, were scattered about the floor, giving an air of confusion and desolation to the place; and on the bed—silent and motionless, as if already summoned from her pilgrimage of misery on earth, lay the hapless victim of the Sorcerer and the Priest.

Her eyes were closed. The very form of her countenance, was distorted and changed. Even the poor relics of former beauty, were vanished from her, now. Saving when the sobs of Aimáta and the women, or the wail of the affrighted child, broke upon the ear, there was nothing to interrupt the silence of the place, but the sufferer's deep, convulsive gaspings, for breath. Her fingers clutched, mechanically, at the empty air; and at intervals, a quick, sudden shudder, passed over her limbs; but, no look of consciousness broke upon the rigid, death-like expression, of her features—no words, no moans escaped her lips. The long— long raving fits, had vanished; and the welcome lethargy of death, was approaching. No greeting, was there, for Aimáta, when she listened for it from without—no greeting, when she kissed the woman's hand, and wept and watched for it, within!

In patient sorrow, they still kept their melancholy vigil. And, so, the hours wore on, and there was no change, until the sun went down upon the ocean; and, then, the eyes of the dying woman —gentle and eloquent, even in the anguish of that fearful hour—opened, once more.

As she observed Aimáta watching by her side, with the child clasped to her bosom, her thoughts wandered towards the days of peril, and she murmured out some expressions of apprehension and affection, uttered to the girl long since, but well remembered by her, at this awful moment. Then, the cloud passed, gradually, from her faculties; and, as she looked from the infant to Aimáta, the desolation of her lot came over her in all its bitterness, and she wept.

The girl's grief and despair, so completely mastered her, that she uttered not a word. So the woman was the first to speak, and in the hollow and tremulous tones of her voice, there was an awful testimony to the agony she had undergone, at the hands of Otahára and the Priest.

"Do not be sorrowful," she ejaculated, "I leave thee wherewithal to remember me, in the days to come, in the infant that is nestled in thy arms! Even, as I have loved and cared for *thee*; so, shalt thou love and care for *him*—Oh Aimáta!, Aimáta! I bore him in danger, I have preserved him in sorrow!—Pity, as I have pitied; cherish, as I have cherished him! For the morning

shall rise; and none shall be near to look upon the infant
kindly, but thee!—Aimáta! Aimáta"!

Here, her voice failed her, and the passionate weeping of the
girl, was all that was now heard. After a long and weary interval, the sufferer's eye brightened with an unnatural light; and
she spoke once more.

"Behold," murmured she, "the spirits of the dead, shall return to earth; and I shall be released, to haunt with them, the
dwellings of my people that I have loved! Sorrow not Aimáta!
Though viewless to thee, though speechless in thy happy presence, I shall watch over thee, still! In thy seasons of loneliness,
thy beloved shall yet be by; to comfort thee, when thou
mournest—to lighten thy heart, though the tear be on thy
cheek, and the word of sorrow be yet passing from thy lips!
Sometimes, at eventide, when the summer stillness is beautiful
on the land, and thy thoughts shall, haply, turn to thy sister
that is gone; remember, Aimáta, that though the form is cold on
earth, the spirit is lingering about thee, yet!—Do not forget me!
From thy childhood, I have loved thee!—Oh Aimáta! Aimáta!
from thy very childhood, I have wished thee well!—Remember
the infant—if *thou* should'st desert him, his portion is loneliness, indeed! But thou wilt not forsake him! He shall live to
drop the flowers over my tomb; and *thy* hand, shall teach him
to scatter them, aright"!

She ceased again. Even her former painful efforts at breathing, were now heard, no longer. One of the native women,
arose from her station at the bed-foot; and, as she bent close
over the sufferer's head, she whispered to her companion, that
the time of the mourning was, already, at hand. It was very dark
in the dwelling, and none thought of quitting the place for an
instant, to seek for a torch; so, they were fain to await the rising
of the moon, to discover if the awful probability, was already

fulfilled. Aimáta took the woman's hand; it was cold and rigid, even now. She spoke to her, and there was no answer; and, as the girl, in bitter anguish, turned from the bedside, the solemn and beautiful moonlight, arose upon the earth.

Gone! Gone! The beauty that the Island had once loved, had past from it, at last. The mortal mission of that noble spirit had ended, and the eloquence of those gentle eyes, was hushed for ever. Of the affectionate woman, of the intrepid mother, of the patient sufferer for humanity's sake, the desolate dwelling held no relic, now, but a wasted corpse. Gone! Gone!

Happily departed! Though the girl that is weeping by thy side, in her innocence, even, of this world's wisdom, shall never think it—thou art happily departed! Thy removal from thy home of earth, is merciful and just! The thoughtless simplicity of thy people dwelt not in *thee*! Thou walked'st among the children of the land, a stranger and unknown; for, thy heart was the unconscious exile, of other and nobler shores! Now, is thy destiny accomplished! Now, is thy glory begun! With that little band, whose natural affection—like thine—nor iron custom could control, nor mortal tyranny abash—with those, thy sister martyrs for their offspring's cause, shalt thou yet be seen (when the mortal loveliness of thy land has perished for ever) triumphant and divine! For, despised as it was on earth, the remonstrance and revolt of the Polynesian mother, is treasured on high; and, when at the Last Day, the groan of a world of people rises to the judgment seat—when the little and the great nation, shall tremble and supplicate together—when man savage and man civilised, shall await their sentence, in the vast unity of common hope and common dread—pleading, like the virtues of Lot, for the salvation of the city of Zoar, the contemned righteousness of the glorious few, shall, haply, atone for the crime of the reckless many, in the Islands of the South!

Gone! Gone! But to be remembered still, though like clouds

on the summer heaven, of what thou once wast, thy departure leave no sign that is eloquent to mortal eyes! Beside Aimáta's, there were other hearts, that, though in silence and in dread, yet loved and pitied thee, like her's. To these, the scenes of thy suffering, shall be as consecrated ground; and the flowers on thy grave, shall be as deities to their affections, in the years to come. In their happiness, they shall think of the days of thy maidenhood. In their sorrow, they shall ponder on thy patience under thy sufferings. For, where misfortune was, thither thou camest as a sister! Where danger threatened, there didst thou watch, a guardian and a comforter, to the last!

Steady and beautiful, the moonlight still shone; and, in the lonely dwelling, the eloquent silence of awe and grief, still prevailed. Sometimes, as the night wind whistled among the trees, the child, in its astonishment and affright, mechanically murmured forth, the few, simple words, that its mother had taught it last. Sometimes, the misery of the young Aimáta, burst forth in a brief exclamation of despair; and, sometimes, the women at the foot of the bed, muttered an invocation to their gods. But these interruptions—momentary in their nature—only tended to make the stillness that followed them, when they ceased, more impressive and profound.

Then—after that first interval of helpless unthoughtful grief, had elapsed—one of the women, departed for the village; and, erelong, there returned with her, others of her sex. The bier was covered with its pure, white cloth, the flowers were scattered over the corpse, and the mourners gathered them together, to watch and to lament over it, until the morning rose.

And the night passed, and the day appeared that was to usher in the internment—that last, worst separation, between living and dead! It was in the first, calm hours, of the morning, that the simple and solemn funeral began. So, the hut was tenantless now; and the garden path, was trodden by stranger feet!

Slowly and sadly, the little procession wended on its way, along the shady avenues, and among the green and lonely glades of that beautiful land! She had loved them in the days of her joy and sorrow, alike; and, amid the loveliest of those forest places, was chosen her sepulchre, now !—Alas! Alas! Idía!

Beyond the natural arena, where the sports on the marriage festival of the King, had been celebrated, there rustled onward, among the trees, one of the most retired, of the forest rivulets of the land. On one of the banks of this stream, where there was a little rising in the grassy and flower-covered ground, the women of the village, had prepared her grave. In the softness of the atmosphere, and in the sameness and obscurity of the prospect around, there was a simple melancholy, that reached the heart, at once—a sadness whose nature was rather to soften and to soothe, than to harrow and to grieve. Between the massive tree-trunks, the view, though confined and monotonous, was, still, full of repose to the eye, and of solemnity, to the feelings. Here, a turf pathway wound elegantly onward, until lost in the forest obscurity of the distance. There, were to be seen, patches of natural vegetation, beautiful and fantastic in form; now, quivering in the fresh, soft breezes; now, sleeping in the noontide stillness, of the woodland atmosphere. No sound from the neighbouring village, ever reached this deep retirement. The billows of the ocean, around, might roar with their utmost fury, but were never audible, here. It was a quiet and a lovely place. If ever the beauty of repose was visible on earth, it was on this spot. Here, was its favourite empire—here, was its loved and its accustomed haunt.

They had interred the body, they had smoothed and garlanded the turf over the tomb, and one by one, they had mourned and wept and then departed. The chill winds of the Autumn evening, were already arising upon the south; yet, still, the young Aimáta lingered by the grave. Loneliness, near the dead that we love, loses all its desolation and terror, to the heart; and, as the girl sat in her forest solitude, fear, had no portion, in the melancholy emotions, within her. In her place of mourning, there was nothing to distract her thoughts— nothing to shame her in her sorrow. So, unconscious of the lapse of time, comfortless, in this her great sorrow, she lingered on, until Mahíné's presence darkened the one ray of moonlight that had penetrated the place; and, then, she departed with the chieftain; and the new-made grave, was left, unwatched to Solitude and Night.

Thus peaceful was the haven, where the troubled pilgrimage of Idía, was destined to end! Thus, was the mortal turbulence, that years on years had worked, at the signal of a moment, hushed into the utterest earthly calm. The poetic passion of the maiden; the glorious courage of the mother; the horror of the death by sacrifice; the anguish of the wizard's poison—all— all the miseries, that the life of earth, had accumulated for her, in its course, had ended here—in a strip of earth, by the side of a forest brook!

Oh, that the night might wear ever onward, in that solitary burial place; for, in life, it often befriended her; and in death, it fits her well! The season of love, it beautified and softened to her heart. The triumph of her hour of travail, it hastened and secured. In the fastnesses of the Lake Vahíria, it delayed her capture, till capture was of no avail; and, now, in her long repose, it made a mourning for her death, the most solemn that mortality can deserve, the most impressive that mortality can desire.

And, now, that thy grave is lonely—that the flowers are scattered on it and left—that the lamentation for thy beauty and thy goodness, has become a habit to the heart—farewell! At last—Farewell! In the hours of the night we found thee in thy youth! In the hours of the night, we leave thee to thy rest!— That rest is Peace!

CHAPTER VII

The revolt of the army

Thus, the days passed on in Tahíti until the winter months
were arrived. The dwellings of Mahíné's village, were, by this
time, many of them, desolate. None sauntered upon the pathways. None wended to their labour in the field. None sought
the amusements, that had power to delight and to occupy
them, once. A change was at hand.

Before the King's dwelling, there watched, with their martial
gear on them, as in the time of war, a handful of veteran warriors. There were none to relieve these guardians of the ruler[']s
safety. From day to day, their numbers were the same; and from
day to day, they performed their office, although it was the season of Peace, without cessation, or rest.

Within the habitation thus ominously preserved, Mahíné,
stood brooding over the danger that beset him, in stern and
sullen despair; and, at his feet, the young Aimáta sat, weeping
and in silence. There seemed a curse upon the inhabitants of
the place, so deep was the gloom, that—from the highest to
lowest—appeared in the demeanour of all.

It was not without cause, that the countenance of the King,
expressed the strongest emotions of depression and despair;
for, with the exception of the little band of warriors who
watched his dwelling, the army and the people, had with one
accord, declared their contempt of his power, and their hostil-
ity to his reign.

On his arrival at Tahíti, no attempt had been made by the infatuated monarch, to restore his lost credit with the discontented levies. The obstinate pride, that seemed, now, to have taken possession of his heart, rendered all attempts to induce him to accede to a timely act of concession, utterly abortive. The claims of the discontented troops, remained unanswered—even, uncombatted. The dignities promised to the chieftains, and the rewards guaranteed to the inferior warriors; now, that he had arrived at the centre of his territories, were still unbestowed. That part of the native army, that still remained faithful to their leader, soon, began to waver in its allegiance. Some unnecessary exercise of severity in the punishment of trivial offences, soon decided them in their course; and they joined the rebellious party; some few, of the King's personal attendants, and old servants, excepted; who still remained true to the royal cause; and still hoped, that their master would awake from his delusion, and act with wisdom and clemency even yet.

On the part of the warriors in revolt, nothing serious or decided was yet done. Among their numbers, were many men, who—villains as they were—practised a degree of moderation and patience, in furthering the accomplishment of their grand design, that astonished their more unwary companions. But these formidable rebels, had learnt an important lesson, from the position of the King. They had discovered, that revolution must be unanimous, to be permanently successful; and they determined, ere proceeding to extremities, to secure, in their bold attempt, the co-operation of the great body of the island inhabitants.

The desire of obtaining the chief power, was not the cause, that actuated the leaders of the revolt, in their ambitious attempt. Vengeance for their wrongs, and attainment of the objects held out to them as lures, in the first instance, by the perfidious King, were the main designs of their present endeavour;

to accomplish which, no means seemed more effective, than the recal[l] of the banished ruler. Some, knew by experience, others, had heard by report, of the exceeding pliability and gentleness of his disposition. From the gratitude of such a man, everything was to be hoped. From his docility, everything was to be anticipated. Rescue him from his exile, and reseat him on his throne, and dignities and benefits innumerable, would flow in upon them. In him, they saw the man, whose nominal authority might be obtained with the utmost facility, to give importance and security, to their worst schemes. There was no fraud, that might not be practised on his credulity—no threat, that might not successfully be used, to overcome his misgivings, and to shake his determinations. To delegate the rule, to one among their own number, would be, they well-knew, to place a tyrant on the throne, whose subsequent removal from his dignity, would be a matter of stern necessity, to all. To hope any more from Mahíné, was utter delusion. All their revolt now wanted, was a purpose and an excuse; and the very man to satisfy these requirements, in the manner they could most desire, was the exiled King.

The lower orders of the populace, were soon gained over. Even, *they*, were incensed against their unfortunate ruler; for, now that he had returned among them, he seemed as utterly careless of providing for their amusement, or of planning for their advantage, as he was of acceding to the claims of that army, whose dauntless bravery, had placed him on the throne. They remembered with regret, the mild and affectionate sway of their former monarch, as contrasted with the proud indifference of the present King, to their wants and wishes. When, therefore, the return of their exiled ruler, was promised them by the rebel chief, they flew to arms in his cause, with as much alacrity, as when they had arisen, in former days, to cast him from this throne.

The plan of the revolt was soon matured. The great body of the insurgents, were to remain in concealment and inactivity, until the success of the more immediate and important enterprise—the assassination of Mahíné was achieved. They were, then, to be divided into two parties—the one, to keep possession of the village; the other, to embark without delay, to rescue the exiled King.

The conduct of the assassination, was delegated, only, to a chosen few. The heads of the revolt, were well aware of the absolute necessity of this serious measure. While Mahíné lived, there was no security for their plan. They might drive him from the island; but, they could not ensure the certainty, that he would never return. To a man of the active and unscrupulous character, that they still believed him to be, the organisation of a formidable band of new adherents, to secure his re-instatement, would be a task of comparative ease. He was too dangerous an enemy, to be permitted to escape. Nothing but his death, could seal their triumph. So, the surprising of the faithful guards, and the massacre of the chief, was fixed for the very day, on which, Mahíné has been introduced to the reader, as sullenly braving, among his possessions, the dangers that beset him on every side.

Turn we once again, for a brief space, to the interior of the royal dwelling.

The apartment, chosen as the seclusion of Aimáta and the King, was, now, occupied also by a third person; with whom, Mahíné was engaged in earnest conversation. For some time, the colloquy was carried on in whispers; but, erelong, as if fired with sudden indignation, the King broke abruptly from his counsellor, and his last words, were uttered in a loud and angry tone of voice.

"Behold," cried he, "I have chosen my part". "If there be danger, I will meet it. If there be revolt, I will quell it, as a King. Is it for *me* to obey? Shall I be a slave in the hands of my people that I rule, to deliver my throne, to a horde of rebels, and my possessions, to a band of husbandmen and thieves? By the greatness of Oro, whom I serve, this shall not be! This evil people, have I conquered for myself, and by myself, alone, will I rule over them, while I live. The faithful, are still left unto me. In the island of exile, I have guards that shall be recalled. As my fathers conquered, so will I conquer, yet. As *they* died in glory, so will I. Though the rabble of the islands, be numerous as the forest trees, I will spurn them and resist them, to the last"!

And, as he motioned the warrior to leave him, the old martial spirit, came over him again; and, the daring and ambition of the chieftain, for a brief period, took the place of the indolence and infatuation, of the King.

But, as Aimáta drew near to him; and, winding her arms round his neck, looked sorrowfully up in his face, the war-club dropped from his hand, the fire departed from his expression, and the passionate fondness of the lover, ruled within him, once more.

"Let us depart", said the girl softly, "Oh, Mahíné,! Mahíné! let us depart and be at peace again. Since she, that we have loved, has gone from us for ever, there has been no happiness, no comfort for our hearts, in this desolate place. While there is time, we may yet escape. There are other lands to live in. There are other people that we may join—I have none in the Islands to care for me, but thee! Should'st thou be taken from me, whom have I left, that I may call my beloved, among the nations of the earth"?

And she hid her face in his bosom, and waited for his answer. But, though his whole f[r]ame trembled with the violence of the emotions within him, he made no reply. So, she arose, and, departing for an instant, returned with the motherless child, in her arms.

"Look on it, Mahíné", she pleaded, "this is the trust that she left me at her death; and how shall I fulfil it, if we remain in peril here? By *her* care, was I preserved for *thee*; and should I not labour for the safety of the child that she loved, as *she* laboured for *mine*? Shall I not preserve it, as the all that is left unto me, of the companion, whose words were as music to mine ear, and whose presence was as the sunshine of heaven unto my heart! Let us leave this place—oh, my beloved, let us make our habitation, where the woods shall be safer to our feet, where our dwelling shall need no guard, and where the weapon of war shall become a stranger to thy hand"!

As she ceased, and knelt to him, weeping, with the child still clasped to her bosom, the chieftain's infatuated insensibility to the dangers around him vanished at the bidding of the still, sweet voice, of affection. With a groan of bitter anguish, he raised the girl from the ground, and advanced towards the door of his abode.

But, even now, he hesitated ere he could quit the dwelling. The conflict between Love and Ambition, had been lulled for awhile, but was not over, yet. An expression of the deepest dejection and melancholy, came over his countenance; and the entreaties of Aimáta, at this moment of important decision, fell unheeded upon his ears. It was a fearful trial, to abandon thus, the throne that he had battled for and won—to live, self-condemned to obscurity and exile, when he had counted so surely, but a brief season before, on a future existence of triumph and renown. Ardently, truly, as he loved the girl, this was a miserable moment, for the conqueror of a battle-field, and the usurper of a throne—a moment, to make the boldest quail, and the most affectionate hesitate, at such a choice as his.

His brief and bitter reverie, had lasted but a few moments, when the clang of weapons, from the outer door, struck upon his ear. He seized his war-club, and listened for an instant. The noise of the fray, sounded nearer and nearer; and, the next moment, one of the King's servants, staggered into the room, covered with blood, to announce the attack of the dwelling, by a band of rebel warriors.

At a sign from Mahíné, the man seized the terrified Aimáta by the hand, dragged her through a secret entrance at the back of the house, and scaling the wall that ran round it, gained, with his charge, a place of safe concealment, on the sea shore, below. Meanwhile, in the front of the dwelling, the King had already placed himself at the head of his devoted band, and, at the first onset, had driven the assailants, without the wall again. But, their triumph was a short one. The number of the rebels, trebled that of the royal party; and, as man after man of the defenders fell, it became evident, that a few minutes, only, must elapse, before the King's dwelling passed into the possession of the leaders of the revolt. At this moment, Mahíné—who was still desperately battling, at the head of his warriors, for his honor and his throne—was forcibly dragged back, into the rear, by two of the last spared of his war chieftains. Spite of his resistance, he was forced onward, in the same direction as that taken by Aimáta and her guardian. A canoe lay ready on the shore, the warriors manned and launched it, and the instant after, the usurper and his bride, were speeding out for the main ocean.

The resistance at the dwelling, was protracted to the utmost, by the few brave men, who yet remained of the adherents to the King, until all chance of further successful opposition to the attacking party, was at an end. Then, the defenders turned, and fled to the mountains; and the assailants rushed, unhindered, into the King's house. The stratagem, by which, the victim had escaped, was penetrated immediately. They hurried to the shore, and launched their canoes; but, the bark that bore the fugitive monarch, had, already, so completely the start of them, that pursuit was useless. And, in bitter disappointment and in-dignation at the result of their attempt, the rebels returned to the camp.

Some hours, were, now, wasted in useless recrimination, among those entrusted with the assassination of Mahíné; and in noisy argument, among the members of the army, at large. Peace, however, was at length restored. The village was, ulti-mately, occupied by one division of the warriors; and the other, started, the morning after, for the island of exile, as determined at first.

CHAPTER VIII

The recall of the banished King

Since the escape of Ioláni, the prisoners had been watched with greater care, and treated with more severity, than before. The fruit of their labours, now became apparent, on the island. Dwellings arose,—pathways were widened—gardens were arranged—groves were planted—trees were felled for timber; and, over the general appearance of the place, an aspect of fertility and comfort was spread, most delightful to behold.

Among the guards, the belief was, that the two Priests had effected their escape in safety, and were concealed among the mountains of Tahíti. Communication of their flight, had, accordingly, been made to Mahíné, and the country had been searched—with what success, the reader may easily determine. Suspicion attached to the banished monarch; but, as no direct evidence of his guilt could be obtained, either by divination of the priests, or investigation among his fellow-prisoners, he remained unpunished; his guards being content, simply, to watch him with greater caution, than they were wont to employ, in the care of his brother exiles.

About noontide, on the day after Mahíné's flight, prisoners and guards were, alike, astonished by the appearance of a fleet of war-canoes, steering direct for the island. As they drew nearer, the amazement of the exiles was much increased, when they observed that the occupants of the vessels were completely armed, as if in expectation of an approaching conflict. Loud shouts were already to be heard from the canoes, of—"the King! the King"!; which, as the rebels landed, were changed into a haughty summons to yield, when the guards of the usurper, showed a disposition to contest their further advance.

A few minutes parleying, sufficed to prove to the prisoners that their liberty was at hand, and to Mahíné's warriors, that the power of their master was at an end. There was nothing left for them, under such circumstances, but to yield; and, as they laid down their arms, the cries were redoubled of "the King, the King"!

But the exiled monarch, had withdrawn himself from the crowd on the beach, at the first appearance of the rebel army. After an eager search, he was found by his unruly liberators, sitting alone, in one of the sea-side gardens; his face buried in his hands, and his whole demeanour, expressive of a melancholy most strange and unaccountable, at a period so glorious as this, for his people and himself.

As they made their obeisance before him, and with the greatest apparent joy and reverence, hailed him as their ruler, once more; he raised his eyes, with a piteous and bewildered expression, towards the countenances of his wild deliverers. At first, he made them no answer. Perhaps, his thoughts, at that important moment, strayed to the hour of his defeat—perhaps to his murdered queen—perhaps to the desolate dwellings and the mouldering skeletons, on the Temple plains; for, he bent down his head, and groaned bitterly. Then, as they reiterated their assurances of future obedience, and their declarations of future affection, he raised himself, and in a faultering and hollow voice, spoke to them thus:—

"Seek ye among yourselves, for a ruler that ye may obey, for I have no part in the beautiful Tahíti, more. Of my people that I loved, there is left but the little remnant, that have shared my banishment here. Of the home that I dwelt in, there is nothing

but a place of ruins, that remains. Ye would have me for your
King—alas! how shall I rule, when my councillors are strangers? How shall I stand forth among the people, when, haply,
none that I know, none that I care for, shall appear in their
ranks? Oh, that I had perished in the battle!—that I had been
cut off in the retreat by night; for, then, had I died with the
beautiful and the brave!—then, had I escaped for ever, the
shame of dethronement and defeat"!

He stopped abruptly; and, again, his head sunk on his
bosom, as the long-restrained tears began to flow from his eyes.
But, among the stern, fiery warriors, around him, there was no
sympathy for the desolate and heart-broken man. His petition
to be left in his banishment, was drowned in the clamour, that
now prevailed on every side. He was born in triumph from his
peaceful retirement; the canoes were manned and launched;
and the few native inhabitants, who lingered on the beach to
watch the departure of the fleet, were all that were now left in
the island of exile.

The system of future government for Tahíti, was fixed in a
few days; for, the more considerable were the exactions of the
rebel chief, the more implicit was the King's obedience to their
will. The strictest retirement—the greatest possible exemption
from all personal responsibility in the affairs of the island,
seemed what he coveted most—what he most obstinately desired, from the heads of the army and the people.

It was settled, that the island should be divided into different
provinces, as usual; but, it was also insisted, that the chiefs set
over them, should be accountable to none, in the exercise of
their power—a privilege never before conceded, for very obvious reasons, to the petty rulers of districts, in the Polynesian
Islands. This bold demand, received, of necessity, the tacit acquiescence of the defenceless King; who, voluntarily,
strengthed the position of his formidable and ambitious coun-

cillors, by appointing, as regent over his own district, the principal chieftain of the army of revolt.

Thus, was peace in the land once more. The weapons of war
were again laid aside; and the husbandman returned to this
labour of tillage, until the next revolution, among his brave, but
thoughtless people, summoned him again, from his quiet
homestead and his simple amusements, to swell the fatal ranks
of bloodshed and strife.

On the morning after the formation of the new government
had been completed, the King left the palace, unattended, and
proceeded—sometimes along the sea coast, sometimes through
the paths of the forest—towards the desolated scene of his rule,
in the days of happiness and peace.

Until this period, he had, uniformly sacrificed his own emotions and desires, since his liberation from the island of exile, to
the requirements of others; however unjust or numerous, they
might be. But, now that he had played in the pageant of others,
his humiliating and unwelcome part, he scrupled no longer to
satisfy the harmless exactions, of his own simple and affectionate feelings. From the moment when he had once more stepped
on the shores of his island home, his heart had yearned towards
the spot, consecrated to him even now,—dreary and solitary as
it was—by the remembrance of the bright and untroubled past.
On the Temple plains, he had rejoiced in his happiness—on the
Temple plains, he would mourn in his sorrow. There, for years
on years, he had lived, the companion of his people, rather
than, the King. There, he would gladly have died, in the homes
of his fathers and among the subjects of his love. Indolent of
disposition and affectionate of heart; in feeling, as in action,
considerate and kindly, without cessation or change; he was a
true and admirable type, of the happier characteristics of his
brethren of the soil. His worst misfortune, was the eminence of
his station. His most dangerous enemies, were his duties as a

King. As a ruler of rank, his life was one long error. As a simple husbandman, his existence would never have been harrassed by a care, or embittered by a single grief.

As, in pursuing his journey, he gained the ruined hut of the sorcerer, the heart-broken monarch, paused by the little creek, in sad and solemn admiration of the loveliness of the place. Turning his eyes towards the desolate dwelling, he observed a solitary man, standing at the doorway. Ever anxious for companionship, ever hoping for consolation in his misfortunes, the King hurried towards the inhabitant of the hut, trusting that the figure he saw, might be one of his fellow exiles, bent upon the same melancholy errand as himself. As he approached, the man raised his hand—Joy! Joy! It was his lost brother! It was Ioláni the Priest!

Of the strange perversity that sometimes marks the affections, a more striking example could scarcely have been furnished, than the King's attachment to a man, so cold and disdainful to him, on all occasions, as his infamous brother. From their earliest boyhood, however, the more unfeeling were Ioláni's attempts to repel it, the more patient and continual, had been the King's proffers of fraternal love. Repulse, seemed but to stimulate his affection; contempt, but to nourish it afresh. And, now, when in the midst of his loneliness, one of his own blood, yet remained to him—now, when the desolate man had recovered a companion, after he had so sorrowfully resigned himself to mourn a loss; his old generosity, his old determination to love, even through the iron obstructions of hatred and scorn, returned, in tenfold power, to his heart. He flew up to the Priest, heaping on him, term after term of endearment, and looking anxiously and fondly on his face, as if in the hope, that sorrow and suffering, that change us all, had changed even the hard-hearted Priest.

"Alas"! cried he, "how have we both grieved—yet, now that

we are met together again, how will we both rejoice! My lands have been restored unto me, my power is mine own again. Thy state—thy rank—thy possessions—they shall all return unto thee! Pomp and glory shall once more by thine! Thy greatness in the land shall be restored!—. Oh, Ioláni! Ioláni! If thou willest it, thou shalt be King—so thou lovest me! So, thou art gentle with thy people; and with thy brother, a companion and a friend"!

The King paused, and looked up, once more, into the gloomy countenance of the Priest. But, Iolani returned him no answer. One moment, he hesitated, and his wild, fierce eye, softened for an instant—the next, he broke from the King, as if, even in listening to this brother, he feared that he had committed a fault; and, calling in tremulous and imploring tones—"Otahára! Otahára"!—he tottered back into the hut.

As the sorcerer confronted the King, his hand grasped Iolani's shoulder, as if to sever the Priest, by force, from the last of his race; and an expression of haughty triumph, gleamed in his sinister eyes. No temporal rank, however proudly maintained, had the slightest influence over the students of the supernatural world; and Otahára motioned the King to be gone; not as a vassal, but as a superior and a lord.

The unhappy monarch gazed for the last time, imploringly, in the face of his infatuated brother; but, Ioláni's eyes were fixed on the sorcerer, alone; and, as in despair and misery, he turned to quit the haunt of the devotees of iniquity, he spoke his farewell, thus:—

"I am bidden to leave thee; but, though I depart from thy abode in sorrow and in shame, I will not forget thee yet! As the morrow dawns, my young warriors shall watch the places round thy prison house; and, if haply thou shalt burst asunder the spells that bind thee now, and thy heart shall yearn, towards thy brother that is gone, they shall comfort thee, and bring thee to my dwelling; for, I am lonely among the people, and, even in thy deepest unworthiness—Ioláni, I love thee still"!

As the last words fell from the King's lips, and he disappeared in the mazes of the forest, Ioláni re-entered the hut. And thus, they parted!—The one brother, in his noble sorrow, to commune with the angel within him; the other, in his wretched degradation, to combat the evil spirit, whose abiding place was for ever in his heart!

CHAPTER IX

Morning and Evening—

The mazes of our tale are well-nigh penetrated. With the morning, whose rising we chronicle—with the evening, whose closing we have yet to relate, the task of the writer ends, and the employment of the reader, is over and past.

On a little island—the outermost of the Polynesian group—are situate[d] the characters, that figure in our morning scene. To this place, the fugitive usurper had retreated with his gentle bride; and here, where wars and tumults were almost unknown, they had made, with the motherless child, their permanent and peaceful abode.

The winter season had now set in. The beach of the islet was deserted, save by tho[se] few fishermen, whose necessary avocations led them to the shore. A gentle rain, had fallen for some days, and the sun shone out—on the morning that we describe—on a picturesque, though somewhat comfortless scene. Many of the lowlands, were, already, partially overflowed; and the peasants might be seen, as the day advanced, hurrying to protect their gardens and their habitations, from the stealthy incursion of the waters. Far, in the woodlands, the streams were swollen and discoloured; and the forest avenues were,—here, turned into damp marshes—there changed into resting-places for decayed verdure. Yet, even now, the influence of the season wrought no violent change in the myriad attractions of the island. The atmosphere, though moist and humid, was hardly colder than in the autumn months, the wild-flowers about the rocks, met the sunshine as gaily as ever and the trees and meadowlands retained, in colour, the beauty that had adorned them in the season that was past.

Turn we, however, from the contemplation of Nature, to the habitations of man. On the high lands and cliffs, are situated, for the most part, the dwellings of the little colony; and, conspicuous among them, stands the pleasant abode of Aimáta and the fugitive chief.

Its door is drawn back, that the sun—veiled in clouds for so many days past—may brighten the cottage apartment, with its welcome and refreshing light. The inhabitants are seated near the entrance. Aimáta's hand is clasped in Mahíné's, her face is turned towards the chieftain, and she listens with rapt attention, to the words that are falling from his lips. At her feet, and occupied with a basket of fresh-gathered flowers, is the motherless child. An air of perfect comfort, distinguishes the interior of the dwelling—from the white rafters, with their lacings of coloured cords, at the roof, to the dry soft grass, that is plentifully strewn over the floor. Before the little party, lie the gardens of their abode; the smooth, fertile plains; and the bright, broad ocean. Around them, are the shady woodlands, and the multitude of the forest trees. Charmed by the delights of their retirement, the inmates of the dwelling, have no hope—no wish, beyond their island seclusion. The life of peacefulness she so lately longed for, Aimáta has obtained; and, its dream of lawless ambition, has vanished, for ever, from Mahíné's heart.

Erelong, the position of the little group is changed; for, the child suddenly abandons his occupation, and climbing with his handful of flowers to the girl's knee, attempts to lure her, from Mahíné to himself. For a brief space, spite of his efforts, Aimáta's eyes are still fixed on her beloved. But, soon, as if some tone in his voice, some particular turn in his half-formed expressions of entreaty, has won its way towards her memory, while it lingers on her ear, her attention wanders from Mahíné, a tear gathers in her eye, and the name that is most sacred to her heart, passes softly from her lips, as she turns an instant from the warrior, and affectionately caresses the child.

If the spirits of the dead, are suffered to walk the earth—and who, that has once loved and once grieved; who that has thought in solitude and mourned in the hours of the night, shall have the heart to deny, or the fortitude to doubt, that the awful permission exists—if, indeed, the viewless denizens of other worlds, may, sometimes, return to the places of the earth, how brightly, at this moment, was accomplished, the solemn promise and prediction of Idía, in that hour of anguish, when she parted from her beloved!

And here—while her existence is untroubled, while her heart, has those sorrows only, whose mission is to soften and to soothe—we quit, in sad reluctance, the gentlest and the best of the Daughters of the Southern Isles! In the homes of her people, her presence was a relief in misery and an inspiration in joy. Haply, in the legend that we have written of her remote and beautiful land, the same brightening and innocent part, may yet, be her's! In the very name—Aimáta, was melody for the companions of her life; may it retain a relic of its old attraction still, for the stranger of another nation and another time!

❧ ❧

The day had dawned as auspiciously on Tahíti, as on Mahíné's islet. But, as the hours grew on, the promise of the morning was not fulfilled in the noon; and, when the sun was waning towards the bosom of the sea, the firmament, saving in the west, was covered with huge, dark clouds; the wind was rising shrill; and a thick, heavy rain, had already begun to fall.

Many of the inhabitants, as the day advanced, quitted their usual occupations in dismay, and watched, in silence and inaction, the progress of the approaching storm. For the most part, the people herded together. Among their numbers, however, were two, who kept this tempest-vigil, in desolate and utter solitude.

Under the scanty shelter of the ruined hut, cowered the Sorcerer and the Priest. During the day, they had maintained perfect silence; but, now, as the evening approached, this taciturnity wore off, in both. At first, they communed in low voices and at long intervals; then, they spoke rapidly and in raised tones; and, finally, the converse of the villains, broke into low and vehement dispute.

At the beginning of the quarrel, the Priest's demeanour was hesitating and humble, and Otahára's, vehement and assured; but soon, the wretched remains of Ioláni's former nature, began to work within him, and his violence of manner and speech, equalled the sorcerer's, erelong. Otahára spoke most; the fury of the Priest as taunt after taunt fell upon his ears, seeming to deprive him of utterance. Regardless of his danger, the wizard, tottering nearer and nearer to his desperate companion, reiterated his insults. Though goaded almost to madness, for a few moments more, Ioláni suffered in silence; until, at the mention of a term of the utmost ignominy applied to him, by Otahára, in tones of the bitterest sarcasm, his patience forsook him, at once; and, uttering a yell of fury, he dealt the sorcerer a tremendous blow, with his clenched fist.

The wizard staggered back a few steps. His face flushed almost to purple—then, turned to a livid paleness. One instant, he raised his hand threateningly in the air—the next, without word or groan, he fell heavily to the earth.

For some minutes, Ioláni gazed upon the dead body. Then, he tottered up to it, and placed his hand upon the heart of the corpse. One instant's attention, convinced him that the Sorcerer was no more. He was alone! His own hand, had wrought on him, the curse that he dreaded most!

He thought on his awe for Otahára—on the abject terror of the man and his power, that, since their first meeting, had possessed him so constantly, as to have become a habit to his heart. He had entered on the dispute with the most degrading sensations of fear and humiliation—was it possible that such an one as he, could have ended it thus?—And, again he passed his hand over the dead man's heart, and strained his eyes over the dead man's face.

Half paralysed with horror, he staggered from the corpse, and peered through a rent in the wall of the hut. The roaring of the waves, and the deep, hollow moaning of the wind, seemed like voices that cursed him, as he looked forth. The first object that met his eyes, on the beach, was the canoe that had born him from the island of exile, and that he had left to fall to ruin, on the spot where he had gained the shore. Even the paddle, lay yet, in its appointed place at the vessel's bow.

The instrument of one crime, before him; the evidence of another, behind him; around him, loneliness; above him, the lowering sky—it was too terrible a misery to be born! He remembered, in his agony of fear, his brother's last words. It was possible, that the warriors might have been sent to watch him, before the appointed time. It was possible, that a fellow-creature might be within hail; even if the King's servant's had not approached the hut. Who might discover him, he cared not; for, solitude was worse than death; so, he called for help.

For a few minutes, nothing interrupted the mournful monotony of sound, in the wind and waves. At last, he heard footsteps without. They came nearer — they passed the door. A spell was over him. He dared not move, or look round. Suddenly, a hand was laid on his shoulder. He turned.

It stood before him!—a living, moving being! It stood before him!—the forest wanderer; the watcher of the storm; the stern, fearful embodiment, of the recollection within him! Speechless and motionless, he gazed on the man; and, speechless and motionless, the man glared back on him, in turn.

Soon, an exulting smile, deepened the deformity of the madman's features. He seized the Priest by the arm, dragged him out upon the beach, down to the very water's edge, and launched the canoe.—the frail, rotten bark, that in the days of its greatest strength, was hardly sufficient for the weight of one!

He made a first and last effort to escape, at this moment; but, the outcast's grip on his arm, loosened not, for an instant. "Out! Out!" cried the madman, pointing to the wide, dark ocean, as the Priest struggled in his grasp—"Out! Out!"— "Eiméo! Eiméo!—I have possessions! We shall voyage merrily, for we love the night; and we laugh at the fury of the storm"!

These disjointed words, fell on the ear of the Priest, as words had never fallen, before. Above the roaring of the waves on the reef—Above the howling of the wind in the forest—Above the wild laughter of the madman on the beach, rose the yell of frenzy and horror, from the astounded villain's lips! His efforts at escape, ceased instantaneously. He might have been a dead man, so stoically did he suffer the torment inflicted on him by the bonds, that the outcast detached from his waist, and passed round the arms of his victim, till the blood streamed from them, to the ground. A low groan burst from him, as the madman flung him into the canoe, and stepped in, after him—but, not a word escaped him, even then.

The sun set in the dark and troubled waters, as the bark floated slowly out to sea. A vacant calmness, had now settled on the outcast's countenance, as he listened, with fixed and gloomy attention, to the solemn dirging of the wind. The spray dashed over him in showers; but, he heeded it not. The paddle fell from his hand; but, he stirred not to recover it from the waves. Slow, as the sinking of the darkness on the earth, was the course of the canoe, as it floated drearily out to the reefs, with its doomed and inhuman freight—slow!—slow! ——

——The End——

✢ LIST OF VARIANTS AND DELETIONS ✢

All variants recorded are deletions except where a single-word lemma has been repeated for identification. "⟨illegible⟩" means only one word has been deleted. The column to the left indicates page and line numbers of this published edition.

5.0	Chapter I [deleted to the left: Iolani and Idía]
5.3	desolation] desolation ⟨illegible⟩
5.11	scanty] insignificant
5.14	other] other ⟨three illegible words⟩
6.3	preserved] preserved ⟨illegible⟩
6.23	marked] intended
7.7	hung] hung ⟨illegible⟩
8.5	off] assisted
8.10	time] being
8.14	delusive] deceitful
8.21	was] was ⟨illegible⟩
8.30	heart!] heart! ⟨three illegible lines⟩
10.24	hut] building
11.4	her] still
11.16	trees] trees ⟨illegible⟩
11.26	is] is alone
11.28	her] her still
11.30	at last] at last ⟨illegible⟩
11.31	her] her at last
11.32	in store?] in store for herself
12.13	girl] girl story-teller
12.15	story-teller] girl
12.18	possession] possession ⟨illegible⟩
13.2	of] of the

13.2	in] in their
13.2	and] and the
13.3	in] in their
13.3	assumed] attemptd
13.7	woman] Idía
13.8	Idía] the woman
13.12	forlornness and] ⟨*illegible*⟩
13.14	recognized] generally ⟨*illegible*⟩
13.15	unknown] ⟨*five illegible words*⟩
13.22	frequently] liberally
14.1	unaccountable] ⟨*three illegible words*⟩
14.16	affectionate to] with
14.18	encounter] encounter now
	have been] ⟨*two illegible words*⟩ + almost this difficult
14.27	those days] to be
14.28	glided] passed
15.3	Idía] Idía, laying
15.20	place] again
15.31	laughing] in a
	unnaturally] manner
16.10	her] there
16.17	investigation of] the
	few] darkest and most
16.18	the] awful
16.19	people] ⟨*five illegible words*⟩
17.5	consequently] almost invariably
17.16	frequent] ⟨*two illegible words*⟩
17.24	Pacific] Southern
18.3	opportunity for] ⟨*nine illegible words*⟩
18.15	law] until now
18.27	as] and
	vengeance] as well
19.4	maidenhood] even now
19.7	Jealousy!] thus!
19.21	befallen] ⟨*illegible*⟩
19.22	grown] ⟨*illegible*⟩

19.23	attempt] ⟨*two illegible words*⟩
19.24	proposal] ⟨*nine illegible words*⟩ her] ⟨*illegible*⟩
19.26	erelong,] on the
20.2	herself] a ⟨*illegible*⟩ help in times of trouble
20.8	and] more
20.12	along] down
20.20	Aimáta] the girl
20.23	slight] strange
20.30	sufferer] she
21.9	sufferer] she
21.21	none] is not
22.9	Idía] the woman
	approaching] yet
22.17	someone] something
22.26	shall] shall
23.12	He was] searching for her still
23.13	She] started
	rise] rise herself
23.29	Priest] but no sign appeared
24.2	wearily] weary
24.7	offspring] the child
24.11	flickered on] over
27.2	Island] Island ⟨*eleven illegible words*⟩
27.5	however] however ⟨*twelve illegible words*⟩
	was] ⟨*illegible*⟩
28.10	disposed] ⟨*illegible*⟩
28.16	elder] elder ⟨*eight illegible words*⟩
28.20	feelings] in form and beauty
28.21	beauty] beauty ⟨*illegible*⟩
29.28	rebels] rebeles
30.7	fugitives] fugitives at once
30.19	wishes] wishes thus
30.24	vengeance] vengeance thus
30.32	passion] passion at once
31.5	had] had not
31.13	dilating] ⟨*seven illegible words*⟩

31.28	high as] it now did
32.15	interference] interruption
32.21	important] frequent
32.25	and] he
33.3	which] which that
33.7	demanding] demanding those tributes
	possessions] possessions that
33.15	attempt] attempt to
33.19	enterprise] enterprise,
34.5	ill-treated] ill treated in the most savage manner
35.21	pinnacle] towers
35.33	observable] observable here
36.3	doomed] doomed and escaped
36.19	in] of
36.23	superstitious] wild
37.4	Tahíti] the island
37.6	communication] communication between that and
37.21	tidings] intelligence
38.12	display] display ⟨illegible⟩
38.14	strangers] strangers ⟨illegible⟩
38.18	safe] secure
38.21	less] actually
38.24	woods] woods ⟨illegible⟩
38.25	her] the
38.26	danger] danger left to her
39.12	organisation] sounding out
39.14	purpose of] purpose to
39.15	band] men
39.17	god,] god, was
39.18	ten] ten English
40.2	Ioláni] Ioláni the Priest
40.4	supplication to] supplication to his renewed interview with
40.10	advanced] progressed
40.13	insurgents] insurgents ⟨illegible⟩
40.13	this] this ⟨illegible⟩

42.7   of] of ⟨*illegible*⟩
43.9   They] They still ⟨*illegible*⟩
43.14   sallied] went
43.15–16 avenues] avenues, for the stresses of Virtue, if ever she
          ventured on the Islands of the South, left no warning
          mark behind them; and the women, kindly as the clime,
          vied with the generous soil, if not in its inexhaustible
          treasures, in its yielding and fertility at least.
43.16   Fresh] Fresh ⟨*illegible*⟩
43.21   were] was
43.21   their] its
44.4   This band of] The appearance of
          had] has
          appearance] appearance that
44.17   human nature] humanity
44.27   with] with the most
44.33   of] of other
45.24   assembly] crowd
46.9   steps] steps forward
48.22   shall yet] shall await ye yet!
49.10   complete] complete in the thoughts of men.
50.22   for,] for the ⟨*illegible*⟩
52.4   those] they
53.7   appalling] apalling
53.30   is] is sufficiently and
55.3   them] them ⟨*illegible*⟩ for the night
55.26   about] about it
55.30   upon,] upon, but
55.31   day.] ⟨*following paragraph deleted*⟩ Little heeding how-
          ever the wide prospect that stretched before him, Ioláni
          paced the smooth promentary in connexcion with the
          agitated and unsettled thoughts. His situation had be-
          come perilous in the extreme. To return unsuccessful
          was impossible yet how should he act? And the previous
          evening his plans had been arranged and
56.9   him] him now

56.16	night!] night at last!
58.4	alone!] alone at last!
61.28	this] that
62.2	its] his
62.6	was] were
62.12	longer] longer there
62.29	length] last
63.10	side] sight
63.14	her,] her, now
64.3	halted] halted successful at last
64.11	his] his ⟨*illegible*⟩
64.15	final] last
64.19	even] yet
65.8	sat down] sat down from
66.16	fiercely] fiercely ⟨*illegible*⟩
66.17	sacrifice] sacrifice even yet
66.23	to] towards
67.17	for] for unbelief
67.29	fresh] the
	performance] performance again
67.31	short] short
68.6	subject of] subject of the
68.12	former] former ⟨*illegible*⟩
69.10	nearer to] nearer towards
69.31	miserable] wretched
70.2	see textual note
71.3	hinted at] hinted at as yet
72.13	was] was ⟨*two illegible words*⟩
72.15	latter,] latter, ⟨*two illegible words*⟩
	and] and without variation
72.17	Priests, the] Priests, some
73.24	words] word
75.7	The] The big
75.24	carnage] carnage, still
76.6	plain] field
76.7	were] was

76.10	back] forth
76.12	conflict] warfare
76.18	where] were
78.13	it] it ⟨*illegible*⟩
78.16	among] of
78.16–17	retreat] fight
78.21	aged] old
79.2	around,] around, there arose
79.7	quit] abandon
79.32	a] a few
80.5	cold] dead
80.6	fly] die
80.7	reach] sight
80.8	refuge] refuge ⟨*two illegible words*⟩
80.12	place,] and by the darkness
80.15	point,] now
80.17	the] fugitives
80.25	women,] women, ⟨*illegible*⟩
80.33	journeying] wandering
	slower] yet
81.5	the] little
81.9	halted] halted ⟨*illegible*⟩
81.28	This] This place of
82.25	entire] utter
82.33	him.] him still
83.22	still] now
85.5	close] slowly
85.19	with] to
86.1	demeanour] demeanour ⟨*three illegible words*⟩ the aspect of his eyes
87.4	in] terror
87.24	arms] arms ⟨*two illegible words*⟩
88.29	face,] face, while
91.1	infant] child
91.6	little] little ⟨*illegible*⟩
91.14	down] down again

92.10   appeared] were
93.2   subject to] under
93.11   subdued] subdued even
          mind;] mind; already
93.21   in the] in our
93.26   tears,] tears ⟨*illegible*⟩
94.2   next] day
          change] change ⟨*illegible*⟩
94.5   her] her mind
94.6   Aimáta] the girl
94.21   discovered] confessed
95.29   period] period as this
96.5   from] of
97.4   remaining] left
97.5   snatched] taken
97.5   him.] him. ⟨*illegible*⟩
          left] left
97.15   moment.] moment. ⟨*illegible*⟩
98.6   past] before
98.16   harangue] message
98.21   address] harangue
99.28   effect] action
100.5   visited by] visited by the punishment of
100.13   observance] ceremony
100.22   him.] him. ⟨*illegible*⟩
101.3   turn] call
101.17   reached] arrived at
102.9   turn] return
104.11   possessed] possed
105.13   address] speak to
          expressions] words
105.27   mischance;] mischance; and
105.30   path] path ⟨*two illegible words*⟩
107.5   heedlessness] incaution
107.18   track,] track, still
108.2   to] to ⟨*illegible*⟩

108.27	loneliness] loneliness ⟨*two illegible words*⟩
109.2	extended] extended ⟨*illegible*⟩
109.14	power] firmness unlikely
109.17	some] a
110.15	had] that
111.4	sympathies] a new feeling
111.5	sprung] arisen among
113.29	custom] custom over the
114.14	entwined] entwined to
114.18	Then,] Then, an
114.31	made,] made by
120.10	strewed] was strewed
121.18	pervaded] pervaed without exception
121.22	as] as an
123.3	each other,] themselves
123.23	and,] and lastly
125.4	intention,] intense
125.7	and] and the
125.20	valley] vally
127.12	the] the carelessness regarding the
	strengthening] strengthening by every means in his
	power
127.15	councillors] councillors ⟨*five illegible words*⟩
127.22	remote] remote ⟨*ten illegible words*⟩
128.2	life] existence
128.4	advent] advent ⟨*illegible*⟩
129.3	faded] passed
130.24	distant] yet
130.25	chase] hunt
131.25	could] could
132.17	halted] as if, at last
132.21	a] a ⟨*illegible*⟩
134.21	man] to
135.7	more] the
135.17	—] — of that ⟨*three illegible words*⟩
135.33	of] for

136.5	attributable] to
136.10	of] Ioláni's
136.13	necessity,] necessity, ⟨*illegible*⟩
137.1	disposed] disposed ⟨*illegible*⟩
137.10	and] surrounded by
	and] that was the night that they determined to
138.2	Priest] Ioláni
138.6	obvious] evident
138.13	course] still
139.1	savage] fierce
139.2	on] over
139.13	dearly] but dearer
139.16	him.] now
139.30	appeared] appeared ⟨*illegible*⟩
140.15	him] even now
141.9	by] the
	invocation] incantation
141.23	where] were
142.31	effort] of
143.9	proceeded] proceeded ⟨*three illegible words*⟩
143.28	obstructions] difficulties
144.13	tone] voice
14.22	him.] without
144.28	forest] above
145.15	faded] faded ⟨*illegible*⟩
145.17	his] the
	deep] deep ⟨*two illegible words*⟩
146.8	earnest] deep
146.23	anger] vengenance
147.13	reason to] comply
147.27	last] last ⟨*illegible*⟩
147.28	him.] he had changed
148.29	child] threshold
149.8	sorcerer] Sorcerer
150.1	for] for —
150.8	being] still

150.14   distance as] was within his power
151.15   length] last
151.21   dread] fear
151.30   thicket] again
152.21   turned] turned ⟨*illegible*⟩
152.22   yet] still
153.1   By] By ⟨*preceded by ten illegible words*⟩
153.6   to] from
153.15   ever] yet
153.19   before] before ⟨*illegible*⟩
154.22   him] attempt
154.25   means] new plan
155.5   then,] then, ⟨*illegible*⟩
155.18   voyage.] And
155.27   over the] beat
156.4   each] one, so long
157.24   people,] people, ⟨*illegible*⟩
157.27   to] to ⟨*eleven illegible words*⟩
160.1   intervals] intervals ⟨*two illegible words*⟩
160.6   approaching] at last
160.8   it,] from
160.9   vigil] yet
160.16   some] old
160.18   moment] still yet
161.4   heard] now
161.11   still] as in the day sof our forest
161.23   my] thy
162.21   for] they
163.2   is] not
163.9   sufferings] in many a ⟨*three illegible words*⟩
163.11   the] very
163.33   was] now
164.14   nature] though
164.22   woodland] forest
164.24   roar] supreme
164.34   loses] looses

165.19   that] that ⟨*two illegible words*⟩
166.1   thus,] thus, ⟨*illegible*⟩
166.2   arrived.] arrived. ⟨*fourteen illegible words*⟩
          Mahíné's] the
167.17   clemency] at last
168.2   ruler] King
168.31   to] their
169.17   dangerous] dangerous ⟨*illegible*⟩
169.26   person] as well
169.28   colloquy] interview
171.15   affection] affection ⟨*two illegible words*⟩
172.15   passed] fell
          possession] hands
172.19   spared] spared ⟨*two illegible words*⟩
172.29   the] the ⟨*illegible*⟩
173.7   length] last
174.13   to] the
174.15   his] fellow exiles
176.10   eyes] eyes ⟨*illegible*⟩
176.18   exile] now
176.26   be] be ⟨*illegible*⟩
177.11   —] — ⟨*illegible*⟩
177.12   of] his
178.15   marks] markes
178.29   Priest] Ioláni at lat
181.2   chronicle] chronicle ⟨*illegible*⟩
181.9   unknown] that
181.13   shore] spot
181.23   myriad] delightful
182.3   colour, the] colour, the ⟨*three illegible words*⟩
182.5   ⟨*two illegible words*⟩ [precedes *Turn we*]
183.19   relief in] sorrow
183.20   joy] joy ⟨*illegible*⟩
183.24   still] yet
184.8   they] both
185.24   might] might

❧ TEXTUAL NOTES ❧

blank   Preceding title page is the following undated
                         comment in pencil not in Collins's hand:
                         "an unpublished manuscript of Wilkie Col-
                         lins about 55000 words. The scene is laid in
                         the Island of Tahiti before its discovery by
                         whites — It is a story of native life, and
                         seems to be quite complete and to have re-
                         ceived its last revision before sending to the
                         printer."
Title page   by Wilkie Collins/ unpublished [*in pencil;*
                         not in Collins's hand]
70.2 prison house.   [*Corresponds to end of ms p. 57, a pasted-in*
                         sheet attached to the edge of a previously cut
                         page with some of Collins's handwriting visi-
                         ble in the gutter. Page 57 begins on p. 69 line
                         6 of this edition with the phrase "gave her no
                         answer" and ends with the phrase "prison
                         house" on page 70 line 2 of this edition. The
                         addition of this pasted-in sheet suggests that
                         Collins may have had some difficulty in con-
                         cluding Chapter V.]

❧ EXPLANATORY NOTES ❧

Book I, part title page	"In secret we met —." From Byron's "When We Two Parted," *Occasional Poems, 1807–1824*, lines 25–28. Byron died in the year of Collins's birth, 1824. Collins was a fan of his work. Edmund Yates, writing in 1879, declared that Collins thought Byron's letters "the best English I know of—perfectly simple and clear, bright and strong"(*Celebrities at Home*, 22). Collins acquired in 1843 the two-volume 1838 edition of the *Life, Letters and Journals of Lord Byron*, edited by Thomas Moore, as Collins's signature on the fly-leaf confirms. A tenuous connection between Collins and Byron was that Beppo, the Italian gondolier and servant engaged by the Collins family in Venice during their sojourn there when Collins was twelve, had been Byron's cook.
6.19	"fastnesses"—strongholds or fortresses; implies the state of being secure or a place not easily forced. It originates in the Old English *faestnes*.
Book II, part title page	Coleridge, "The Pains of Sleep" (1803, 1816), lines 21–26; first published with "Christabel." Coleridge was a friend of Collins's father, who painted a portrait of Coleridge's daughter, Sara. Coleridge's addiction to opium was well known, and William Winters in *Old Friends* (1909) retells a story from Collins that on one occasion, when Coleridge arrived at his par-

Book II,   ents' house in some distress, the young Wilkie
part title page   Collins had to secure some opium for him
(*cont.*)   from the local apothecary. The event made a
                         lasting impression on the youthful writer.
27.12   Steeps—high promontories or cliffs with per-
                         pendicular faces or slopes.
44.1   On the entertainers of Polynesia see William
                         Ellis, *Polynesian Researches*, 2 vols. (London:
                         Fisher, Son and Jackson, 1829) vol. 1: chaps.
                         11, 12. Also see Melville's *Typee*, *passim*.
89.19   wended—to go forward or proceed; to journey
                         or make one's way from the archaic Middle
                         English form of the Old English *wendan*. Re-
                         placed by "went."
114.19   heiva—Ellis explains that the heiva was
                         danced by men and women, the headdresses
                         of the latter decorated with "fillets of *tamau*, or
                         plaited human hair, and adorned with wreaths
                         of the white sweet-scented teairi flower. The
                         arms and neck were uncovered, the breasts or-
                         namented with shells or coverings of curiously
                         wrought net-work and feathers" (I:298). They
                         danced to drum and flute music, occasionally
                         outdoors but often under the cover of spacious
                         pavilions constructed for public entertain-
                         ments. The heiva often followed athletic
                         events, beginning in the evening and lasting to
                         dawn. See Ellis, *Polynesian Researches*, I:298–
                         99.
Book III,   Thomas Gray, "The Bard" (1757), III.1, line
part title page   100. Collins altered the punctuation from the
                         original, which read, "The web is wove. The
                         work is done." Collins favored this Pindaric
                         ode based on the tradition that Edward I or-
                         dered all of the bards executed after his con-
                         quest of Wales. Collins owned a copy of Gray's

	Poetical Works (1821) with plates by Westall; the date of Collins's signature in the volume is 8 January 1840.
121.16–122.28	wrestling—on wrestling as a popular Tahitian sport, see Ellis, *Polynesian Researches*, I: chap. 11.
136.25	canoe—for a detailed account of the variations and history of the Polynesian canoe see Ellis, *Polynesian Researches*, I:163–77. Collins incorporates the canoe into the plot of *Iolāni*, especially at its end.
154.7	levies—armed men drafted to fight in an army.